JONAH LOOKED FROM ELIZA BACK TO LEVI. "AM I MISSING SOMETHING?"

"*Ja*," she said. "You missed telling me who we might be hiring. It won't be him."

Levi stepped forward. "I see you still have a strong temper. What happened to your leg?"

She glared at him. "Nothing for you to be concerned about." He stood. She sat. They stared each other down.

Jonah, never one for drama, held up a hand. "Someone needs to explain what's going on. I take it you two know each other."

"We do," Levi said before she could spit out the words. "We used to be close. Walking-out close."

"We broke up," Eliza managed to say. "End of story."

Jonah watched her and then turned to Levi, his expression changing. "So, you're the one?"

Also by Lenora Worth

The Memory Quilt

The
FORGIVING
QUILT

THE SHADOW LAKE SERIES

LENORA
WORTH

ZEBRA BOOKS
Kensington Publishing Corp.
www.kensingtonbooks.com

ZEBRA BOOKS are published by

Kensington Publishing Corp.
119 West 40th Street
New York, NY 10018

All Kensington titles, imprints, and distributed lines are available at special quantity discounts for bulk purchases for sales promotion, premiums, fund-raising, and educational or institutional use.

Special book excerpts or customized printings can also be created to fit specific needs. For details, write or phone the office of the Kensington Sales Manager: Kensington Publishing Corp., 119 West 40th Street, New York, NY 10018. Attn. Sales Department. Phone: 1-800-221-2647.

First Printing: December 2022
ISBN-13: 978-1-4201-5247-0
ISBN-13: 978-1-4201-5248-7 (eBook)

10 9 8 7 6 5 4 3 2 1

Printed in the United States of America

CHAPTER ONE

"Doc, will I ever be able to walk straight again?"

Eliza King gave Dr. Samuel Merrill a pleading stare, her heart as heavy as the cast on her left leg. She'd never get on a ladder again, that was for certain sure. "I miss my horses."

She missed her mobility, too. She'd been home from the hospital for two weeks now. Still remembering the excruciating pain of falling from a ladder onto the hard floor of the stable alley, she tried to block the awful sound of her bones breaking and a shivering shock moving through her system.

Today, she'd come back for a checkup, so the doctor could make sure the cast was still secure and doing its job. She was ready to go home without this infernal cast, but that would take a few more weeks.

The Shadow Lake Inn, once a massive Colonial mansion, was nestled in a cove near Lake Erie, Pennsylvania, and always had a lot of visitors during the fall. The leaf-lookers would fill the woods and walkways and have the inn's employees hopping to keep up with the restaurant and the guest rooms. The inn would be so busy in the next few weeks. She had picked a bad time to get hurt.

But when was there a *gut* time? The inn her family had inherited from a kind and loving *Englisch* couple had become her world. Her sisters, Abigail and Colette, worked hard in the main house while she maintained the stables and gardens. Abigail's husband, Jonah, had become a big help. He'd do fine while she was laid up, but Eliza needed her animals. She'd always gotten along with animals better than people.

"Doc?"

The gray-haired *Englisch* doctor patted her arm and smiled. "Eliza, you have been impatient since the day you were born. Even though I didn't deliver you, I've taken care of you most of your life. But this is serious. You shattered your leg with that fall, you had surgery to repair it, and it will take time to heal."

"You know how things are at the inn," Eliza said, wondering how Abigail and Colette were handling the hustle and bustle without her. Fall—her favorite time of year—had come in vivid reds and golds. Jonah was trying to take care of the horses, of course. Her brother-in-law was *gut* with the animals, but since Daed had cut back on helping around the stables, Jonah had taken on even more responsibility in this first year of his marriage to her older sister, Abigail.

Eliza needed to be with her horses, but it wasn't possible to do any actual work in the stable. Over the last week or so, she'd mostly sat on a cushioned bench with her leg elevated. "How long, Doc?"

Mamm sat in a chair by the window. "Eliza, you heard the doctor. Surgery is serious. Your bones were pinned back together. Healing will take time." Looking up at Dr. Merrill, Mamm said, "She will follow your directions. I'll make sure of that."

Dr. Merrill nodded. "Your mother is highly qualified to take care of you. Being a trained midwife does come in handy, and Sarah, you go beyond just helping with births. I appreciate your keen interest in all things medical."

"And I appreciate all your *gut* advice through the years," Mamm replied with a smile. "So let's go over the details regarding our instructions for Eliza."

"At least six to eight weeks in the cast, then a cane or walker, and a lot of physical therapy."

Eliza let out a sigh. "That's the whole autumn season."

Mamm shook her head. "You've already passed two of the weeks, so you're coming close to halfway there."

"You can sit and read and rest, Eliza." Dr. Merrill smiled again. "You will have other seasons."

Eliza knew the doctor had her best interests at heart. "I don't want to get an infection or cause more pain. I'm thankful you helped me and found a competent surgeon. I'll do my best to stay off my leg."

"You must," Mamm said. "You asked for over-the-counter medicine, but I'll mix up a batch of herbal ointment to ease the itching and dryness and soothe your muscles."

"And remember, Eliza," Dr. Merrill said, "if the pain increases, don't be brave. We can send you a prescription."

"Can you send me a helper?" she quipped, glancing at her mother's soft smile.

The doctor, so familiar with her family history and her love of books, sat down behind his desk. "I know a man who's good with horses. He's Amish and he recently returned to Shadow Lake. He's looking for work. He's also a farrier, so he can make sure Samson and his mares are happy and healthy. I've had him out to my farm to work with my horses."

"But I have a stable with spoiled, picky animals," she reminded him. "And unlike you, my place is not a fancy ranch with lots of helpers."

"I do have a great staff," he said with a grin. "They could use some advice from a taskmaster like you, however." Placing his hands on his desk pad, he chuckled. "I know Samson is a handful."

Samson was the big gray Percheron—and her favorite. Rosebud, Sunshine, Pickles, and the pony, Peaches, they all needed her.

"I can't abandon my animals, Doc."

"You won't be abandoning them. You can visit the stables as long as you keep this leg elevated as much as possible. I could arrange for a wheelchair."

"*Neh*," Eliza said, shaking her head so fast, the ribbons on her *kapp* shook. "I'll rig up a small buggy. Peaches can give me free rides to the stables."

"That's my Eliza. Innovative and determined." He wrote out some orders and handed them to her. "Don't overdo it. If you do, your leg might not heal properly and then, yes, you could walk with a limp."

"Crippled?"

"We don't refer to it in those terms. But you wouldn't be completely disabled."

Eliza would get well. A lot of people depended on her, and she wouldn't let a broken leg get in the way of her responsibilities. Meanwhile, she'd do what she had to do. "You can send this man over, Doc. We need the help. You can give Jonah all the information, since he'll have to show the man around." Then she tossed out, "But if I don't approve of him, we'll find help elsewhere."

Levi Lapp stopped at the end of the lane leading up to the Shadow Lake Inn. He'd never dreamed he'd return here one day, not after that terrible night six years ago.

The night he'd made the worst mistake of his life.

But when Dr. Merrill called him yesterday and told him he was needed, Levi couldn't say no. He'd come back to Shadow Lake for two reasons—to find work closer to home, and to ask Eliza King to forgive him.

But he couldn't have imagined those two goals would merge into something he wasn't prepared to do—face his indiscretions.

His *mamm* always said, "*Gott* will find you, and He will redeem you."

Well, Mamm, *you were so right there.*

Gott seemed to have a sense of humor, too. Or a sense of justice.

Levi reckoned it was time to face his past, head-on.

After Dr. Merrill called him, he'd told his friend he could make the introductions himself. The doctor had been too busy to argue with him. Now here Levi was, about to start working for the very family he'd dishonored in a foolish attempt to impress his friends during Rumspringa.

His running around days were over now, and he'd returned to his faith. But he'd been away from home for years, doing his work in various Amish communities. When his *mamm* had gotten word to him that Daed was ailing, Levi had hurried home. Now he'd stay for the rest of his life. His *daed* had died three days after he returned. Levi needed to take care of his family—Mamm and his younger siblings, James and Laura.

After a month of piecemeal work here and there, he couldn't turn down this opportunity for a possibly permanent job.

You need the work, he reminded himself. *Don't be a coward.*

Levi clucked to send Rudolph, the gentle reddish brown quarter-horse he'd raised from a colt, back onto the gravel lane. Rudolph really did have a furry red nose, with a white streak of fur moving up that noble nose to shoot across the top of the gelding's head. Children loved him and Rudolph loved humans. Maybe he would help Levi win over Eliza again. Dr. Merrill said he knew the Kings very well and that they needed help right now. Not sure what had happened, Levi knew enough about medical privacy rules to realize there was no point asking questions.

Rudolph was *gut* at dealing with hurting humans, but Levi wondered if *he'd* help Eliza or if she'd send him packing.

He went on up the lane, taking in the canopy of fall trees in various colors ranging from golden yellows and bursting oranges to russet and burgundy splatters here and there. Fall was here, the air crisp, sending the hot winds of summer away and replacing them with clean, fresh cold breezes.

He sent Rudolph trotting toward the stables, hoping to avoid the historic Colonial-style inn where the three King sisters would surely be bossing everyone around. He smiled at that thought. Those girls were different—more independent and a little more progressive than most of the Amish girls he'd met.

Eliza had a mind of her own—the one time he'd tried the wrong moves on her, she'd let him have it with a fist to his stomach and a promise that she'd knock him out if he ever came near her again. Somehow, she'd forgotten the Amish did not approve of violence. But who would blame her? He'd been too fresh, and she'd put him in his place.

To calm his nerves, he took in the view of the lake below the bluffs, then turned to glance toward the inn. A huge old place, steeped in history, and still thriving thanks to the King family, who'd taken it over after the *Englisch* couple that had hired them left it to Eliza's parents. He'd spent a lot of time here at singings and frolics and during church, where he'd glance across the aisle to find Eliza's golden-brown hair and beautiful hazel eyes. Her eyes reminded him of the changing leaves—so many different colors, going from gold to green, depending on her mood.

He prayed she'd be in a *gut* mood today.

Levi pulled his custom-built wagon up close to the open barn doors. He didn't have a sign on his wagon, but it was equipped with whatever he might need to shoe a horse or clean up an existing shoe.

After he'd checked Rudolph, he left the horse and wagon by the open doors to the stables. His heart hammered, his hands sweated, his head filled with regret and apprehension, and just a dash of anticipation. Surely, Eliza's bad feelings for him would have softened by now.

Then he heard her voice.

"I don't like this, Jonah. A stranger working with Samson. You know how Samson is, ain't so?"

The man answered her. "I was a stranger and *Englisch* at that. You accepted me."

"But I trained you," she said. "I was able to watch you and help you and correct you." A pause, a sigh. "Besides, you were a fast learner, and I had to keep you away from Abigail."

"*Ja,* you sure did all those things."

Her laughter, like the sound of tiny bells chiming, hit Levi square in the midsection, somewhere in the vicinity of his heart. He remembered that voice and that laughter. He also remembered her tears.

He'd embarrassed her, hurt her feelings, and if she hadn't stopped him, he might have done something he would have regretted. He regretted even thinking of such a thing now. Not that he'd ever force himself on a woman, but kissing Eliza had brought out too much need in him. And her, too, obviously. Their strong reaction had scared both of them. Her fear had turned to anger. His fear had turned to shame.

He was going to need a lot of courage to go into that stable and face the woman he'd tried to seduce when they were both seventeen. Eliza was no longer a child.

But he was no longer that kind of boy either. He'd changed and grown; the events of his life had left imprints on his heart. Eliza King had left a big imprint on his heart.

He would never be that stupid again.

Eliza wished she could get up and move around. If she ever got out of this cast, she would certainly dance a jig. Her *daed* would be appalled, but that's how she felt in her head. Her leg had to heal before she could even walk again. Why had she decided to search the rafters for an old basket? They had plenty of baskets in the inn's storage room and at the cottage where her family lived, but she'd wanted this particular one to use for making a show-stopping fall arrangement for the lobby of the inn. She never found the basket, but the old ladder had broken a rung when she'd stepped back, and down she'd gone. Just thinking about it now made her shiver.

"Where's the ladder?" she asked Jonah, hoping he'd burned it.

He glanced around in the midst of cleaning Sunshine's stall. "I'm going to repair it. Meantime, I've ordered a new one from the hardware store in town. A sturdy one made with tough metal so the rungs can't break."

"*Denke*, Jonah."

"That old thing wasn't safe, and I'm pretty sure I mentioned that several times."

"You did, but I was in a hurry and took my chances. I have learned my lesson, for sure."

Her brother-in-law had become her confidant during the last year. Jonah understood her in the same way he understood her older sister, Abby. Except he loved Abigail with all his heart and had done much to prove it. He even knew how to deal with their younger sister, Colette. Jonah had given up the outside world to become Amish. As if *Gott* had known exactly what this place needed, a *gut* strong man to help them with the never-ending chores. And to make her lonely sister happy. He'd changed his name to the one Abigail had given him—Jonah from the lake. He'd gone through hours of study with the bishop and her *daed*. Those two men were his best friends now.

Jonah had washed up on the shore with no memory in the early spring of last year. After he'd remembered who he was and taken care of some dangerous people, he'd come back to stay.

Eliza wished she could find someone like Jonah. She loved him as a brother, but she wanted someone to love as a partner. Jonah was a *gut* brother-in-law. Eliza wished a man like Jonah would show up for her. But she feared she might become the *alte maidal* of the family.

After a few tries during her Rumspringa, she'd given up on love. She preferred horses and books now. There was that one boy, that one night, that wouldn't leave her mind and made her reluctant to get close to anyone. Maybe because she'd messed up things with him so badly.

"Hello, Eliza."

And just like that, the very man she'd been thinking of was standing there in the open doors of the stables, his silhouette shadowed, his shoulders broad now, and his voice deep. But it was a voice she could never forget.

"Levi Lapp," she said from where she sat on a bench with cushions all around her and her broken leg up on a pillow, "what are you doing here?" Her mind reeled at seeing him again after so many years—years when she'd tried to forget him completely.

"I'm your new hired help," he said as he stepped forward, giving her a chance to see his rugged face and that shaggy light brown hair that she'd once wanted to tame. She'd thought she'd be able to tame him, too. That had not worked out. After they'd broken up, he'd left.

But her heart began to beat too fast, reminding her that he was now back in a big way. Just like their brief relationship, this would not work either.

Jonah turned from mucking the stall and walked up to him. "Hello. Levi?"

Levi nodded, confirming what she hoped wasn't true. She'd hoped she might be seeing things thanks to her pain medicine.

"*Ja*," he said, his eyes dancing from her back to Jonah. "Levi Lapp. We talked on the phone."

Jonah's smile brightened. "You're right on time."

"*Neh*," Eliza said. "He is in the wrong place, and this is not a *gut* time. Any time with him is not a *gut* time. There is no way I will allow this man to handle or take care of any of my animals. Not now. Not ever." She crossed her arms over her chest to protect her heart, then looked Levi square in the eye. "And that is final."

Chapter Two

Jonah looked from her back to Levi. "Am I missing something?"

"*Ja,*" she said. "You missed telling me who we might be hiring. It won't be him."

Levi stepped forward. "I see you still have a strong temper. What happened to your leg?"

She glared at him. "Nothing for you to be concerned about."

He stood. She sat. They stared each other down.

Jonah, never one for drama, held up a hand. "Someone needs to explain what's going on. I take it you two know each other."

"We do," Levi said before she could spit out the words. "We used to be close. Walking-out close."

"We broke up," Eliza managed to say. "End of story."

Jonah watched her and then turned to Levi, his expression changing. "So, you're the one?"

Levi waited for her to speak. "Go ahead. Tell him, and then I'll be on my way."

"He's the one," she replied. "It was a long time ago and I handled it."

Jonah shifted closer to Levi but kept his eyes on Eliza. "Do you want me to deck him?"

Eliza blinked. "What does that mean?"

Levi's smile held some heat. "He's willing to knock me out on your behalf. Are you two together?"

Eliza managed an unladylike snort. "*Neh*. He's my over-protective brother-in-law, who used to be *Englisch* and worked as a detective. He helped put away a whole cartel of bad folks. Do not make him angry."

She almost laughed at the shock on Levi's handsome face. "I've been away too long. Things have changed."

"That's right. You don't belong here," she retorted.

Jonah let out a long-suffering sigh. "She's right about me. I was once angry and full of vengeance. Then I met Abigail."

"Abby? You're married to Abigail?"

"He is," Eliza replied, glad to have Jonah on her side.

But then Jonah said, "I am. But I don't condone violence anymore. Except—if Eliza wants me to knock you to the floor on her behalf, I will. If not, we need your help and you come highly recommended. But if you two are going to go at it all day long, we can't hire you."

"Eliza?" Levi asked. "Do you want him to hit me? Will that make you see that I'm not a boy anymore and I regret what I did? If so, I will gladly take the hit."

Eliza couldn't believe this was happening. She'd often dreamed of two valiant men arguing over her. Maybe one of them would win her heart and the other would be a friend or protector. Things always ended happily, no matter.

Now that it was coming true, the dream stung more than it burned. What should she do? Levi hadn't tried to force her that night. He'd only kissed her. A kiss she still remembered, but one that had shaken her to her sneakers. She'd panicked and overreacted to his determination to make their first kiss a passionate one.

"Answer him," Jonah encouraged. "If you are afraid of him, I'll make him leave. We don't have all day, and we certainly do not have time for you to overthink this."

"I'm not . . . overthinking," she replied, *thinking* about a lot of things. "I do not want you to hit him, but I do not want him here."

"Then I will leave," Levi said.

He turned to go, but before he made it to the open doors, a big roan horse with a tuft of chestnut hair right over its nose stuck its head inside the door and neighed.

"Rudolph, how did you get in here?" Levi said, his voice devoid of any surprise.

"Is that your horse?" Eliza heard herself asking. The animal was beautiful. "A quarter horse with an unusual nose."

"He's a big baby," Levi said, looking impressed that she knew the breed. "And he manages to stroll off sometimes, wagon and all."

Eliza knew animals. "Or maybe someone just left him unhitched so he could graze?"

"He didn't leave the wagon behind," Jonah pointed out.

Levi shrugged. "I left him hitched to the wagon. He never runs off, but he's known to go strolling. He's smart enough to turn that little wagon around, but I reckon he wanted to see what all the fuss was about. He knows a stable door when he sees one. He might like a carrot."

Sure enough, Eliza saw a small work wagon still hitched behind the curious horse. "Oh, I didn't see that."

Levi motioned for Jonah. "Will you help me unhitch him from the wagon, so he can move more freely? He's restless after driving around this morning."

Jonah nodded and the two men went out to loosen the

many straps and tugs involved in a hitched wagon. Like heavy belts, each strap had to be unbuckled and unwound to free the wagon from the horse. Rudolph threw his mane back, his impatience obvious, but once the two men backed the wagon away and released the long shafts, he relaxed. That made Eliza smile. But when her eyes fell across Levi's fine features and heavy muscles, she snapped back to stare at the rafters.

"This is my worst nightmare."

Rudolph finally pulled free and stepped into the dark entrance to the stables, his nose twitching with interest. Eliza fell for the horse but ignored the man.

"I can see why you named him Rudolph," Jonah said as the men entered and stood to the side. "He has a red nose."

"And he thinks he's a reindeer," Levi said with a smile.

A smile that went straight to Eliza's heart. To counter it, she grabbed the chunks of carrots and apples she'd brought to feed the other horses and held one out to Rudolph.

Rudolph walked right up to her and nudged her with his red nose.

"He likes you," Levi said, a triumphant smile on his face. Then he turned and glanced around the stables. "What a nice place. Rudolph and I could easily work here, in spite of it all."

Jonah lifted his chin and sent Eliza a stern glance. "I'll show you around."

And off they went, like two peas in a pod, while Eliza sat, unable to chase after Jonah and tell him to stop.

She watched Rudolph and rubbed his nose each time he lowered his head to her. "Why did he come here of all places? He's been away a long time."

Rudolph's eyes widened but he gave her no answers.

"Do you spend a lot of time with him?"

Of course he did. The gelding seemed lovable and compliant while the man seemed dangerous and different than she remembered. She didn't want to remember. She could call one of her sisters to come help her back to the house, but they'd only ogle Jonah and ask too many questions.

When the men returned, laughing like old friends now, Eliza stopped petting the big horse that seemed to like her, and stared at Levi. "You made sure he'd come in here, didn't you?"

"I might have loosened the reins and left it up to him. He did bring our wagon with him, and as you can see, we are a full-service company. I'm a licensed farrier and I know my way around any kind of horse. I've worked all over Arkansas, Missouri, Ohio and Pennsylvania. Some say we're the best."

"You've obviously traveled a lot," Eliza pointed out. "Which gives me hope that you won't linger here too long."

Jonah held a hand over his lips, but she saw his grin.

She glared at him. "This is not humorous."

Dropping his hand, he said, "I think Levi and Rudolph will fit right in around here."

"You would." She shook her head. Rudolph did the same.

"What do you think, Rudolph? I will leave it up to you."

The magnificent horse lifted his head and tossed his mane, his dark eyes focused on her. Then he leaned down and nudged her cheek.

Eliza had never been able to turn away a horse.

"Rudolph can stay."

"He can't without me," Levi replied, his tone soft with hope. "Eliza, I promise I will not do anything to . . . disrespect or upset you. I need the work."

Jonah gave her a beseeching glance. "I have talked to Levi, and we have an understanding. He is sorry for how he treated you and he hopes to make amends. What if we do a test run and give him two weeks to prove himself? If you still don't want Levi here after that, we'll send him—and Rudolph—on their way."

Levi watched her.

Rudolph nudged her.

Jonah waited.

Eliza sat silent, a thousand reasons to say no running through her mind, while the obvious reasons to say yes shouted out to her.

Rudolph stomped a foot and shook out his mane, his dark eyes still on Eliza. It was as if the horse knew all her fears and her failures and still wanted her to know he liked her.

She let out a sigh and shifted her leg. "I'm tired. I'd like to go back to the *haus* now." Then she said, "Two weeks. Stay away from me and we'll see. You can stay in the carriage *haus* apartment. Jonah knows where it is. He'll take you there."

"Not yet," Levi said. "First, I'll get you home and settled in."

"*Neh*, someone else can do that. Did you not hear what I said? I want you to stay away from me."

Jonah gave her a no-nonsense glance. "I'm busy. Abby and Colette are busy. Your parents have gone to town. Want me to call Matthew or the front desk?"

"I can do it," Levi said. "Don't be so stubborn. I have room in the back of my wagon."

"All right," she said, her energy fading fast. "Jonah, will you at least carry me to the wagon?"

Jonah stepped forward, but Levi beat him to it and with a gentleness she had forgotten, lifted her up into his arms. His brown eyes were so close, she could see the bits of black in them.

"I've got you, Eliza," he said, his words like a whisper on the wind. Then he turned and carried her out through the doors and gently set her against the canvas-wrapped equipment inside the open wagon. "Hold on tight."

Eliza couldn't speak. Her heart had flared with a longing so strong, she wanted to cry. He sounded so sweet and gentle, so kind and caring. Why had he come back to torment her?

She glanced up as he and Jonah rehitched Rudolph to the wagon they'd just painstakingly freed him from earlier and saw her brother-in-law watching her.

"Eliza, are you sure you're okay with this? Levi says he'll have to take on other stables to make ends meet—for his family. So he won't be around every day. He's moved back home because of them, so he won't need to stay in the carriage house."

She nodded. "I will have to be okay with this now that you've explained, won't I?" Then she lowered her head. "I'd heard his *daed* passed. I'll be fine. I'm not a naive little girl anymore, ain't so?"

"You are not," Jonah replied. "And as Levi said, he is not that boy anymore. He says he's changed, and I believe him. I mean look at me—think how much I've changed since I came here. We should give him a try—if you feel okay with that."

"Two weeks," she said. "But he's already broken the first rule. He didn't stay away from me at all." She glanced at Levi. "We need his help, though."

Jonah nodded. "We do need help, but I don't want you to be worried or uncomfortable."

She thought about that. Levi and she had been so young, so inexperienced, and back then she had been awkward around other people and uncomfortable. Now, her heart twisted in a conflict between the past and the future.

But she'd asked *Gott* to send them help. And here that help stood, looking hopeful and sheepish.

"I handled it then, Jonah. And I surely will handle anything that I don't feel comfortable with now."

Jonah turned and said something to Levi; then he went back inside to clean stalls.

Levi glanced at her and then got up on the wagon and clicked the reins. Rudolph walked sedately toward the cottage on the backside of the property, the fall leaves dancing around his hooves like colored butterflies.

Eliza held tight, as Levi had suggested, her knuckles turning white with anxiety. Levi Lapp was back in her life. And there wasn't a whole lot she could do about it. For now.

CHAPTER THREE

Levi followed the path to the white cottage up on the hill, a place where he'd spent a lot of time as a youth. It felt odd to be back here now, in a home that was at once both familiar and different.

He stopped the wagon by the front porch and took in the beauty of red and burgundy mums and round orange pumpkins clustered in a pretty basket on the wide steps. Then he hopped down and came around to help Eliza.

"I can manage from here," she said, gritting her teeth as she tried to stand.

He held her arm. "*Neh*, you can't."

Levi lifted her up quickly, before she could make a move. She felt as if she weighed less than a bushel of corn. "You're in pain, Lizzie."

She let out a gasp. "Don't call me that."

He didn't answer. That had been his nickname for her once, and she'd only allowed him to use it. But things had changed. He carried her up the steps with firm determination, while he breathed in the clean scent of her gold-streaked light brown hair.

At the top he was met by her two sisters, staring at him

as if he were a giant lizard. "Abby, Colette, *gut* to see you. Where should I put your sister?"

Abigail took over, rushing to open the screen door. "On the sofa where the big pillow can prop up her leg."

Levi went to the long blue sofa and placed Eliza as carefully as possible in one corner, then tugged the pillow toward her. Then he noticed the set of crutches leaning against the wall.

"I'll do that," Abigail said, taking the pillow from him to place it underneath Eliza's cast-bound leg; her green eyes moved from him to her sister. "What are you doing here, Levi?"

"He's our new hired man—for the stables," Eliza said, her frown showing her distaste. "Your husband hired him."

"Without telling you?" Colette asked as she brought Eliza a cup of water and ignored Levi.

"He told me he'd talked to the man and liked his credentials. I didn't think any more of it until Levi showed up, ready to take the job."

"And yet, he's still alive," Colette retorted, her gaze drilling a hole through Levi.

"Jonah offered to knock him to the floor," Eliza told them with the sweetest smile on her pretty face, her hazel eyes flashing a dare. "But he refrained."

Levi glanced from sister to sister. "And he also gave me another warning after I offered to bring Eliza home. He told me he used to be good at undercover work, so he'd be watching me at all times, and if I made one wrong move . . . let's see, how did he put it? Oh, I'd regret it greatly."

"Jonah has embraced our non-violent ways," Abigail said, glancing at Levi. "Which is something to be thankful for at this moment."

"I'm thankful," Levi said. "For the job, and for Jonah's sparing me a black eye." He held his hands out, palms up. "I have apologized to Eliza for my past actions. I need the work. Since Daed passed, I'm needed here at home to help my *mamm* and my brother and sister. I hope to call on all the local farms with my farrier wagon, help anyone who needs my expertise. I'm *gut* with animals."

"Just like our sister," Colette said with a smile. When Eliza glared at her, the smile disappeared.

"Of course," Abigail said. "We were so sorry to hear of Linden's passing, Levi. It's *wunderbar gut* that you came home to help your *mamm*. And we could use your help as often as possible. We're about to get busy around here with lots of tourists visiting. The horses need new shoes and Jonah always needs help with their daily care. Eliza is usually in charge of that, but as you can see, she is disabled right now. She fell and broke her leg—a bad break that required an operation."

"You had surgery?" he said, glancing at Eliza, his expression both concerned and shocked.

"*Ja.*" She looked down at her hands, the memory of her painful fall as real as the day it had taken place. Just as the memory of Levi's kissing her with too much passion had stayed with her. "I miss my work, my animals, even the chickens and goats. I even miss working in the restaurant and kitchen. My accident couldn't have happened at a worse time, and now things have gone from bad to worse."

Was she going to cry? He wouldn't be able to handle that. He'd always had a soft spot for tears. And he surely remembered hers when they'd so clumsily kissed each other and she'd panicked. Maybe he'd panicked, too. Had it been a mistake coming here?

But when she lifted her head, her eyes were clear and bright. "I have agreed to let Levi work here on a trial basis for two weeks. He has agreed to leave me be during that time."

"Oh, so how's that going?" Colette asked, her shrewd

gaze sweeping the room. "I mean, seeing as how he carried you into the house and all."

"He broke that rule," Eliza admitted, her gaze fixing on Levi. "But Jonah was all messy with muck and . . . I didn't want to disturb you two. Are Mamm and Daed back yet?""

"Still visiting, thankfully," Abigail said. "But they will be back soon, and we'll have to . . . explain this. We were about to eat a light supper. Levi, would you like to stay?"

Levi was starving, or maybe that was just nerves. He should leave, get home, and check on his own animals. "I . . . uh . . ."

"*Neh*, he has to hurry on home," Eliza said with what could have been a growl. Obviously, she was thinking the same as he. "He insisted on bringing me home, and he has done that. Let him leave."

"But he's been so kind to you," Colette replied, pure innocence brightening her features. "It would be rude to send him home when he's standing right here, and the food is on the stove and ready."

Eliza eyed her sister, clearly not inclined to agree. Colette stood still, maintaining her sweet pose. Colette had always been sweet, but she was a dreamer if Levi remembered correctly. She'd grown up since he'd last seen her. With vivid blue-green eyes, and strawberry blond hair, she was a real sweetheart. But Levi only had eyes for Eliza.

Abigail made the decision. "We will feed you and send your *mamm* some of the chocolate layer cake we made. It's a ten-layer."

Levi knew his *mamm* would appreciate the cake. But should he stay? Did he want to stay? "Eliza?"

She looked at him, sighed, crossed her arms. "Why not? You've already ruined my day, so you might as well continue on. I'll just eat over here in the corner."

Levi didn't know how to react. "I guess I should go wash up."

"I'm sure you remember the water pump outside," Colette said, pointing to the back door just off the shiny clean kitchen. "We'll put supper on the table."

Levi nodded and went out back to clean up, not sure what had just happened to him. But he did remember the determination of the King sisters.

He was in it now—in for the long haul.

Eliza might be worried about being around him all day, but truth be told, he was terrified to be around her, too. He'd hurt her feelings once by being too forward when she hadn't been ready. He hadn't really been ready either. Now she had the power to torment him all day long. But it would be a sweet torment—he'd missed her way too much. He'd have to handle himself better, this time around.

Eliza sat stewing while her sisters fussed over serving cold chicken and potato salad with corn bread and peas. It looked like they were putting on a feast. Now they were bragging about the ten-layer chocolate cake they'd made today, actually two cakes—one for home and one for the inn. She missed helping with such tasks. They'd cooked the layers on a griddle like hot cakes and then stacked them one at a time, pouring rich chocolate frosting over each layer to make everything stay in place. A beautiful cake as long as the layers were all perfectly round.

Ten-layer chocolate cake was her favorite, and a Shadow Lake Inn specialty ever since Abigail had perfected it a couple of years ago.

Levi walked back in, his light brown hair shimmering with water drops, his shirtsleeves rolled up to show his muscular arms. Pushing a hand through his hair, he placed his straw hat on a peg by the door.

"Can I help?" he asked Abigail.

Her sister shook her head. "*Neh*, we've got it. Jonah will join us soon. We walk over and have meals with Mamm and Daed once or twice a week."

"You and Jonah live on the property?" he asked, looking ill at ease.

"They built a home on the other side of the inn, with a view of the big lake," Colette explained. "That's where they met—on the lake. Jonah kind of washed up there, and Abigail decided to keep him around."

Abigail hushed her imaginative sister. "It's a long story, and one we won't go into right now."

"I'd like to hear it one day," Levi said, glancing over at Eliza.

"You'll be around Jonah all day on days you work here," Colette said. "He'll tell it to you."

Levi laughed at that, then glanced over at Eliza. "Are you joining us?"

She pointed to her leg. "I really do eat here every night, because of this."

His gaze went from her to the kitchen. "What if I pull up a chair and a stool with a pillow to prop your foot up? Then you could eat at the table."

Eliza blinked, surprised at his thoughtfulness. "I suppose I could try that, *ja*."

She saw her sisters exchange speaking looks.

Levi pulled an upright, cushioned chair to the table and then he found a stool by their *mamm*'s chair. "This should work."

After propping some pillows on the stool to elevate her leg properly, he came over to where she sat. "I'll carry you to the table."

"*Neh*," she said, holding up a hand. "Doc Merrill told me to practice with the crutches."

Levi nodded and helped her stand. Then, her face turning red from exertion and embarrassment, she took the wooden crutches and put them under her arms. Holding her head high, she hobbled and shuffled over to the table.

Once she arrived at the chair Levi had set up, she wobbled and tripped. Levi caught her as the crutches went slipping and sliding, one going across the table and narrowly missing the potato salad, and the other one clattering nosily against the old, hooked rug.

Levi held her so she wouldn't stumble again. Eliza grabbed his arm to steady herself, which brought them face-to-face, staring into each other's eyes.

Just as Mamm and Daed came hurrying through the back door.

"Someone needs to speak," Daed said, his dark eyebrows going up. "What is going on here?"

They all started talking at once.

Abigail: "Supper. Just supper."

Colette: "*Kumm*, we were about to eat."

Eliza: "Levi has returned."

Levi: "It's *gut* to see you, Abe and Sarah."

Jonah came through the front door and did a scan of the entire room, amusement twisting his features. "Ah, looks like I'm just in time."

Eliza pulled away from Levi after they'd all spoken, her hands grabbing for her chair, her heart pumping from exertion and well, from being in his arms.

"Levi fixed up a place for me to sit," she explained to no one in particular.

Mamm took it all in, and as usual summed things up rather quickly. "So I see."

Daed turned to his wife. "Will you explain?"

"*Ja*," Mamm said, patting Daed's arm. "Abe, we have company for supper, and you and I should wash up before the cold chicken gets colder."

Hurrying Daed to the sink, she then turned to Levi. "It's so *wunderbar gut* to have you back home, Levi. Please, find a seat and let us eat the meal my three resourceful daughters have prepared."

"Two, Mamm," Eliza said, her words a little breathless. "I didn't help."

"And yet, you managed to make it to the table," Mamm said, her smile as serene as ever. "We are certainly thankful for that."

Eliza smiled back, a shaky twist of her mouth. Then she blurted out the rest. "Oh, and Levi is our new part-time farrier and stable hand."

Mamm looked at Daed. Daed looked at Levi, then Jonah, before he turned his gaze on Eliza. "We were only gone a few hours." Then he shook his head and sat down and closed his eyes.

Eliza said her silent prayers along with everyone at the table, hoping the Lord would forgive her for her bad thoughts. But when she opened her eyes, her whole family was staring at her as if she'd gone daft in the head.

And maybe she had. Levi Lapp was here in her kitchen and soon he'd be working in her stables. Her world, which she so liked to manage, was as out of control as a runaway horse. She couldn't catch up. Breaking her leg had been awful, but she'd been prepared to get through her recovery, to work toward healing.

But now this. The one boy she'd fallen for, the one

person she remembered with such intensely good and bad thoughts, had come home.

Now he'd taken on work here at the inn.

How would she make it through fall knowing Levi was back, and knowing she had no control over the matter?

CHAPTER FOUR

As usual, the sisters gathered after supper.

They used to gather in Abigail's room the moment their parents had retired to bed. But Abigail had moved out and Eliza had taken her room.

So they gathered earlier now. Each time Abby and Jonah came over for supper, they'd finish cleaning up and then go upstairs to chat.

But Eliza couldn't get up the stairs anymore, so Mamm had put a small bed in the sewing room downstairs. Surrounded by quilts and swatches of colorful fabric, Eliza felt as if she'd landed in a giant cushioned chair. The room did have a small washroom to the side that came in handy for all sorts of things. Right now, it allowed her to stay clean, and with help from Mamm or one of her sisters, wash her hair.

Being around animals for most of the day made her want to be clean and sanitized before she went to bed. That had not changed.

Now, Abby and Colette lovingly helped her bathe and made sure her hair was clean, tidy, and combed before they braided it into a long tail on one side of her head, so she could sleep.

Abby sat back. "I'll have to go soon, but I wanted to know how you really feel about Levi being back."

"Supper went well," she said on a dry note. "I mean, after Daed stopped staring at us all."

"Poor Daed," Colette replied. "He can't figure out his daughters."

"It was awkward," Abigail said as she tugged at the blue starburst quilt covering Eliza. "Almost as awkward as me sneaking around to see Jonah."

"Daed and Mamm always know when one of us is up to something," Eliza replied, smiling. "But I'm not up to anything. I plan to avoid Levi. He'll be handling my horses, so I have to be nice to him."

"But you don't have to be around him all the time," Abigail said.

Eliza saw concern in her sister's eyes. "Abby, you know me. I will be okay. I'm not going to follow him around, but I miss my animals, so I plan to check on them every day, regardless of Levi Lapp. I'll pretend he does not exist."

"That could be a *gut* thing," Colette said under her breath.

"You think I might harm him?" Eliza glanced at both her sisters. "We were so young. We both overreacted to . . . to our feelings for each other."

Abigail took her hand. "Eliza, it is scary when you have strong feelings for a boy, for a man." She lowered her gaze. "I know how I felt with Jonah. He took my breath away, but I was terrified of what could have happened between us."

"But you both showed restraint," Colette said. "Thankfully, the man married you, and now . . . well . . . you are definitely in love."

"I am at that," Abigail replied with a dreamy expression, her eyes bright. "I thank *Gott* every day for my Jonah."

Then she stared at Eliza. "Are you willing to forgive Levi?"

Eliza twisted the frayed threads of the quilt draped over her little bed. "I was mad at him for such a long time because he pushed me too far that night. But . . . I did sneak out into the garden with him, and I did kiss him back."

"But he tried more?" Colette asked, clearly curious.

"He did, and I stopped him cold."

"He'll be remembering that, for certain sure," Colette replied.

"I'm sure he is." Eliza shook her head. "I think I've been mad mostly because he never tried to apologize back then. He just left without a word. As if he didn't even care one way or the other."

"He could have been ashamed," Abigail said. "Boys are just as terrified of passion as we are. Men are just as terrified, too. Finding a soul mate, a lifetime partner, someone to share your life with, requires a lot of things, including every emotion you've ever felt."

"I'm feeling a lot of emotions right now," Eliza admitted. She shrugged. "Levi is back. That is the way of it. *Gott*'s will be done."

"So you're going to be friends with him again?" Abigail asked as she stood to tuck Eliza in.

"Of course not," Eliza retorted. "I'm going to watch him like a duck on a June bug but treat him as if he's invisible."

"You've been around my husband too much," Abigail said. "You're learning his slang."

"That's not slang," she corrected. "It's just a saying you can hear anywhere out there in the *Englisch* world."

"Too bad for the June bug," Colette said through a giggle.

"Too bad for Levi Lapp. He is the June bug," Abigail said, laughing.

"I won't harm him," Eliza replied as she sank into the pillows. "But I will watch him while I'm ignoring him."

"I'm not sure that's really possible," Colette said. "I'm so glad I don't have *man* troubles."

"What about Matthew?" Abigail asked. "You've been walking out with him for a while now."

"That's all we do," Colette said. "He's a bit shy."

"So the boy you like is the opposite of Levi?" Abigail asked.

"*Ja*, I suppose he is," Colette said. "But I'm in no hurry and neither is he. We both work here, so there is that. Not a lot of hope for the future."

"Are you saying you and Matthew don't want to work here the rest of your days?" Eliza asked, glad they'd moved on to someone else.

"*Neh*, I'm not saying that." Colette shrugged. "But we do have dreams for a *gut* life."

"Don't we all," Eliza said, fisting her covers. "I'm tired. I have a lot to think about."

Her sisters stood. "You'll be thinking about being kind to Levi, I hope," Abigail said. "He's lost his *daed*, remember."

"I told you, I'm going to ignore him but in a nice way."

"We'll be around," Colette told her. "To help you ignore him, that is."

"You are the best sisters ever," Eliza replied, sleepiness overtaking her. "*Gut* night."

After her sisters left, she lay there, watching the moonlight play across the wall while she remembered the boy she'd thought she'd love forever.

That boy was gone. This Levi was new and different and . . . tempting. So tempting. She wouldn't give in to that temptation. That would be a horrible mistake.

But he had been pleasant and kind during supper. He'd complimented them on the meal and talked with Daed and

Jonah about everything from farming to the stables, to the maintenance of the inn. They'd talked about the orchard, and he'd offered to help pick apples. That was nice because the crop was overflowing this harvest.

Levi Lapp was no longer a clumsy, confused boy.

And she was no longer a naïve, confused girl.

They both knew more about life now, the good and the bad of life. And of love.

She had to find it in her heart to forgive him, somehow.

And maybe, she needed to reexamine why she'd blamed him for so long, too.

Levi showed up the next morning right on time. Horses didn't like to wait for their food and grooming. He'd told Jonah he'd check their shoes, apply new ones as needed, and work with him to make sure their hooves were clean and healthy.

He found Jonah in the stables, mucking out stalls. Always a fun job, but Jonah hummed as he worked. The man seemed content and happy. Levi longed to feel the same.

"*Gut daag*," Levi said, walking toward Jonah.

"Morning," Jonah replied. "I'm still learning Deitsch, so bear with me."

"You were once *Englisch*," Levi said. Jonah and the others had told him of how Jonah had come to stay here. "Was it hard to give up that world out there?"

Jonah shook his head. "Not as hard as you'd think. I needed a place like this, after what I'd been through. And . . . love has a way of making our decisions for us. I fell for Abigail, even before I knew about my past, and that was that."

Levi nodded. "Hmmm. You make it sound so easy."

"It was anything but," Jonah admitted. "Of course, I'm happy now."

Levi glanced around and then back to Jonah.

"She usually comes out here later now," Jonah said.

"Who?"

Jonah had read Levi easily enough from his amused expression. "You were wondering where Eliza is, right?"

"Maybe. I wanted to protect myself if need be."

"She used to be waiting here for me each day, but since I've taken over a lot of the responsibility, she comes later and takes over while I do yard work or fix what needs to be fixed."

Levi looked up and down the long alley between the stalls. "This is a nice place. Clean and tidy. Eliza always did demand tidiness."

"You two knew each other a long time before you left?"

"We did. Grew up together, attended school together, played together. She's *gut* at baseball, by the way." He stopped when Jonah laughed. "Started walking out together. She was my *aldi*—girlfriend." Levi shrugged. "I always thought it would be Eliza and me, forever."

"And then you did something stupid," Jonah finished.

"*Ja,* I did."

"We'd best get you set up," Jonah replied, obviously knowing when not to ask questions. "I thought you could take the space in the back of the barn. I cleaned out a corner for you to set up your tools and supplies while you're here."

He showed Levi the area. "It's by the doors for light and air, and it's near the small corral we fixed up this past year. Rudolph can hang out there while you work."

"This will be fine," Levi said, admiring Jonah's dedication and attention to detail. "A *gut* place away from the animals and stored hay to do my work."

They heard a shuffling at the other end of the long alley.

Levi looked up to see Eliza moving slowly toward them on her crutches.

When she wobbled, he stepped forward, but Jonah caught his arm. "She has a lot of pride."

"I should remember that about her," Levi said, leaving her to walk by herself. But it pained him to see her like this, struggling, hobbling, hurting.

Now she had him to contend with as well. He'd be kind to her by avoiding her as much as possible.

So he went out the back door, walked around front to where he'd left Rudolph grazing, and brought his wagon and equipment around to his little corner of the giant barn and stable.

After he let Rudolph out into the corral, he turned back toward the barn, ready to get started on reshoeing Samson.

And found Eliza sitting on her bench, which had some-how been moved from the front of the barn to the back. She looked pale and tired, but she had her leg propped up on a pillow, with another pillow supporting her back on the long wooden bench.

"I see you came to visit," he said. It would be rude not to acknowledge her presence.

"I came to make sure you know what you're doing," she replied, glancing over his shoulder rather than looking directly at him.

"I know what I'm doing, Eliza," he retorted. "I went to school, and I did my time as an apprentice with a farrier who demanded nothing but perfection. Kind of like you."

"You have a sense of humor," she replied, not smiling. Then she let out a sigh. "Where did you school and train?"

He squinted, trying to ignore her burnished hair and the scent of honeysuckle and lemongrass—probably from her goat's milk soap. "I went to school in Ohio, just a six-week course because I don't have the education to go further. But I did find a good apprenticeship in Lancaster County. I learned hands-on there, and also worked with a thoroughbred farrier down in Kentucky."

"Bluegrass country," she said with a smile. "That must have been exciting. Thoroughbreds are amazing creatures."

Impressed that she knew about thoroughbreds, he figured she must have studied up on them. She'd always loved being around horses.

"Exciting and different," he replied. "Thoroughbreds have to be pampered and protected. They are expensive animals."

"Aren't all horses?"

He grinned and realized they were actually having a conversation. "*Ja*, I reckon they are at that."

Levi also noticed Jonah was nowhere in sight. Giving them time to get reacquainted, or getting out before the sparks started flying?

"So you've traveled far and wide, ain't so?"

Levi stopped organizing his knives and brushes and turned to face Eliza. "I guess you could say that."

"Must have been nice to just up and leave, travel around, and come up with a career. I wonder how that feels."

Levi felt a fight coming on. Well, that didn't take long. "Are you asking me, or maybe you're condemning me, chastising me, wondering about me?"

"All of the above," she said, her hands crossing over her lap like a shield. "I've been right here, Levi. Right here, wondering while you've been *wandering*."

"Oh, *ja,* I can see that," he retorted, ready to do battle. He owed her nothing. He only asked for forgiveness. "What have you been wondering about, Lizzie?"

She lifted up as much as her cast would allow her. "Wondering why you left without a word, nothing, no apology, no explanation, no thought for the future we'd talked about. You left me with nothing, Levi. And now, I feel nothing."

Levi stopped his busywork and leaned back against a counter. "What did you feel before, Eliza?" he asked, his voice low and whispery. "Because I was never sure with you."

"You needed to be sure?" she asked, her voice cold and firm, her eyes misty.

Levi shut his eyes and asked for patience. He'd hurt this woman, and now he'd have to wait for her to forgive him. "*Ja*, I still want to be sure."

She shrugged and shifted to find her crutches. "Well, you can be sure of this. I don't want you here, and I'll be glad when you're gone again. And this time, I won't wonder about you at all. Ever again."

CHAPTER FIVE

Eliza hobbled up the alley, stopping to pet the horses and check on each of them. Silent, she stopped near Peaches and fed the little filly a carrot, then turned to watch as Levi talked to Samson while he led him out to where he'd set up his equipment.

"We'll start by cleaning your shoes, boy," he told the massive gray horse. "We all need our shoes cleaned, now and then, kind of like Jesus washing people's feet. It makes us feel better."

That was a compelling sentiment, she thought. Even if Samson didn't understand, she sure did. Being kind counted in her book, but she had to remember she planned to ignore Levi.

Jonah came walking up to her with a bucket. "So this is you ignoring him, huh?"

She shot her brother-in-law a frown, thinking Abigail must have mentioned that to her husband. "I'm making sure he doesn't damage our workhorse."

"Eliza, the man comes highly recommended," Jonah reminded her. "We were in a pinch and *Gott* provided an answer."

"*Gott* does things His way," she said, wondering why

Gott had seen fit to bring Levi back to torment her. Mamm would chastise her for even thinking such thoughts. "I'll have some questions for him one day."

"Who? Levi?" Jonah smiled. Her brother-in-law liked to get her riled.

"*Neh*, I don't need to ask that one anything."

"We don't question *Gott*," Jonah pointed out. "At least, you've told *me* that many times."

"You are right." She stood balancing on her good leg while she used her crutch to keep her casted leg steady. "But how can I not question his being here? Of all people, Levi?"

"Maybe *Gott* has a reason for that," her brother-in-law suggested. "Levi seems to want to make amends."

"But I'm not ready for that, or for him." She let out a sigh. "I'm just making sure he handles Samson properly."

"Let him do his work," Jonah said. "You should go and rest."

"I don't want to rest. I want to observe. If I don't like the way he cleans Samson's shoes, I'll let him know."

"Don't go making trouble."

"I don't make trouble. I'm particular, is all."

Levi glanced around from where he stood shaving down Samson's left hoof. "You know voices sure do echo in this place. I can hear you."

"*Gut*," Eliza said. "Then you know I mean business."

Levi grinned and went about his work, still talking softly to Samson as he bent his knees and positioned his lower legs around the horse's big hoof and leg; then he leaned forward and gently worked the long narrow rasp like a grater across the bottom of the shoe. "You're got some chips here, Samson. We can't have that. You have to look fancy, right? You're the king of this stable, ain't so?"

"He's not a *bobbeli*," Eliza said on a droll note. "You don't have to talk to him like that."

She'd die before admitting Levi's words had touched her. Samson *was* the king around here. And she loved to spoil the big draft horse.

"He needs some pampering," Levi called. "I think I can make these shoes work for a few more weeks."

"Don't forget the hoof dressing," she replied as she inched closer.

Levi kept his head down and focused on his work. "Got a new supply."

"Did you clean out the frog?"

"*Ja*, Eliza, I did. Want to come and smell his hoof to be sure?"

"Whew, *neh*," she blurted before she could stop herself. Cleaning out around a horse's shoe was never pleasant, especially the part of the hoof called the frog because of its shape once it was cleaned. A dirty frog was a perfect place for thrush to develop. The soft flesh on the upper hoof had to be scraped and peeled, but this had to be done with a delicate hand so as not to harm the horse.

"What kind of knife did you use? You know, the frog can be damaged if you dig with the wrong knife."

Levi steadied Samson's big leg on a foot-tall hoof stand, then started filing the front of the shoe and hoof smooth before he finished up the bottom. "I used a curved hoof knife and a regular blade knife, same as I always do, and I'm going to powder the frog on his left hoof. He had a bit of thrush."

"Are you sure it's thrush? Did you get it cleaned properly?"

Levi stood and released Samson's right leg, then gave her a bemused stare. "Eliza, I've been a farrier for six years now. You need to trust me. I know what I'm doing."

Eliza stiffened her spine and tried to appear aloof, but she did wobble a bit. "I have to see that for myself."

Jonah, pretending to do busywork, started chuckling. "Eliza, you're itching to *do* that yourself, I believe. Which is not possible for you right now."

She frowned again and glanced between him and Levi. "I miss my work."

Levi finished the right hoof, then stood and stretched, and stared at her. "You might as well sit there on the bench so I can hear you telling me how to do everything without both of us shouting."

Jonah's eyebrow lifted and he gave her a smirking smile. "Shall I escort you to the bench?"

"I can manage," she said. Then she told Levi, "I'm here to observe and make sure you do right by my horses."

Jonah shook his head and moved to the far other end of the barn.

Levi put his hands on his hips, the farrier apron he wore making him look like someone out of the Wild West. "I plan to take *gut* care of them, I promise. Samson and I are already friends."

"Samson likes anyone who feeds him."

Levi dropped his hands. "I'll finish up with him, and then maybe you and I can have a chance to visit."

She settled on the bench, trying to be proper and distant, like one of the heroines out of the books she read. "I don't have time to visit."

He cleaned his hands and then gathered some more tools. "Oh, so you're busy today."

"Very."

"Are you busy right now, sitting on that bench pestering me?"

"I told you, I'm observing."

Levi's dark eyes swept over her face. "And what do you see, Eliza? What do you see when you observe me?"

Levi waited for her to answer. For someone who seemed to want to avoid him, she was spending a lot of time watching him. And it wasn't all because of the horses, as they both very well knew.

She averted her eyes, but not before he saw a shadow of doubt replace her aloof expression for a moment.

"I told you—I'm here to make sure you can handle my stable."

"Your stable is in the best of hands. Jonah is a big help, and he knows what he's doing as well as I do. You'll have to *kumm* up with a better excuse than that, Lizzie."

She tried to stand and wobbled. Levi steadied her. Eliza lifted her chin in defiance. "I am not an invalid."

"I never said you were."

He held her there, their eyes meeting, and for a moment he was back in time, trying to be a man when he was still a boy. He'd messed up so badly, he'd left to hide his shame.

And to spare her any further embarrassment.

"Lizzie . . ."

"I need to get back to the inn," she said, grabbing her crutches. "I've dawdled out here with you long enough."

Disappointed, he said, "So you're finished watching me work?"

She struggled with her crutches but managed to balance herself before she toppled over. "I think you'll do for now, *ja.*"

Aggravated, he backed away. "*Gut*, because I'm not an apprentice anymore. I don't need to be watched and corrected. I like my work and I take pride in it. So if you allow me to get on with it, I think you'll find your horses will be happy. So happy they might even smile and show you their teeth."

She glared at him as she maneuvered a slow turn on her crutches, her broken leg lifted so she didn't put weight on it. "I've never seen any horse that happy."

Levi's anger dispersed as he caught a little movement that might have been a smile. At least, her pretty lips twitched a bit.

"I'd be glad to take you to the inn," he offered, wishing he could do just that.

"I need the exercise," she replied. "And you need to get back to work."

"Yes, ma'am."

She gave him a frown over her shoulder, then turned and managed to make her way out of the stables, her spine straight, her head high, in spite of the sound of crutches dragging.

Levi shook his head and went back to where Samson waited. "Your human is like a temptress in a teapot, Samson."

The big horse shook his mane and looked up the aisle, then he whinnied softly.

"*Ja*, I like her, too," Levi replied. "But the woman sure does not want me around."

Jonah came by with a wheelbarrow full of fresh straw. "You and Eliza work things out?"

"*Ja*," Levi replied. "She's still mad and I'm still wishing I'd found work elsewhere."

"Don't you love those King sisters?" Jonah said with a chuckle.

"Hmm. I don't know about that," Levi replied. "I had forgotten how stubborn that particular one can be."

"Stubborn runs in the family," Jonah said. "But I have found that once they get past us being us—when they fall in love—they are all in, as the *Englisch* would say."

"You, my friend, have many tales to tell, I'm for certain sure," Levi replied. "At least you and Samson like me."

"Keep at it," Jonah said as he moved on. "Soon she'll be bringing you lemonade and cookies."

"That'll be the day."

Jonah chuckled and kept walking. And he kept smiling.

Well, he would. He got the kind, sweet King sister. Abigail treated everyone with compassion. She'd even married an *Englisch* which showed true compassion.

An *Englisch* who'd fallen for an Amish woman and changed his life to be with her. Jonah seemed right at home here. He even spoke *Deitsch* now and then.

Levi had come here hoping to change Eliza's mind, not her entire way of living. Was that too much to ask?

He glanced toward the heavens.

"I'll have to wait on the Lord for that answer, Samson."

Samson snorted, his dark eyes all-knowing.

"Now let's get back to you and your delicate frogs, shall we?"

Eliza had broken out in sweat by the time she'd made it to the inn. A few more weeks and she'd have this cast off. But what would she find then? Would she be able to walk properly again? Or would she have a limp the rest of her life?

Pouting and tired, she shuffled into the employee room and sank down on the old couch by the window, immediately putting her leg up on a pillow. Which gave her a perfect view of Levi leading Rosebud out into the new corral. She could see him there with the mare at the corner of the fence.

Levi was gentle with the animals. She couldn't deny that.

She also couldn't deny the way he'd looked at her when he'd asked her what she saw when she observed him?

That had thrown her, shifted her, caused her to doubt

herself. Which only made her more determined to ignore him. Because she'd seen a new side of him. A man fully grown and comfortable with himself, not a clumsy schoolboy who only wanted to show off for his pushy friends. Levi had become a true gentle man. A gentleman. And a fine-looking one at that.

Colette came in and looked at her, surprise in her blue-green eyes. "What are you doing?"

"I'm sitting," Eliza said. "What else can I do?"

"Moody, are we?" Colette asked. Then she sat across from Eliza. "What happened?"

Eliza shook her head. "Levi is a pain."

"Or rather Eliza *was* a pain?"

"I was perfectly pleasant, considering."

"So you managed to ignore him, *ja?*"

"I've discovered the man is hard to ignore."

"Really, now."

She saw Colette's grin and the beaming interest in her younger sister's eyes. "Really. I had to ask questions, of course."

"Of course."

"He is *gut* with the animals. Samson didn't even flinch when Levi filed his hooves. He even got the frogs cleaned and freshened."

"I'd hate that job," Colette said with a delicate shudder. "I've seen where horses walk."

"It's best for the horse," Eliza explained. "A necessary task, and Levi certainly has experience. That much was obvious."

"But you hounded him, didn't you?"

"I had concerns."

"I can imagine."

Eliza glanced at her sister. "*Denke* for being so sympathetic," she said sarcastically.

"I'm being very supportive," Colette said. "Would you like something to drink, some food, maybe, to get rid of that crankiness?"

"I'm not cranky." Eliza rubbed at her cast. "I just want this thing off, but what if I can't walk or ride or anything?"

"You'll be able to walk," Colette said, real concern in her eyes now. "But Doc did say you'll need therapy to walk comfortably again."

"I can't limp, Colette. Not with him here."

"Are you being vain?" her sister asked.

"*Ja*, because I liked the way I walked before, and I especially enjoyed riding my horses."

"You should be able to ride."

"What if I can't get on a horse by myself?" she asked, lowering her head.

"Then I'll lift you up," a male voice said from the doorway.

Levi stood staring at her, his eyes as black as night, his face holding a determination that took her breath away.

"You shouldn't stand around listening to people's conversations," she said, embarrassed.

"I just walked through the door. I was told I could get a meal here."

"Is it dinnertime already?" Colette said, getting up. "I'd better get out front. Levi, wash up and we'll bring you a plate. You can keep Eliza company while she eats."

"*Neh*," he and Eliza said at the same time.

Colette shook her head. "Either you eat together, or you starve. Maggie has a sick child, so she had to stay home, and I'm too busy to serve you both at different times."

Eliza knew a maneuver when she saw one, even if she did feel sympathy for their kitchen help. "I can wait."

"We might run out of food."

Another ploy. "Then I'll go home and find something."

She tried to stand, but Levi shook his head. "*Neh,* I will wait. You need to eat to keep up your strength, and since you don't want to share a meal with me, I'll wait. I can make my own meal once I get home."

"But that will be hours," Eliza replied, showing her true colors. Then she sighed. "Colette, bring us some food. If we're eating, we can't talk with our mouths full. That should work."

Levi glared at her, then turned. "I'll wash up."

Colette looked from his back to her sister's face. "This is going to be so much fun."

"What are you talking about?" Eliza asked.

"Oh, let's see. Fall is in the air, and love in the air, and . . . I just love the holidays."

"You make no sense," Eliza said, wishing she could get up and run out the door. Wishing she'd never taken Dr. Merrill up on his offer to send them help.

Levi returned, smelling fresh and clean, his hair damp from a face washing. "I'm starving," he said. Then he smiled at her, the beam of it leaving her blushing. "It'll be nice sharing a meal with you, Lizzie. You know, out there, I ate many a meal all by myself, sometimes out on the road with only a small grill to cook a big steak. This will be a *wilkom* change."

Eliza wanted to say something witty and snarky, but she didn't have the heart. "Well, you're in the right place for the best home-cooked meals, that's for certain sure."

"And the best company," he replied, his smile taking her breath away all over again.

Suddenly, having Levi back didn't seem so bad after all.

CHAPTER SIX

"I meant what I said," Levi told her while they enjoyed chicken and dumplings and snap beans. "I'll help you get up on a horse if you need me."

She almost snapped back that she'd never need him. But something in his words curled like a ribbon around her heart and tugged at her with a silky softness.

"I don't know if I'll be able to ride again."

"And why wouldn't you?" he asked while he buttered a huge slice of corn bread. "If your leg heals and you go through physical therapy, you should be okay."

"The doctor can't promise that. My fall was bad. He mentioned limited mobility or loss of mobility."

He put down his bread. The fear in her eyes made Levi think about how strong she was, how stubborn and determined she became when she set her mind on something. She'd have a hard time not being perfect. He also noticed how pretty she looked there with the sun streaming around her. Her hair shimmered like dark gold and her eyes sparkled like crystals. She was still prim and tiny, but he saw the steel in those eyes, and he saw the woman she'd become. Eliza would not accept being helpless in any way.

"What happened?" he asked.

"An old ladder out in the barn. I needed a basket and so I climbed it, knowing it was rickety and unstable. You know me—determined."

"I do know you," he said, his eyes on her. "But I want to get to know this you—the grown-up Lizzie."

She gave him a prim frown. "Why do you insist on calling me that?"

"You were my Lizzie once."

She moved her fork around her food. "Well, as you noticed, I'm grown now. I'm Eliza. I'm . . . I'm doing all right."

Then she looked down at her leg, propped on a chair. "Or at least I want to be Eliza again. I want to walk, and run, and ride my horses. That's what I want."

Levi finished his meal, then sat staring at her. "Then let me help you. Let me do whatever needs to be done to make you that strong, spirited Eliza again."

She gave him a surprised glance. "What could you do?"

"I can take you for long walks. Help you up on a horse. Make sure you do your exercises. Make sure you eat healthy and do what the doctors and therapists tell you to do. I can be here with you, Eliza. As a friend and a helper. Would that be all right with you?"

Eliza's eyes widened, her lips parted in a gasp, but nothing came out. For once, the woman was speechless.

Ah, the sweet silence of just sitting together.

Short-lived.

"I don't need your help."

"Who around here will help you then?"

Colette came back with refills for their tea and apple crisp for dessert, her gaze bouncing back and forth between the two of them with keen interest.

"There," she said, clearly not wanting to leave. "What else do you two need?"

"I need to go to the *haus*," Eliza said. But she didn't move.

"I need to have my head examined," Levi said. But he didn't move.

Colette frowned and then she smiled. "So finish your meal before it gets cold and then . . . continue on."

Levi waited a beat for Colette to leave the room; then he leaned over and started eating again. After he'd had a few bites, he drank some tea and sat back. "Everyone here is busy. Who will take you to therapy?"

"I'll call the taxi—the one that serves the Amish community. That's how Mamm got to the hospital and back when I was there for a week or so." She didn't want to remember those days. "Sometimes, *Englisch* friends gave her a ride, or Jonah would take her by buggy to the bus station. There are ways, you know."

"A taxi?" He rubbed his chin. "Will the driver help you in and out? Wait for you to finish? Buy you ice cream?"

He remembered she loved ice cream.

"I don't know," she said, twisting her corn bread into shreds. "I'll worry about that when I get my physical therapy schedule."

"If you let me help, I can fit it into my work schedule," he replied.

"You'll be busy, too, Levi," she retorted. "Working here, helping your *mamm*, going back and forth. I can't see you having much free time."

"My *mamm* lives on the other side of town, near the hospital."

"That doesn't help much."

"But I can drop you off at therapy, go see Mamm and help her with anything she needs, come back and pick you up, and have you home before suppertime."

"You've thought this out."

"*Ja*, I think about a lot of things when I'm working with the horses."

"Hmm."

"You don't like my idea."

"I have Mamm and Daed and Jonah and Colette, even Matthew or Henry. Henry has a car."

"But all of those people are busy. They have their jobs here, big or small. I can come and go since I'm my own boss."

"But I'm paying you for your time."

"I won't charge to take you to the doctor, Lizzie."

She looked affronted. "I wasn't offering to pay you. I told you, I'll be all right."

"Well, think about it." He spotted the apple crisp Colette had left on the table. "I don't mind at all. I'd like to spend time with you. Alone."

She lifted her head, her chin jutting out. Levi realized he'd said the wrong thing.

"I don't want to be alone with you, Levi. Not ever again."

Then she stood, stumbled, her eyes misting over. "I need to get back home. I'm tired."

He reached for her. "Lizzie?"

"*Neh*, don't call me Lizzie," she said, pushing him away. "Don't make plans on my behalf. You can't, Levi. We can't."

He watched as she struggled with her crutches. "You really can't forgive me, can you?"

Eliza stopped and stared over at him. "I've had a lot of time to think, too, about what happened that night. I wanted you to kiss me. I wanted you to hold me."

Shocked, Levi felt a thread of hope. "But?"

"But when you did, it frightened me, scared me, made me feel . . . not myself, as if I had no control."

"And you like to be in control," he said, understanding at last.

"*Ja*, I like things my way, in my own time, on my own

terms. It's a flaw, I know. We're taught that everything is in *Gott*'s own time, that He is the one in control."

Confused, Levi stared over at her and saw the fear in her eyes. "So you're not afraid of me—you're afraid that if you let go of your feelings and lose control, you will have sinned?"

"*Ja*, and I can't. I won't do that."

Colette, who always seemed to have perfect timing, came rushing back in. "Are you done then?"

She took one look at both of them and nodded. "I think you are. Eliza, I'll walk you to the cottage."

"*Denke*," Eliza said, her eyes on Levi. "I need to rest, and I'm sure Levi has work to do."

Colette sent him a questioning glance, but he didn't move. He couldn't. What had he done? Why had he gone and ruined things?

Finally, he said, "I do have plenty to keep me busy, and plenty to think about while I'm working."

Then he watched as Eliza hobbled away on her crutches, her sister hovering in a protective manner beside her.

Levi sank down on the chair and held his head in his hands, his prayers scattered and incoherent. Had he been wrong to take on work here, in the one place he should have stayed away from?

Then he felt a hand on his shoulder.

He looked up to find Eliza's father staring down at him.

"Ain't it 'bout time you and I had a talk, young Levi?"

Levi nodded, his stomach burning with shame and regret.

"I'm ready."

Colette waited as Eliza managed to get herself up the porch steps. Eliza stopped, caught her breath, and sank onto one of the hickory rocking chairs lined with floral cushions.

"Sister, are you okay?" Colette asked in a kind way.

"Do I look that bad?" she retorted. "Because you actually sound worried."

"I am worried," Colette said. "What happened back there?"

Eliza held her head with one hand. "I confessed something to Levi I never wanted to admit."

"And what was that?"

She glanced around to make sure no one was about. "I never realized why I panicked that night—the night Levi kissed me."

"You panicked over a kiss? I thought it was more."

"I thought it was more, too," Eliza said. "I'd never kissed a boy before, so I wasn't sure what to expect. I mean, I'd read books, but it's different when it's real and it's me kissing a boy."

"So did you like the kiss or hate the kiss?"

"Both," she admitted, her heart hammering like a beating drum. "I wanted to kiss Levi, and then when it happened, I felt so many things, confusing things, forbidden things."

Colette lifted her gaze and stared into Eliza's eyes. "You felt . . . desire?"

Eliza bobbed her head. "Only I didn't know what that was at the time. How could I know?"

"How could any woman know?" Colette said. "Mamm told us about how babies come, but she never explained much about falling in love. We saw that with Jonah and Abby. You remember?"

"I'll never forget," Eliza said. "It's a longing that is a puzzle, a hurt that makes you feel good, a need that you can't explain. Do you feel like that with Matthew?"

Colette tugged at her *kapp* strings. "I might. I mean, I could. Matthew is shy and he's never tried . . . to kiss me."

Eliza was almost glad to hear that. "Being attracted to someone sure changes your whole perspective on love and life and the birds and the bees."

Colette smiled, and then she started giggling.

"You find this funny?"

Her sister sank down on a stool beside the rocking chair and took Eliza's hand. "Well, the birds and bees just get on with their courtships. I think humans should do the same."

"But it's frightening, these wild feelings," Eliza said. "It makes me understand why Abby snuck out at night to go see Jonah."

"But they didn't—"

"I know that. He was respectful and Abby showed restraint. But sister, what if . . . I couldn't show restraint?" She shrugged. "Remember how Deborah Buell walked out with a boy and then she was taken away to live with her widowed *aenti* because she was pregnant?" Shivering, she said, "I don't want to have to live with Aenti Miriam."

"Nobody wants that," Colette agreed with a grimace.

Their *aenti* tended to be overly judgmental and bitter in a big way.

"You won't have to do that because you're smarter and more cautious than Deborah Buell. That girl flirted with any boy who looked at her straight."

"I've only ever kissed one boy," Eliza said. "I blame him and myself, and now . . . he's back and being nice to me. I don't like it."

"Well, we've already established that you aren't so much mad at Levi as you are confused. Maybe you should talk to Mamm about this."

"About what?"

They turned to find their mother standing inside the

screened door of the cottage, her hands on her hips and her eyes on her daughters.

"Someone better tell me why you're out here deciding if you should talk to me."

Levi watched as Abe brought the coffeepot to the table and poured two cups. Then Abe slid Eliza's untouched apple crisp over and picked up the fork Colette had left on the dish and started eating.

"This is *gut*, ain't so?"

Levi stared down at his half-eaten dessert, his appetite gone now. His stomach roiled and burned. He'd hurt Eliza yet again. "It tasted fine."

"So why do you look like you swallowed a pickle?" Abe asked in his quiet, formidable way.

"Because your middle daughter hates me," Levi retorted, his tone almost a croak.

"Oh, that. I see." Abe gave Levi a glance that showed he did indeed see just about everything. "Does she have reason to hate you?"

Levi felt the piercing heat of a father's love and wrath. "I kissed your daughter once long ago and it went bad. I made a mistake and now . . . she will never forgive me."

Abe nodded, his dark eyes flaring for a brief moment. "Did you mean to do harm to my Eliza?"

"*Neh*, I only wanted to kiss her because I cared for her and wanted her to be my wife one day."

Abe let Levi's words settle for a couple of beats. "Did she agree to this kiss?"

"She seemed to, but then we both got confused and . . . she slugged me in my midsection and told me never to do that again."

Abe lowered his head. "That does sound like Eliza. She

likes to be the one in control of any situation, but she should not have reacted in such a violent way. Unless you deserved such action."

Levi stared into Abe's wise eyes. "She just told me that right here at this table—told me she likes to be in control and that she had some sort of panic attack, a fear of being kissed. She got mad all over again because I offered to help her while her leg is healing. She refused me and said she didn't want to be alone with me."

"And now you are frustrated and even more confused."

Levi grunted, feeling sixteen again. "*Ja.*"

Abe finished his meal, his manner so calm, Levi couldn't tell if he was angry or not.

Finally, Abe said, "I can only tell you that women need to be needed, and women need to have some sort of control over their lives. We follow certain rules in our faith, guidelines that teach a man to honor his wife, and also teach a woman to honor her husband. There are some within the community who don't do that, but instead, use *Gott*'s word and the Bible to control each other. I don't believe you are a cruel or unkind man, Levi. I believe you and Eliza were not ready for the kissing part of your walking-out time."

"I reckon you're right there. I messed up, didn't I?"

"You made a mistake, a miscalculation. And then you walked away. You left."

"Another mistake?"

"Could be."

"So she's angry that I crossed a line and now she's angry because I left?"

"Could be."

"Does she hate me?"

Abe stood and smiled. "Eliza harbors no hate in her heart. She is kind and sweet, but she has her own ways.

She had to figure this out for herself. My advice to you is this—stay the course. Don't push but don't walk away, because leaving again will only hurt her more."

"But Abe, she doesn't want to be around me."

"Then don't be around her. Just be near her."

"And you are giving me your blessings."

"*Neh*, I'm giving you a chance to make up for your mistakes, and to show my daughter you have the best of intentions toward her."

"That's a tall order," Levi said, standing.

"But it will be worth the trouble, *ja*?"

Levi had his doubts, not about Eliza being worth the trouble, but about his being able to pull this off. He nodded all the same. He was talking to Eliza's father, after all. "I will do my best."

Abe seemed pleased with that response. "Women are a constant mystery, Levi. That's part of the fun."

"I'm not really having fun," Levi said as they walked toward the stables.

Jonah came out and waved to them, and they walked over to join him. Then they got into a lively discussion on the merits of marriage, family, and life.

Levi finished his day in a better mood. He'd shoed two horses and cleaned up his workspace. He wouldn't want tidy Eliza to complain about any messiness in her stables.

He knew what he had to do to win Eliza's heart.

He had to go big and court her in a proper way, show her he had staying power no matter how she acted. She was a lot like her beloved animals. Timid but tough, afraid but with courage, a bit skittish, and always ready to lash out at anyone who messed with her.

Just be near her.

He'd have to go with Abe's advice for now.

CHAPTER SEVEN

"Eliza needs to discuss something with you," Colette blurted to their mother. "I'll go start supper."

Mamm glanced from Eliza back to Colette. "I have a pot roast in the oven and creamed corn on the stove."

"I'll check on it and slice the roast then."

Colette, ever the domestic daughter.

That left Eliza sitting there with her hands in her lap.

Mamm sat down on the stool Colette had left spinning.

"Eliza, you look *baremlich*. Are you in pain? Does your leg hurt?"

Eliza knew she must look terrible, her hair falling down, her skin shimmering with sweat. But she refused to cry. She was alive and had a family who loved her. She'd focused on those blessings for years, but now she doubted herself . . . and her true feelings.

"I don't know."

"Talk to me," Mamm said in a soft, soothing voice.

Eliza could no longer hold back. "I'm upset with Levi."

Mamm's gentle expression turned into the same kind of face Eliza had seen on a mad hen. "What has he done?"

"Nothing." Eliza didn't want to get Levi in trouble. "He

offered to drive me back and forth to my upcoming therapy sessions."

"That was kind of him," Mamm said, relaxing a bit. "So why are you upset?"

"He said it would be nice to be alone with me."

"*Ach vell*, I see." Her mother took her hand. "You're still not ready for that, ain't so?"

"I might not ever be ready for that," Eliza admitted. "It went so wrong last time."

"Because of the *schmunzla*?"

"Definitely because of the kissing," Eliza replied. "We broke up over a kiss—something that's supposed to bring people together."

Mamm nodded. "I understand. Eliza, you realize kissing men is okay as long as you respect yourself and our faith, *ja*?"

"*Ja*." She was acting like a young schoolgirl. And after all the sweet love stories she'd read, too. Maybe her problem had been depending on books to learn about falling in love, rather than getting accustomed to the real thing.

"That's why I ended the kiss and our . . . time together," she explained. "I felt so out of control, uncomfortable, and almost sick. *Daremlich*." Dizzy. The same way she felt now.

Mamm nodded again. "All of those feelings are normal when you're falling in love, Eliza."

"I didn't think I was *that* in love." But hearing the truth from her *mamm* made Eliza feel much better. She mustered up her next question. "Did you and Daed kiss a lot?"

Mamm smiled, her eyes going dreamy. "We didn't at first, mind you. He was older and I was afraid in the same way you sound afraid. But your father was gentle and patient, and by the time we had our first chaste kiss, I was already in love with him."

"You didn't deck him?"

Mamm looked confused. "I wish you wouldn't repeat Jonah's *Englisch* words."

"I decked Levi. I mean, I punched him in the stomach."

Mamm put a hand to her mouth and let out a giggle. "And yet, he's back here trying to make amends."

Eliza nodded. "He kissed me and I . . . kissed him. I've blamed him for so long when really he did nothing wrong."

Then Mamm turned serious. "You have every right to defend and protect yourself if a man is trying anything you feel uncomfortable with—I mean anything from going too fast in a buggy, to drinking alcohol, abusing you in a physical way, or touching you in a way that makes you feel uncomfortable. Never forget that."

Eliza nodded. "It wasn't like that with Levi. I fully participated in the kiss, Mamm, and . . . I liked kissing him. We both messed up and panicked. He left town and I turned to my animals and books. It was a fine arrangement until he came back."

"*Ach*, so you'd rather dream of Levi in your head and wonder what might have been than see him in the flesh and think about what could happen now?"

Eliza didn't like the way this conversation was going. "I want nothing to do with him now. Why can't I make him and everyone else understand that?"

Mamm's expression remained serene and neutral, her most infuriating expression in Eliza's mind. "I think what you need to know is that finding a soul mate, a helpmate, a husband, is one of the joys of life. You are wise to be aware of the powerful feelings love can arouse, almost every emotion you'll ever feel—joy, hurt, happiness, anger, fear, courage, longing, desire, acceptance and awareness, and so much more."

Eliza didn't know how to respond. She'd surely felt

most of those feelings every time she was near Levi Lapp. Even now.

"What should I do?"

Mamm smiled and stood, then offered her hand to help Eliza up. Eliza didn't mind putting her hand in Mamm's. Mamm had the strongest, softest hands.

"I think," Mamm said as they moved inside, "you should just be near Levi. Just let him do his work. Don't try so much to ignore him, because we all know you're not doing a very *gut* job of that, and this is just his first day at work here." Mamm glanced out toward the stables and the lake beyond. "If he's back to stay, you and he have all the time in the world to get reacquainted, to decide how you want things to be between you."

"Fall will last forever," Eliza lamented while she hobbled to the sofa. "I will learn to ignore him better."

"Fall will shift to winter, and I'm thinking your strong feelings for Levi Lapp, both *gut* and bad, will shift, too."

"I don't think so."

"Eliza," Mamm said with a sigh, "patience is a virtue. Just be patient and thankful we've found a man who knows his work, a man who was willing to come help us, despite these mixed-up feelings he has for you."

Eliza shook her head as she dropped onto the sofa seat. "I don't think he has feelings for me. He only wants forgiveness so he can keep his job."

Mamm looked at Colette, who been watching with eager eyes, and shrugged. "I tried." Then she turned away from Colette and back to Eliza. "Wait. I have a solution. I know what you need to do."

Both of her daughters lifted their heads. Hope filled Eliza's heart. Could she avoid the stables? Go visiting far away? What had Mamm decided?

"You will make a quilt—a forgiving quilt."

That was not the solution she had expected.

"I don't like making quilts."

"Eliza?"

Guilt colored Eliza's face. She shouldn't have snapped at Mamm. "Why, Mamm? Why would I want to make a quilt?"

"Remember how Abigail handled her confusing feelings for Jonah? She made a quilt to show his memories and really, to show her feelings for him. It's all there, and it tells a story."

Colette's eyes flared with excitement. "You can do this, Eliza. Each time he does something nice for you, you put it on the quilt."

"That will take all fall!"

Mamm smiled and placed her hands together, beaming at a job well done. "Exactly." Then she clapped her hands. "Now let's get the meal on the table. Daed will be here soon."

"I can't wait to tell Abigail," Colette said. "She'll help you and so will I. This is the best idea."

"And I'm sure I'll be available," Mamm said. "As well as Aenti Miriam."

Eliza looked up in shock, until she saw the twinkle in her mother's eyes. Then they all burst out laughing.

Colette shrugged. "I was really looking forward to that showdown."

"It might happen yet," Mamm said. "She's planning to come here in October and stay for the Harvest Festival."

A few days later, Levi walked into the modest farmhouse his *mamm* still lived in. The neat ranch-style house was long and narrow but had three bedrooms and a washroom. His *daed* had kept the place up and built a root cellar they used to store food and where the family could hide if a tornado came up. The kitchen was to the right of the front door and a big living room was on the left, with propane lamps in each corner. It still hurt to walk in and not find his *daed* sitting in his rocking chair reading either the Bible or *The Budget* newspaper.

But as usual, he found his *mamm* in the kitchen, cooking over the old stove. "Levi, you're just in time. Go wash up and by the time you get back, supper will be ready. I've made smothered pork chops with rice, field peas, and biscuits."

Levi grinned. "I am hungry, for certain sure."

He passed James, or Jamie as they called him, when he went down the hall toward the room that served as a laundry room and bathroom. Jamie sat at a small desk in his room, reading.

"*Bruder*, what have you learned today?"

Jamie squinted through his glasses. "I'm studying improvements in agriculture. We need a tractor."

Levi had heard this kind of talk before. At fourteen, Jamie had big dreams and big ideas. "And we also need money to buy that tractor." Then he ruffled Jamie's dark, thick hair. "Wash up for supper."

Jamie nodded, and without looking back up, said, "*Gut* to have you home, Levi."

Levi was glad to be here.

They could use a decent tractor, but in accordance with the Amish tenet that members must avoid anything fancy from the *Englisch* world, they could only drive the tractor on dirt, not the road. Having a used, stripped-down machine would help with their small acreage. Daed had planted corn, beans, tomatoes, greens, and peas in the spring, then in fall, turnips, broccoli, and cabbage, along with other fall crops.

That produce, along with the hunting they did, provided food for them all year long.

Mamm sewed dresses and aprons for Amish women to bring in her own cash. She had been patiently teaching his twelve-year-old sister, Laura, how to sew, too.

Laura came rushing up the hallway, her coppery hair braided and pinned up. "Levi, John-boy is so big now. You need to see him."

"I'll check on your goat after supper," he replied, tugging at her *kapp* string. His siblings were all grown-up now. He'd missed out on so much, including helping his *daed*. Though his *daed* had encouraged Levi to strike out, the guilt Levi felt at leaving home stayed with him day and night. No one knew just how sick his father had become, and once they learned, it was too late.

How could he ever have thought he'd find something better out in the world than what he had right here? The only saving grace was that now he could help here at home and do his farrier work, too. That would bring in extra income so Mamm could rest more.

He finished washing up, his mind considering the guilt he carried like a heavy anvil. He'd come home for so many reasons, but he didn't know if Eliza could be one of them. She wasn't comfortable around him. She did not want to be alone with him. Didn't she know he'd never do anything to hurt her?

Then he remembered Abe's suggestion.

Just be near her.

Would being near her help both of them or make things worse? Well, he really had no choice in the matter. He needed the job and he needed to become grounded in the Shadow Lake community again. So far, he'd managed to focus on work rather than Eliza. Since he had other jobs, he'd only seen her two times this week.

Two awkward times, but he had to admit it was nice to be around her again.

Mamm watched him as he entered the kitchen, her dark eyes bright with interest. "How did your day at the inn go?"

He let out a huff of breath. "Workwise, not bad. I like Jonah and I love the inn. That always was a peaceful, beautiful place, up on the bluffs by the lake."

"And what else?" Mamm's eyebrows lifted. "Have you talked to Eliza at all?"

He could never hide anything from his diminutive but fierce mother. "Now that's another story," he said. "Maybe we can talk some after supper."

"I'd love nothing more," Mamm said. "Let us eat."

The gentleness in her eyes countered the hint of worry he saw there. His *mamm* wasn't that old, but losing her beloved Linden had aged her considerably. Levi wanted to make things right for her, but how could he do that when he couldn't even make things right with the girl he'd thought he'd be married to by now?

How could he get this anvil off his chest once and for all?

Chapter Eight

"John-boy is a healthy billy goat," Levi told his sister an hour later as he and his siblings went to finish their chores. "He's done his job around here."

Laura made a face. "Mamm explained that to me. I want no part of it. I'll just wait for the kids to arrive. They are so adorable when they dance and play."

"Probably for the best," Levi said with a chuckle. He was glad Daed had spared John-boy from being sold off or slaughtered at a young age. Laura had taken to the goat the day he was born. Now he was the big buck of the goat pens.

And a constant pain in the neck. The mature buck liked to jump the fence and run wild. But Laura could always find him and bring him home, a rope loosely tied around John-boy's neck.

"He's glad you have returned," Laura said as they fed, watered, and checked on all the livestock. They had two milking cows, as well as two nanny goats that had both had kids and were now in their prime milking years.

Levi liked living off the land, and he also loved being able to keep horses shod and safe so they could do their jobs, too.

Eliza knew her horses well, and he appreciated that she loved animals as much as he did. He appreciated a lot of things about Eliza.

While he and Laura separated the kids from the two nannies—Peony and Rosie—so Laura would be able to milk the does in the morning, Jamie took care of the cows and chickens.

Then Levi stood at the back fence in the same way Daed used to do and watched the sun setting over the trees to the west where Shadow Lake lay nestled near the bigger Lake Erie. Where Eliza was probably just finishing her supper.

Would he be able to do this? Work near her and not pester her? Could he hide his feelings for her? Could he do what he needed to do to provide for his family, and to seek forgiveness? He needed forgiveness for more than just a kiss.

He really needed forgiveness for leaving after that kiss. For deserting his family and the life he'd had here in Shadow Lake. But he'd gained a whole new perspective upon returning here. This was home. He wasn't running away again.

Laura came up and laid her hand on his forearm. "Are you glad to be home, Levi?"

"So very glad, sister." He patted her hand. "We'd best get in and get washed up and ready for quiet time."

Laura bobbed her head. "I have a new book to read."

"That's gut."

"Mamm has mending to do."

"Always."

"Jamie draws, writes, and studies. He's so smart."

"You're smart, too."

Then Laura said something that hit him in the stomach.

"I hope you and Eliza get back together. She used to sit with me when I was little. I miss that."

Levi turned to his sister, surprised she remembered Eliza. "I miss that, too, but it might not work out between Eliza and me."

"It will if it's *Gott*'s will, Levi."

Then his wise little sister turned and skipped back to the house, leaving Levi to watch the sun disappearing behind the foothills and bluffs, allowing the sky to shine in deep blues and vivid pinks and creamy yellows before the gloaming hit the fields and valleys.

Just be near her.

It will if it's Gott's will.

What more could he do but be still and wait?

Eliza was tired of being still.

She'd always been restless, needing movement and action to keep her content. She could sit and read a whole book, but then she'd get up and clean her room, scrub down the hallway floors, or bake a pie.

Her sisters did much the same, but their energy came from doing domestic tasks. They enjoyed them, while she went through them out of duty.

There was another difference between Eliza and her sisters. An *Englischer* who returned to the inn year after year had once told her, "Eliza, you are just not a people person."

Truer words had never been spoken. People made her uncomfortable and nervous. She wasn't timid, but she enjoyed solitude and her alone time. Even as a child, she'd find places to hide so she could read or watch the birds out over the water or gaze at the clouds and imagine them in any way she chose.

But once she'd found her way to the stables with Daed, she knew where her best work would be—with Samson and the rest of the horses. She loved the milk cows and the few goats they had, but the horses had always been her favorites.

Now she missed jumping up on Samson and riding him around the hillsides and pastures or taking him down to the shore to give him a workout.

Sitting and watching life go by was not easy.

But Mamm wanted her to begin a quilt. Ugh.

She'd always helped make quilts out of duty, nothing more. Though she admired the handiwork, Eliza never had the urge to create her own quilt. But the idea was out there now, and she'd have to make the effort or look like a dolt. No man would want a woman who couldn't quilt. Not that she needed a husband to complete her, but she'd never say that out loud. What was it about squares of old material being pieced together that seemed to draw women together?

Was it to impress their friends? Or maybe the memories created by friendship and laughing and remembering with each stitch, the way Abigail had helped Jonah remember?

But she had to make a quilt to forgive a man, not in the hope of marrying him. Once, she'd dreamed of marriage. What young girl didn't?

Now, she was content. Well, she *had* been content until Levi had walked not only back into her life, but into her stables of all places.

She could still be content.

Yet here she sat on her cushioned bench, inside the stables, watching as Jonah and Levi performed their daily chores.

Two weeks had gone by, and she hadn't talked to Levi directly since that day in the kitchen when he'd offered to take her to her appointments and physical therapy.

Her next checkup with Dr. Merrill was at the end of the following week. Would Levi offer to go with her? Other than a wave and a smile, he'd managed to ignore her all week. She had asked for that, of course.

Reminding herself she had to come up with some quilt squares for the next quilting frolic, Eliza pulled out the sketch pad Abigail had given her. Abigail loved to draw and doodle, and she was gifted at applying what she'd drawn to her quilt patterns.

Eliza stared at the blank white paper and let out a sigh.

She was so deep into seeing nothing, she jumped when a small red porcelain pot filled with yellow mums appeared in front of her nose.

"What?" She glanced up with a glare to find Levi standing there, his hand extending the pretty fall flowers.

"For you," he said. "My *mamm* sent it." Shrugging, he went on. "She heard about your fall and your surgery."

Eliza took the plant and touched the bright flowers. "That was thoughtful."

"My *mamm* is a thoughtful person."

"And you are the delivery person."

"Of course." He gave her a look that hovered between longing and reluctance. "I have to get back to work. Pickles— the shy one—does not like getting new shoes. And here I thought all women loved new shoes."

Eliza actually laughed. "I have boots and sneakers—in every color."

"I've noticed," he replied, giving her a tip of his hat.

So no asking her to talk to him, no telling her he was truly sorry, no offers to help her in any way. *Gut*. He'd learned how to let her avoid him. He'd also learned how to avoid her.

Sort of.

Eliza sat with the cute cluster of potted mums in her

hands, trying to ignore the confusion slipping through her thoughts. They'd actually had a decent conversation with a bit of flirtation. She bit back a full smile. Then she placed the mums by her side and sketched out a very primitive rendition of the lush yellow flowers with bright red centers. Abby would help her fill in the colors and shapes.

This would become the first panel of her quilt. A small bouquet of brilliant flowers, given to her in a kind gesture from Levi and his *mamm*.

She'd accepted, because, well, she liked Levi's *mamm*. And his siblings. He came from a nice family.

Eliza glanced up from studying the mums as if her life depended on it and saw Levi looking at her. The minute their eyes met, he turned and went back to work.

There. There it was. The look in his eyes before he'd pivoted indicated he might have finally taken the hint and given up on asking for her forgiveness.

There went the quilt idea, too. She'd have to break the news to Mamm and her sisters before they got their hopes up. And she'd ignore the trace of disappointment buried in a hidden spot within her heart.

It was better this way. Maybe being still could work to her advantage after all. But being still also meant being alone and lonely.

"You still need to make the quilt."

"Mamm, please." Eliza had explained how Levi had been avoiding her, not speaking to her, mostly just coming to work and going home. He wasn't asking for forgiveness or anything else. So what was the point of a quilt?

"Don't *please* at me," her mother said that night after supper. "This is a *gut* way to learn forgiveness and also to ask for forgiveness, Eliza."

Eliza's neck stiffened. "I don't need to ask for forgiveness."

"I think there could be some on both sides," Mamm replied as they finished the dishes. "Now let's sit down and see what panels you have so far."

Eliza gathered with her sisters in the living room, a pout plastered on her face. Daed and Jonah were out on the porch discussing the weather, as usual. There was a definite crispness in the air.

About as crisp as the exchanges between her and Levi now that he'd taken her seriously and was leaving her alone.

Abigail and Colette stared at her, waiting.

"Well," Colette said, impatient. "Let's see what Levi did to try and win you over."

"He hasn't done a whole lot," she replied, kind of mad about that. "He gave me the mums that are in the kitchen window."

"So pretty, and they will grow and flourish. You'll need a bigger pot." Colette was always so optimistic.

Abby nodded. "That's an easy panel with an easy pattern." She glanced at the red pot in the window, and in about ten seconds had drawn the pot and flowers and handed the sketch back to Eliza. "You'll only need a square for the pot and some circles for the flowers. Then half circles for the blossoms. That will make a passable resemblance of his peace offering."

"It wasn't from him. His *mamm* sent it."

"Right," Colette said with a smirk. "His *mamm* sent it."

"She might have," Mamm said, giving them all the Mamm look. "But he delivered the potted mums with a flourish, so that is a great start to your quilt, Eliza."

Eliza's sweet feelings for Levi deflated. "He tricked me."

"He did not," Colette said. "He delivered a gift from his *mamm* and . . . from him. It's nice."

"Nice." She let that word roll around her mind. "He never once asked me to forgive him."

"Sometimes being nice is an indication that a person has gotten over the past," Abigail replied.

The mums were nice. They added to the brightness of the kitchen, and they'd work great in the big basket out on the front porch. The basket she'd had to find, the basket that had caused her to fall down the ladder so she must now endure being around Levi almost every day.

"*Ja*, so nice."

She wanted to pout but that would be immature. Instead, she thought of ways she could be nice to Levi and give him a taste of his own medicine.

"It's well over his two-week probation period, and you haven't sent him away," Colette pointed out. "So you'd better get going on that quilt."

Abigail nodded. "Jonah says he's the best help you've had in the stables. He has no problem with Levi continuing to do our farrier work."

"I guess I don't either," she admitted. "The horses are happy and healthy and we're getting the daily work done much faster now."

Mamm clapped her hands together. "*Gut*. I like a calm stable, and I'm sure your father will be happy to know things are settling down."

"Okay, I'll make the quilt but that doesn't mean Levi and I will become all chummy."

She'd add her own kind deeds to the quilt, too, to prove that she'd taken the high road and treated him in a gracious way.

That would be nice all the way around. And it would prove she could be forgiving, too.

Even though she still thought she didn't need forgiving.

CHAPTER NINE

"Are you going to sit there all day?"

Levi watched Eliza's face, probably looking for signs of a tantrum. She refused to give him the satisfaction. And she also refused to be nice about it. She had been waiting on the porch for someone to *kumm* and take her to her checkup. Anyone but him. Why did everyone else suddenly have important things to do?

"I don't want you to be my driver."

"You have no choice," he reminded her. "As fate would have it, your *mamm* has a birthing, and your sisters are busy with the early leaf-lookers, so they can't help or spare anyone to help. Your father is unable to take you all the way to the hospital and besides, he wants to stay here to oversee the gathering of the final fall harvest—apples, corn, turnips, cabbage, and your favorite, brussels sprouts. And Jonah has to oversee just about everything else."

He stopped to give her a calm, steady stare.

"I don't care for brussels sprouts."

"*Ach*, she speaks."

"I can speak, and I don't need you to chaperon my trip to the doctor."

"So you'll walk?"

"I can call a cab."

"I won't let you go alone. I promised your *mamm*."

This was a trap. Her mother wanted them together, obviously. So all that forgiveness that neither of them really needed could be given.

If she agreed and just got it over with, would everyone leave her alone?

"I suppose since I don't have a choice, you can come with me. But do not bother me."

"I won't be a bother at all. You won't even know I'm there."

She doubted that. Levi was hard to ignore. He'd become a big, strapping man, strong and muscled. Not that she'd been ogling him, of course.

"Do you want me to drive you in the buggy?"

She thought about that. "It might be quicker to call a cab, but it is a *wunderbar gut* day."

The air was crisp and fresh, with a hint of late fall. October had arrived and soon and the Harvest Festival would come, then on to Thanksgiving and Christmas. He knew the inn was always decorated to reflect each holiday.

"I checked the map. It's ten miles to the hospital where Dr. Merrill has an office. I can make that easy with Sunshine and Rosebud."

He stopped, staring at her again. Then he let out a sigh. "But we'd be alone, and you don't want to be alone with me."

Eliza tried to show kindness, even if her heart was pounding like a hammer against an anvil. He did sound rather dejected, almost melancholy. "I think a cab would be better. I will need help getting in and out, if you don't mind." He smiled at that. "I don't mind one bit. I finished early today, so I have time to take you."

"So you planned ahead?"

"I planned just in case," he replied. "You don't need to overthink every action I take, Lizzie."

"Don't I?"

"Are we going to argue all day, or do you want to get to the doctor so you can get that cast off?"

She did want the cast off. She hated it with every breath she took. It was hard, itchy, and ugly and . . . she sounded like a big baby. But she was afraid of what she would find when her leg was free again.

"I want it off, and if it takes you getting me there, then I will go. By taxi."

"I'll go into the inn and have Henry call one for us. Are you ready?"

"*Ja*." She wasn't ready to spend the rest of the day with him. Mamm usually escorted her to the checkups. But Mamm had a busy life, too. Would it hurt to spend a little time with Levi?

She glanced around and didn't see anybody coming to her rescue. So she allowed Levi to help her down the porch steps and across to the portico on the back section of the inn, where taxis came and went to accommodate guests who'd flown in to see the fall colors.

He settled her and her crutches in one of the high-backed rocking chairs that were coveted by all the guests because they provided a perfect view of the bluffs and the lake.

Eliza had never actually sat here, rocking. Even with her stiff leg, it was relaxing and beautiful. She lived in a lovely place, but she had taken it for granted before her accident. Now she couldn't wait to roam around the grounds again and enjoy life.

Every part of it except for the man waiting with her.

Levi decided to stand. Then he leaned against one of the broad round columns holding the porch up. Then he settled against the sturdy white railings lining the long porch. Skittish, restless, nervous.

Same as she felt. Eliza was glad others had gathered on the porch this morning. An older couple holding hands while they both rocked to the same rhythm. A young mother and a toddler.

The little blond boy giggled and pointed. "Leaf, leaf."

"Lots of leaves," his pretty mother said. "We'll play in them when Daddy comes."

"Daddy?"

"He'll be here soon."

Eliza's heart did a bump and longing filled her soul. Would she sit with a child here one day, explaining the changing leaves to him or her?

She looked up to find Levi studying her, then quickly glanced down the lane, searching for the cab.

Suddenly wishing she'd canceled her appointment after all.

Because she wasn't sure she wanted Levi there when the doctor told her whether or not her leg had healed properly.

What if it hadn't?

"Are you nervous?"

Levi could feel her apprehension lasering around the compact taxi. He'd never known Eliza to be afraid or fearful, and right now, he wanted to hold her hand and comfort her.

But that would be a big mistake. He'd done his level best to avoid her for days now, but when her *mamm* had pulled him aside after he'd just finished work and asked if he'd been serious about taking Eliza to the doctor, he'd readily agreed.

"I appreciate this, Levi," Sarah had told him. "I have to go to the Mast house. Twins, and they are coming fast. Much as I wanted to, I can't go with Eliza today."

"I'll take care of her," he'd promised Sarah. "If she'll let me."

Sarah had laughed at that. "I wish you the best on that."

Now here he sat, riding in the back of this cab with the one person he'd tried so hard to stay away from.

She glanced over after his question. "What do I have to be nervous about? Just this leg and whether it will work properly or not."

Levi tried to comfort her. "Getting that cast off should be exciting. You'll be able to move around more and get back to doing the things you love."

She nodded, one hand grasping the loose strings of her *kapp*. "*Ja*, I can't wait."

He tried a different tactic—getting her riled. "Well, try to stay calm. You're just all sunshine and happiness. It's getting on my nerves."

She glared at him, the heat in her eyes overtaking the fear he'd seen there before. "I am fine. I told you I could do this on my own."

"You don't want to be around me ever, right?"

"*Neh*, not ever. Well, maybe just not today. I wish Mamm could have come with me. Or maybe Abby."

"Eliza, do you think I'd do anything to upset you today of all days?"

She studied him in her Eliza way. Direct and right on target. "I should hope not."

"I'm going to get you where you need to be, and I'll be waiting for you when you're finished. And then, we'll find some ice cream. Do you still like a chocolate-vanilla mix?"

Eliza's worried expression changed to an awestruck smile. "You remembered?"

"How could I forget?"

Eliza settled in her seat. Then she turned to glance at him again. "I'm afraid, Levi."

"Afraid of what?" he asked, hoping it wasn't him. He didn't want her to be afraid of him. He'd never known this woman to be fearful of anything.

"Afraid my leg will not work the way I want."

Well, she had a right to worry, and he couldn't reassure her because he didn't have the answers. Instead, he'd try to distract her.

"You'll have therapy. The doctors know what they're doing, Eliza. And Dr. Merrill made sure you had the best orthopedic surgeon in the area. Your *daed* told me that."

"*Ja*, Dr. Merrill had been *wunderbar gut* to me. He'll be here today with Dr. Crane. They'll tell me the next step."

She giggled. "The next step—literally."

Levi laughed with her, glad to see her smile. "You made a joke. That's a positive sign."

"I'm still nervous," she said. "I don't usually get the jitters, but then I've never had a broken bone or surgery until now. I guess I can mark both off as not much fun at all."

"I know I can't go in there with you since I'm not family," Levi said. "But I'll be waiting right outside. And then, no matter what, ice cream."

She nodded, her eyes getting misty. "*Denke*, Levi." She glanced out the window. "It's nice to have you with me."

Levi lifted his eyebrows. "So . . . you're beginning to like me again, maybe a little bit?"

She smiled and held her thumb and forefinger a fraction apart. "Maybe this much."

He laughed at that. "I'll take it."

By the time they'd made it to the hospital, they were laughing and talking about her being able to ride again.

"I can beat you," she said as the cab pulled up to the drop-off doors of the towering building.

"I can still ride a horse, Eliza."

"I can still beat you in a horse race, Levi." Then she whispered, "But Mamm frowns on that, so we can't let her find out."

Levi nodded and paid the driver, then came around to help her out. After she had her crutches in the right positions, he walked with her into the hospital and got her to the proper waiting area.

When the nurse called her in, Levi stood. "I'll be right here, remember?"

"I'll remember." She gave him one more futile glance back, her fear still there, back, then disappeared behind the double doors.

And he became the nervous one. He couldn't handle seeing her in pain or afraid. She might not appreciate his concern, but he couldn't help worrying.

He prayed everything would work out. If not, Eliza would be devastated.

But he'd still be here to help her get through it.

"So, Eliza, how does the leg feel?"

Eliza looked up at Dr. Crane, who stood tall like a real crane, and then back to Dr. Merrill who was not as tall, but a strong force in her life. Dr. Crane and an assistant had just sawed her cast off. Her leg felt chilly in the cool hospital air.

"It feels light and free," she said, sitting on the examining table. "But how will it feel when I put weight on it?"

"You'll need to use the crutches for a while yet," Dr. Crane explained. "If it hurts too much to put weight on your leg and you try anyway, it will swell, and you'll have to go back to staying off the leg for a while."

That didn't sound promising. She'd hoped she'd be able to walk out of here without the aggravating crutches. "Can I give it a try?"

"That's next," Dr. Crane said. "Let me help you off the table."

"I'm ready." She took a breath. She wasn't really ready, but she was glad to be free of that cast.

Carefully, he held her arm as she slid off the paper-covered table. "Lift your foot up slowly so we can gauge the extent of your pain."

Eliza did as he'd instructed. Dr. Merrill held her on the other side. She didn't know whether to laugh or cry. This was a big moment.

"Okay," Dr. Crane said. "Lower your leg slowly and tell me how it feels once your foot hits the floor."

Having the cast off made her feel disoriented, but she did as he'd suggested and tried to get her balance. Then she pressed her foot down on the floor.

And pain shot through her leg. "Ouch. That's not pleasant."

"It'll take some time," Dr. Merrill told her. "Patience and time, plus your therapy sessions."

Dr. Crane let her stand on her own but stayed close by. "You might walk with a limp on that left leg for a while. You'll feel strange and probably swing your hip to avoid the pain."

That didn't sound good.

"But try to learn how to straighten your leg again, slowly and without forcing it. You don't want to do any new damage to it."

"*Neh*, no damage. I've had enough of that."

"Okay, then. Put your full weight on the left leg."

Eliza slowly lowered her leg, but the minute her foot touched the floor, she wobbled and cried out. "That hurts."

Dr. Crane glanced at Dr. Merrill. "It will take time, Eliza. But you can do this. I'm going to give you a cane to help you keep your balance while your leg is getting back to normal."

"Why is it hurting?" she asked, wishing she could walk normally again.

Dr. Merrill helped her to a chair. "Your leg has been through a trauma, and so have you. The body is an amazing thing. It can heal but that healing starts in your brain, where you tell yourself you can do this. I know you're worried about having a limp, and you will for a while. But one day, you'll wake up and you'll be walking normally again."

"Are you sure?" she asked, feeling like a baby.

"We're positive," Dr. Crane assured her. "Your mother has some amazing salves and lotions that you can use on your leg to help it heal more quickly. And I'll give you an instruction sheet on your therapy and your at-home exercises. Do the work to help your leg heal."

"I will." She didn't mind hard work. She wanted to be able to walk normally again. "*Denke,* both of you."

Both doctors smiled. Dr. Crane patted her on the arm. Dr. Merrill handed her the cane a nurse had brought. "Don't let this scare you. It's part of the healing process."

Eliza stared at the cane as if it were a snake. "I guess I can fight off bears with it."

"I don't recommend that, but yes, it would come in handy," Dr. Merrill said, grinning. "Now I'm going to take you back to that nice young man who brought you. You didn't tell me you had a boyfriend."

"I don't," she quickly amended. "He's a friend who is helping out while I'm healing." Then she added, "I believe you know him since you recommended him. Levi Lapp."

Dr. Merrill chuckled. "Levi got the job? He's a mighty good friend to bring you here and pace in the waiting room. I'd say that man thinks of you as more than a friend. I didn't realize that was Levi."

Eliza couldn't speak. She only nodded and tried to walk, but her leg didn't want to work. Reluctantly, she took the crutches, along with the cane.

Dr. Merrill brought her instruction papers and the offending cane out with her.

Levi whirled and hurried toward them then greeted Dr. Merrill before taking the cane and papers. When he saw her on crutches, he looked deflated but then he smiled. "Ready for that ice cream I promised?"

She wasn't sure she could eat, but she didn't want him to pity her. "I'll race you to the ice cream truck."

Dr. Merrill shook his head. "I think she's feeling better after all. Enjoy your ice cream. And Eliza, mind your therapy and come back for your follow-up appointment. Your appointment schedule is in your folder there."

"I'll do as you say," she replied. "*Denke.*"

After the doctor had gone back through the double doors, she felt her resolve slipping.

Levi didn't say a word. He just opened his arms.

Eliza reached for him and let him pull her close. Then she sobbed against his shirt and silently thanked her *mamm* for asking Levi to come with her.

CHAPTER TEN

"Better?" Levi asked later as they sat eating their ice cream at a bistro table outside the Shadow Lake Ice Cream and Shakes Shop. After Eliza had cried in his arms, Levi wanted to protect her even more.

She'd held tight to him for a moment that ended all too soon. Then she'd stepped back and straightened her spine. "Give me the cane."

She'd been determined to walk to the waiting cab, but it had been torture for Levi to watch her struggle, trying to keep her weight off her healing leg.

Now they sat quietly in the fall air, eating the ice cream he'd promised her. Eliza had picked at hers at first, but then she must have realized she was hungry. She was tearing into it now.

She sniffed and took another bite from the cup of vanilla and chocolate swirl he'd brought out to her. "Much better. But I can feel my leg swelling."

"We'll be done soon, and I'll call another cab," he said. "You'll probably need to keep it elevated for a few more days."

"I know. It feels so strange, lighter but exposed. I haven't looked at the scars yet."

Levi took a spoon to his butter pecan treat. "Was it horrible?"

"You mean, when it happened?" She nodded. "It was bad. Jonah knows some CPR and he was able to get me settled and put a splint on it, but I knew from his expression it was bad. I felt the bone pop when I hit the stable floor. Then Mamm and Abby came running and I heard sirens and I don't remember much after that."

"You must have gone into shock."

"I did. I woke up a few times and Mamm was always there. She told me I'd need surgery. I was so afraid but . . . I knew *Gott* would protect me."

"You have a strong family, Eliza."

Her head shot up. "You called me Eliza."

"That's your name."

"But you've only used my nickname."

"And you didn't like it."

"*Denke* for being thoughtful."

He smiled, thinking he saw a hint of disappointment in her eyes when he called her by her true name. Maybe she liked being called Lizzie more than she let on.

"Do you want to take one of your pills?" he asked while they finished their treat.

"*Neh*. I will when I get home. It's been a long afternoon."

"And you've been a trooper."

She looked uncomfortable. "I'm sorry I fell apart. You must think I'm acting like a *bobbeli*."

"There is no shame in reaching for a friend, Eliza. I came with you to offer support . . . and I'm glad you turned to me."

"I am glad I had someone with me," she admitted, her ever-changing eyes holding a hint of longing and regret.

But that hint disappeared like a puff of clouds. "Just to carry all the paperwork and that infernal cane."

She still had her wit, he noted. He liked that about her. Strong and stubborn, but so pretty, even with tear-swollen eyes.

But he had to ask. "Even if it's just me here with you?"

"Even so," she said with a saucy grin. "I've had a meltdown, as the *Englisch* say, in your arms. I reckon we can be friends again."

Levi did a fist pump. "Now that is a miracle."

She laughed at his antics. "And . . . we've been alone together for four hours now."

"Are you still afraid of me?"

"I was never afraid of you, Levi. More confused and hurt, and afraid of what could happen between us."

"I'd never hurt you, Lizzie." He wanted to take her hand but refrained. "And I only want *gut* things to happen between us. If that means just being your friend, so be it."

She glanced up and giggled. "You can't unlearn that habit, can you? Calling me Lizzie."

"Apparently not."

"Since we're friends again, I don't mind."

He grinned, thinking he'd won points with her, at least. Having her in his arms again would remain a special moment for him, even though she'd sobbed all over his shirt. They finished their treats; then he used his business cell phone to call a cab. Soon they were on their way toward the inn.

She glanced over at him. "You don't have to escort me to the cottage."

"I *will* escort you to the cottage," he replied. "You're in pain and you're tired. My *mamm* would not be happy if I just left you by the curb."

She shook her head. "You are persistent, Levi."

"I promised your *mamm* I'd take care of you."

"Oh, so fear of my mother is why you're shadowing me."

"That and . . . before she took off to deliver the twins, she invited me to stay for supper."

Eliza was too tired to argue about his staying for supper. Mamm would want to thank Levi for stepping up, but Mamm had also made sure he and Eliza would be alone to talk and make their peace. Eliza would look ungrateful if she asked him to leave.

When they arrived home, the *kinder* buggy sat waiting by the portico. Peaches stood hitched, but the pony impatiently tossed her fluff of white mane.

"What's this?" Eliza asked Levi.

"Your ride to the cottage. You don't need to walk all that way on your sore leg, and you can't hop that far."

"I have the cane."

"*Ja*, but you need to practice in small measures, and it's a good hike up that slope to your cottage. Peaches asked to be able to give you a ride. You don't want to disappoint your pony, do you?"

"Oh, Peaches asked, did she?"

Peaches snorted and gave them a doleful eye roll.

Levi bent his head, his eyes lifting to Eliza. "I think she's ready."

"This is silly."

"Shh. You'll hurt her feelings."

He paid the cab driver, then helped Eliza up to the tiny buggy. There would barely be room for both of them on the padded seat. Which only reminded her of how she'd felt in his arms earlier.

Safe. Protected. Comforted. Content.

Being in Levi's arms again while she sobbed out of both

relief and frustration would be a memory she'd hold forever in her heart. As mortified as she'd felt, she'd missed those strong arms and that amazing smile. She'd also missed the way he always made her laugh and how he tried to take care of her.

Maybe her pledge to never marry had been hasty.

Or maybe she was being hasty now, already thinking beyond friendship when the thread between them was still delicate and easily frayed. She should have stayed strong and cried when she was alone. Wasn't that what strong women did?

But today, she'd been so disappointed to feel more pain in her leg. She realized she still had a long way to go to get well. Just thinking about trying to make her way up to the cottage made her hurt all over.

"You are kind, Levi," she said. "When did you decide on this little prize?"

"When we were waiting for the cab. I made a quick call to Henry while you went inside the ice cream shop to wash your hands."

Embarrassed at her awkwardness, she said, "I took so long, you probably had plenty of time to arrange this. It would have taken me an hour to get up that hill."

"You only have to get into the buggy now," he said, sweeping her into his arms before she could protest.

Her cane dangling from her hand, she tried to hold on. "Levi!"

"Did you have a better idea?"

She looked into his eyes and felt her heart slipping away. "*Neh*, I suppose I didn't."

Then she turned away, the emotions roiling inside her making her wish she hadn't eaten so much ice cream. But these emotions were about more than getting her cast off or enduring pain all over again; they were also about the way Levi made her feel. This day had been both a joy and a torment.

Levi had been with her and . . . she'd find a way to put this on her quilt. The ice cream, the pony ride to her front door, the sunshine and beautiful, colorful trees.

She didn't know how to capture the way he'd held her close, and she'd never dare put that on a quilt anyway.

But she had forgiven him a little bit and she had to finish that quilt to please her *mamm* and her nosy sisters. Would Levi ever see it? Not if she had her way.

Levi carried her up to the waiting buggy and got her settled in the small, cushioned back seat. He untied the reins, waved a thank-you to where Henry and Matthew stood on the big porch, and turned the buggy toward the path to the cottage.

While the hill wasn't that high and had a few dips, he figured this was the best way to get Eliza up to her home. And he'd get supper in the process. A day worth all the excitement.

He'd have the memory of her being in his arms to send him to sleep this evening. Or keep him awake all night.

Now he tried to keep her spirits up by chattering away to Peaches. The pony trotted along in a high-stepping, proud way. The animal loved Eliza and Eliza loved this little pony.

Levi hummed and told Peaches what a nice pony she was. "I appreciate your help today, Peaches. I'll bring extra treats for you tomorrow."

"You are spoiling that pony and me," Eliza said, a smile in her words. "But I have to admit, I feel like a queen. I'm prideful, but don't tell anyone."

"Sometimes, you can show pride," he said over his

shoulder. "You had a hard day and you handled things in a courageous way. You're strong and you'll be fine. I'm going to help you get your mobility back."

"You're going to help me? You keep saying that, but seems you have a lot to do already, Levi."

"I can find time for you, Lizzie."

She didn't respond with one of her quick comebacks. Had he made her angry again? He didn't liké being around angry Lizzie.

He pulled the little buggy up to the porch and halted the skittish pony. "Peaches, don't go anywhere. I'll get you to your evening feed, don't worry."

When he came around to help Eliza down, she held up a hand. "Please don't carry me. My sisters are sure to be looking out the window."

He nodded. "Let me lift you down, and you can do the rest."

She didn't argue but gripped his arm like a lifeline.

When Levi let her go, she held on to the buggy while he found her cane. "Can you make it up the steps?"

"I can and I will."

Grit. The woman had grit. Stubborn to the bone. She'd want to be tough now because she'd caved in earlier. Probably hated that he'd seen her like that. He needed to focus on her pain, and not how great it felt to hold her in his arms. If he moved too fast, she'd bolt faster than Peaches hearing a firecracker.

He wished he could explain that when she opened up to her feelings, it only endeared her to him more. He'd do anything for Lizzie. If she'd let him.

Right now, he watched as she held her head up and managed to lift her bad leg up onto the steps, then used her cane so she wouldn't put too much weight on her left leg.

It pained him to watch, but he understood she had to do this her way.

The Eliza way.

He waited until she reached the door, then hurried to open it.

"Eliza?" Her mother came running and hugged her tight. "I was so worried."

"I'm fine, Mamm," Eliza said. "We stopped for ice cream."

Colette put her hands on her hips, then glanced from Eliza to Levi. "Ice cream. Well, that's nice."

"It was nice," Eliza replied. "Levi has to take Peaches back to the stables, but I understand someone invited him to supper." Her gaze fixed on her mother.

"I did," Sarah said with a pleased smile. "We're having baked chicken and mashed potatoes."

Eliza glanced back at Levi. "You'd best hurry. Jonah and Abigail will be here too, and Jonah loves Mamm's baked chicken."

"I'll be right back," he said, making haste. He liked baked chicken himself.

But even more, he liked being around Eliza and her family. He'd already told his *mamm* he might be late tonight. So once he got Peaches taken care of, he could relax and enjoy being near Eliza again.

Just be near her.

That seemed to be working for now. Today had been downright pleasant despite the challenge of her healing leg. They'd been alone together, and he'd respected her, as he always would. Never again would he try to move too fast into a relationship with Eliza King.

But how long could he go on, just being near her and not being with her as more than a friend?

CHAPTER ELEVEN

"Have you added anything else to your quilt?" Abigail asked Eliza after supper. The men were out on the porch, discussing the inn, the livestock, and the crops, as always.

Eliza heard them laughing. Levi fit right in, which should make her wary. Instead, it made her glad. He needed *gut* role models in his life and Daed and Jonah would be a blessing to him.

Bringing her attention back to her two curious sisters, she said, "I'm pondering, but I think I'll put in two cones of ice cream, even though we had ours in cups, and a buggy ride with Peaches."

Colette poked at her arm. "Will you show your new cane?"

"*Neh*, I don't think that can add to any forgiveness on my part." She glanced out the window again. "I'll show Peaches and the buggy. That's all anyone needs to see."

"But not the whole story," Colette replied, her eyes wide.

"The whole story is not for everyone to know, and the cane is not pleasant to remember."

"But you are walking with it," Abby reminded her. "Is it better than the cast and crutches?"

"Slightly," she admitted. "But it's awkward and I feel like everyone is pitying me."

"People are concerned, but you are doing great. Your healing time is not over yet," her sister replied.

"*Neh*, not yet. I have much to do to be able to get back to normal."

She thought about how she'd fallen into Levi's arms there in the waiting room. That would be her secret. Her sisters would take that gesture and run with it until they had her standing in from of the marriage minister.

"I have the flowers, the ice cream, and Peaches," she said. "That's a start. The panels will be square and colorful."

"This will be another primitive like Abby's," Colette said. "Soon, we'll be famous for making primitives, a new Amish custom. The *Englisch* will be all over that."

They all smiled because the inn depended on *Englisch* curiosity to bring in a big tourist crowd almost year-round.

Eliza couldn't have her private musings hanging on display in the beautiful Colonial-style inn, right there with the antique cabinets and sideboards. The place had enough interesting historical features and a great restaurant to keep their guests happy without her adding fodder for their discussions. Abigail's quilt covered the chenille spread on her marriage bed. It was that intimate.

Hers would be different. Just a way to let go of her pain and fears and find a way to be Levi's friend. Maybe she'd keep it in her room—on the hickory rocking chair. Or lying across the wooden chest at the foot of her bed, a place where she stored special things.

"I don't think it will be exactly like Abby's." Her sister's quilt would become a family heirloom because it told the tale of Jonah slowly getting his memory back and showed how he and Abigail had fallen in love. Eliza's was more of a task presented by her mother to encourage her to forgive another human being. "I want the squares to depict things Levi has done for me—gestures of kindness that lead to trust."

"Ah, so that's what you two have been up to—gestures of forgiveness and trust," Mamm said after she'd stopped at the bottom of the stairs to catch her breath.

Mamm had a way of sneaking down the stairs when they were chattering like magpies.

Eliza lifted her chin and glanced at her mother. "That is what you suggested, so I'm marking each considerate thing he's done. Buying me ice cream and planning ahead to have Peaches waiting were both thoughtful gestures."

"Not to mention, taking you to get your cast off," Abby said with a prim smile. "You didn't tell us much about that."

"Nothing to tell," she said, hoping her expression didn't give her away. "The docs both told me what I need to do and when. I'm to start exercises here at home and then go to the physical therapy office at the clinic in town, where someone can supervise me to be sure I'm doing the exercises correctly. That should take a few more weeks." She winced as she positioned herself on the old worn couch. "I'll need to buy us a new sofa. I've just about ruined this one."

"The sofa is fine," Mamm said, coming to tuck a shawl around Eliza. "Let me see the leg."

Eliza hadn't shown her scars to anyone. Only the doctors had seen them. Now her mother lifted her dress and held her leg still while she studied the long slash along her calf and lower thigh, a scar from the break and the surgery. "We'll need to watch this for any signs of infection, and we can wrap it so the scars will settle down. I don't expect any problems because I know you'll keep it clean, and you'll be protective of it while you get readjusted to walking again. My herbal salves will help minimize the scarring."

Eliza nodded, afraid to voice her feelings. Each time she glimpsed her leg, the memory of intense pain shot through her. She wished she could forget. She wished she could walk without assistance.

All in Gott's time.

"Are you in pain?" Colette asked, her hand touching Eliza's.

"*Neh*, I'm just concerned," Eliza admitted. "Mamm, what if my leg never heals properly?"

Mamm gave her a stern glance. "Why wouldn't it? Did your surgeon say that might happen?"

"*Neh*." Eliza rubbed the puckered scar. "It's just I thought I'd be able to walk better once the cast was off."

"These things take time, remember?" Mamm patted her leg. "Dr. Merrill warned you of that. The hardest part is over. You had surgery and you've worn the cast. Now it's time to heal. You'll be fine. Don't borrow worries."

"Focus on your quilt," Abby suggested. "We have our quilting frolic planned for next Friday. You can start your panels then."

"I am not a quilter, not like you," Eliza pointed out. "I'm not sure I'll do the quilt justice."

"You need something to take your mind off your leg," Mamm replied. "Start your exercises tomorrow. I'll help, and Levi has offered—"

"I can do it without him," Eliza snapped, and then wished she hadn't. Now they were all three staring at her with raised eyebrows.

"I mean he has a lot to do every time he's here, and he's also trying to help his family. He told me the barn needs repairing and he's the only one who can fix it, of course. To save money, he can't hire anyone."

"We can send people," Abby graciously offered. "Levi is one of us now, and his *mamm* is so sweet and kind. How can we ignore them?"

"I wasn't fishing for help," Eliza said, not wanting to sound selfish. "I suppose he'd appreciate the offer though."

Mamm pursed her lips and thought. "I'll talk to your *daed* and Jonah. Matthew and Henry will help, too."

Soon they were busy planning out how and when this could happen. With the fall festival a few weeks away, they'd best make haste.

Eliza sat listening and adding comments here and there, but she couldn't help glancing out the window to watch Levi leaning against the porch railing, talking and laughing at her father's sage wit. He did fit right in. Too much so.

She'd have to keep her distance. It was that simple. She'd slipped up today and let him see her pain, her longing, her weaknesses. That would not happen again.

She took one more glance, remembering how polite he'd been at dinner, how he'd thanked Mamm for wrapping food for him to take home, how he'd nodded to Eliza before Daed invited him to sit a few minutes on the porch. It all seemed so easy and natural, but Eliza could feel the subtle manipulation of her parents as they welcomed the man she'd once thought she loved. Did they want her to forgive Levi? Or did they want her to marry Levi?

Did she mind their gentle nudges?

What did it matter? Just now, she wasn't able to do much of anything. She'd have to continue to accept that Levi was a friend, connected to her by a tentative fragile thread that could twist and break at any moment.

She didn't want to break that fragile thread by letting things go any further between them. They'd missed their one chance at love and a future together. Now they'd have to settle for being around each other as friends.

When the door opened and he entered, Eliza gave him a quick glance, then looked down at her hands.

"I'll be going now. Didn't want to forget the food you're sending to my *mamm*. She'll be so thankful."

"We also want to offer you our help fixing your barn," Mamm said. "Eliza told us you needed to make some repairs."

Levi looked confused and then he looked embarrassed, his gaze hitting her with a hint of disappointment. "That's not necessary. We'll get by."

Daed touched Levi's arm. "I think my wife and daughters have made up their minds, and if I know them, they won't let this go until we load up our tools and supplies and head over to your place to get your barn ready for winter." He glanced at Mamm. "Ain't so?"

"It is so, just as you said," Mamm replied, her hands on her hips. "Connie and I are friends and I'd like a *gut* visit with her while you all work on the barn. You'd be doing me a favor, Levi. Getting out of the house to go visiting is always a joy, and I haven't had a visit with Connie since . . . well . . . since your *daed* passed. Will you allow me that pleasure?"

Eliza watched as Mamm worked her persuasion on Levi. The poor man never knew what had hit him. "I guess she could use some company these days. We'll pick a day and make it happen."

"*Gut*," Mamm said, clearly satisfied. "Now you'd best get home before Connie worries about you."

Levi nodded, then glanced at Eliza. "I hope your leg will continue to improve."

"*Denke*," she replied, aware all eyes were on her. "And *denke* for being my escort today. I appreciate your help."

He nodded and took the bag of food Abby handed him, then left.

Eliza dropped her gaze again, wishing she'd never climbed that ladder. Then she wouldn't have to deal with a thousand different emotions, a messed-up leg, and being around the one man she'd tried so hard to forget. One wrong move and her life had changed in a matter of seconds.

Her family dispersed when she kept her eyes down. Jonah and Abigail said their good-nights and left. Mamm and Daed headed to their chairs to rest and read.

Daed let out a sigh as he settled. "Eliza, how do you feel?"

She finally glanced up. "I'm not sure. I'm glad to be done with that cast. My leg feels light and free, but still tender. Mamm doctored the scars. I hope to continue to improve."

Mamm gave her a sweet appraisal. "Some scars take longer to heal than others. Please be careful."

"I will." She laid her head back against the pillows, her mind spinning from dreams to reality and back. She did have invisible scars that had festered too long. Maybe she could use this time of being still and getting her strength back to heal those scars, too.

Colette finished the dishes and then came and held her hand out. "I'll help you to bed, sister."

They must have all passed a lot of speaking looks, showing they understood she needed some time alone.

Because she was tired and confused and had so many things to think about, she hoisted herself up and took her sister's hand. Then she went to her temporary room with as much dignity as she could manage with her cane.

After Colette had helped her into her nightgown, kissed her on the forehead, and then left, Eliza lay there in the moonlight remembering how being in Levi's arms again had felt so right and so vastly different from the last time he'd held her.

There were some things that couldn't be stitched into a quilt. Holding Levi was one of those things. Trusting Levi was one of those things. Forgiving him might be easy, but where would they go from there?

She thought about today and how he'd been so kind and protective of her, how he'd held her so carefully but so close. Things she would have scoffed at a month ago.

She'd keep today's memories intact and private, to replace the old memories she'd carried, examined, and rearranged until she really couldn't figure out why she'd been so upset with Levi in the first place.

As she drifted off to sleep, Eliza had two goals. One, to get her mobility back and walk normally again. And two, to find a way to truly forgive the boy who'd left and to accept the man who'd returned.

They would be near each other, and they would have time to get to know each again, and that counted for something in her mind. That counted toward a hopeful outcome wrapped and stitched in true forgiveness.

CHAPTER TWELVE

A week later, after making sure the inn and the stables were taken care of, the family loaded up tools and supplies and headed to Connie Lapp's house. It was a Wednesday, a slow day at the inn. Henry had brought in a part-timer to staff the lobby, and Edith, the cook and boss of the kitchen, had brought two of her daughters to help with the cooking and serving. Abigail and Colette had baked ahead and made sure all stations were covered.

They really wanted this outing.

Eliza did, too, but she was nervous. How would Connie feel about all of them congregating at her house? Mamm had talked to her, of course. They'd sent messages back and forth with Levi.

Levi knew they were coming, and he'd assured her his mother was both touched and excited. She rarely got visitors.

So there was a joyous party atmosphere as they clambered into the buggies and headed out.

Eliza sat in the back of Jonah and Abigail's buggy, while Colette drove the other, with Mamm and Daed in the back. They'd loaded up food and drinks and planned to stay until the barn was renovated. Eliza would be with Levi's family once again, and all day at that. She marveled at how she used to take spending a day with his mom and the *kinder* for granted. She'd never imagined it would all end so abruptly. Now his siblings were almost grown. James was fourteen and Laura was twelve.

"Are you excited?" Abigail asked over her shoulder as they took off. Samson was trotting along and enjoying being on an adventure, while Sunshine snorted and acted affronted at having to leave the barn and her corral.

"I am," Eliza admitted. "It's *gut* to get out on this fine fall day."

"And you're feeling better," Abigail said. "Mamm said you've been doing your foot and ankle exercises."

"She makes sure I do them at least two times a day, but the swelling has gone down, and I can walk better now."

They were all relieved to know that. But Eliza still had trouble with soreness. Mamm had encouraged her to stand and walk on the leg as much as possible so the atrophy in her calf and upper leg would slowly go away.

Eliza was almost there, and her worry about never walking straight again had eased a little. Levi had helped, as promised. He walked with her out on the flat part of the yard by the stables. They talked about the animals, of course. And about her blurting out how the Lapp barn needed repairing.

"I'm happy your family is going to visit Mamm, but you didn't have to make the men work during the visit."

"And how else could four women visit, if we don't get the men out of the house?"

"Ahh, an ulterior motive."

"*Neh*, just some women time. A small frolic while the men do what they do best—fix barns."

"Mamm will be so happy about that," he said. "I've been meaning to get to it, but it seems my work is never done."

"I hope you will all be pleased," she'd told him.

It had been quite some time since Eliza had seen Levi's family. She had managed to avoid Levi's mother after he'd left. Then she'd just broken her leg when they got word that Linden had passed, so she'd missed the funeral two months ago.

"Connie will not judge," Mamm had told her when she'd voiced her worries. "Don't be silly. Just be kind and participate in the conversation. Levi seems content, and that is all any mother wants for her children."

They made it over to the other side of the small community in a few minutes. Too fast it seemed, but Eliza enjoyed the cool breeze and the soft fall sunshine playing through the riotous orange, yellow, and red leaves. A perfect day for work and a meal afterward. Eliza hoped Levi's *mamm* and siblings would be happy to see them. She'd do her best to make Levi's *mamm* see that she no longer held ill will toward him. And she only hoped Connie held no ill will toward her.

Levi came out on the porch when they arrived. *"Wilkom."*

Eliza gingerly dropped down from the buggy, careful to keep her still-healing left leg from hitting too hard on the soft grass. She smiled and waved, her expression colored with anticipation and apprehension.

Levi went down to meet them and help with the supplies they'd brought. His *mamm* came out on the porch and held her hands to her mouth; James and Laura were right behind her.

"This is so *wunderbar gut*," Connie called out, clapping her hands together.

"She's been cleaning and cooking all week," Levi told them as everyone got out of the buggies and the men settled the horses and buggies near the barn.

When the men returned, his mother greeted them and thanked them again.

"*Kumm, kumm,*" Connie said, waving everyone onto the porch. "It's so kind of you all to do this. Levi works so hard, he barely has time to take care of this place, too."

Laura hugged Eliza. "It's so *gut* to see you."

His little sister remembered Eliza taking time with her and James. She always made them laugh, and often brought suitable books for them to read.

James stood back, his glasses falling against his nose. The boy was timid, but he had a *gut* heart. He smiled shyly when Sarah greeted him.

"This means the world to all of us," Mamm said.

Levi lowered his head, feeling the weight of Mamm's innocent words. It had always been hard for him to ask for help. But the King family made it easy. They just took charge and made things happen. They worked hard, no doubt, but they were also well-established and had a big income to back them.

Now that he thought about it, he'd always felt beneath Eliza's status. Even years later, what did he have to offer her? When they were young, they had big dreams, but they'd never actually talked about how marriage would work. Would she want to leave her family and move in here with his? Could they afford to build a new home near his *mamm*?

Too much to consider today. He'd have to keep working and make a name for himself before he had anything to offer Eliza.

He'd work hard today because it meant he'd be near Eliza for most of the day. Away from the stables and his busywork there. They'd share a meal together, and his *mamm* would be talking about this generous visit for days and weeks to come.

Time was all he had to offer Eliza right now. That realization left a burning in his heart. But all he could do was enjoy each moment and pray he'd find a way back to her. Truly back to her.

Mamm took them all inside and insisted on giving them a snack before the men headed out to check the roof on the barn and fix the old rickety doors.

Abe motioned to James. "*Kumm*, young James. We need you to calculate for us. My eyes are too old to read figures."

Levi gave Eliza's father a slight nod. James beamed with pride as Abe patted him on the back and talked to him while they enjoyed their refreshments.

After *kaffe* and cookies, Levi smiled at Eliza. "I think it's time for us to get out there and get to work. Mamm's got a ham baking and red potatoes with green beans on the stove."

"We brought some side dishes and dessert," Abigail said, holding a casserole dish, while their mother carried a cake.

Colette and Matthew took a few moments to chat while Henry was introduced to Levi's *mamm* and shown around the small, neat home Levi had grown up in.

While the others were all talking at once, Levi pulled Eliza to the side. "You were walking pretty well out there."

"I'm getting better," she said with soft smile. "The foot and ankle exercises have helped, and I have other standing exercises to do so my leg will relax and regain muscle tone."

"I'll be waiting to give you a ride to your therapy next

week," he said. "And Eliza, *denke* for doing this. It's much appreciated."

"And your *mamm*?" she asked. "How does she feel about having me here?"

"She feels fine," he said, confused. "Why wouldn't she?"

She shot a worried glance toward the others. "I'm the reason you left, Levi. She has to remember that."

"*Neh*," he said, shaking his head. "I told her everything and explained it was my fault. She and my *daed* gave me a strong lecture right before I left. She does not blame you at all for me leaving. That was my decision."

He wanted to tell her he'd dreamed of leaving anyway, and what had happened between them only gave him an excuse. But Eliza would take that the wrong way. She'd think he'd been planning to leave rather than marry her. He'd hoped she'd go with him, but after their breakup Levi had realized he couldn't make Eliza leave her family. Now he saw that more than ever.

"I'm relieved to hear that," Eliza said. "Not that you got in trouble, but that your parents didn't blame me."

"You did nothing wrong," he said. "Now I have to get to work. But Eliza, Mamm is happy that you and I have made our peace."

She nodded her head. "I'll make sure to visit with her. I was so afraid."

"You've never been afraid of anything," he said, chuckling.

"I have a lot of respect for your *mamm*," she said. "I'd better go help with finishing up the food."

"We will talk later," Levi told her. "Alone maybe."

He glanced up to find Abe staring at them. He wanted to tell Eliza she wasn't the only one afraid. But he had work to do and something to prove—to all of them.

* * *

A few hours later, the small red barn had new roof shingles and a clean, sturdy place to store hay for the winter. The old doors had been replaced with new wood and new hinges and a strong black iron latch. The few stalls had been cleaned, tightened, and secured, and the fence behind the barn had been mended.

Levi finished washing up, then glanced at the barn. It was tiny compared to the inn's stables and barn.

"*Denke*," he said to Abe and the others. "I couldn't have done this without you."

Abe had supervised because Sarah said the young folks should do the actual work. "Many hands, Levi. Many hands make work go faster, ain't so?"

"It is so," Levi agreed. "I'll ask for help more often. This means the world to Mamm."

"I, for one, had fun," Henry said. The *Englischer* had worked as hard as anyone. "Nice to have a day off from the front desk and get a good meal all at the same time."

Abe chuckled as they all finished cleaning up and walked toward the long back porch where the women had set up the food on the table Levi had built for just such meals. "Now I understand why Henry volunteered so eagerly."

"After working all morning, I sure am hungry," Jonah said, his grin big. "I have to admit, Amish women know how to cook."

Abe laughed. "*Ja*, and it's *gut* that you can work off that food."

Levi slapped Matthew on the back. "*Denke*."

Matthew nodded. "I came for the food and to visit with Colette."

Levi gave him a nod. "Seems food and women go hand in hand. And men love them both."

"True." Matthew looked around to find Colette. "You never know with girls. Colette is a constant mystery. I've cared about her since we were *kinder*, but it took her a while to catch on."

"So, you two are walking out?"

"*Ja*, now and then. One day I plan to marry her," Matthew said with the voice of confidence that only young love could bring. "She just doesn't know that yet."

"I wish you well on that," Levi replied as they went up the steps to find their chairs.

He remembered thinking the same thing about Eliza. Could that happen now? Could they find their way back to each other and take friendship to the next level? Would Eliza ever consider marriage, or would she want to remain friends only?

If only he didn't have so little to offer her. Maturity had taught him a lot of things, but he'd never stopped to consider how Eliza might react to marrying a pauper.

Just be near her.

Again, that sage advice played through his head.

Today, he'd been near her and the whole family as well. Nice, but he really wanted to be alone with her. Not to make any moves on her, as the *Englisch* would say, but because time had mellowed and matured their wild teenage urges.

Neh, this time he wanted to talk to her, laugh with her, and make her smile, to listen to her book talk, and see the dreams in her pretty eyes.

When he got to the table, his *mamm* glanced up at him. "Find your seat and let's have our dinner. We have a feast."

"It sure looks *gut*," he said, grinning. "*Denke*, ladies."

"We have had the best time," Sarah said. "We helped Connie with a beautiful quilt and did some mending while we caught up on the events of life." Glancing around, she said, "We should do this more often. The inn keeps my girls so busy, I sometimes forget we need to get away every now and then."

"You are *wilkom* here anytime," Mamm said, joy shining in her eyes as she fussed over the food and brought out the steaming hot biscuits she'd baked. The food smelled like home to Levi. This group felt like home to him.

He glanced at the people around him and knew he'd never leave Shadow Lake again.

Mamm seated Eliza by her side, across from Levi. He was thankful for that. Eliza shot him a quick glance, her expression full of anticipation and something more. Contentment maybe?

At least this way he could see Eliza across the table. So close and still not yet his to marry. But he planned on remedying that somehow. They'd *kumm* a long way since that first day weeks ago when she'd told him he wasn't *wilkom* in her stables. But they still had a long way to go before things could work out between them.

He'd need another kind gesture to move their relationship along.

Books. Eliza loved her books. He'd do some asking around and find one that would show her how much he adored her. He'd helped her leg to heal; books could make her feel better, too.

Having decided that, he said his silent prayers along with the others, and then they all dove into eating and talking, laughing, and enjoying the blessings of a fine fall day.

He'd find some books for her. She'd enjoy reading them and he hoped they'd would remind her of him.

But in his heart, Levi knew he'd have to find a lot more than just tokens to win Eliza. She'd expect more. Somehow, he would have to find a means to also offer her the kind of life she deserved.

CHAPTER THIRTEEN

Something had changed.

Eliza couldn't put her finger on it, but Levi hadn't sought her out to talk privately, as he'd said he'd do. Thinking over the day, she couldn't find anything she'd done to upset him. Maybe asking about his *mamm*'s feelings toward her?

Would that have brought back painful memories for him?

Had he left because of her, or was he forced to go after he'd told his parents the truth, that he and Eliza had broken up because he'd tried to hurry their romance? Could he have been angry because they'd blamed him and reprimanded him?

Eliza wished that long-ago night could have turned out differently. If they'd just talked about their feelings, they would be better off today. And possibly married.

But that was just a dream now.

Connie Lapp had welcomed her with open arms, and Levi had seemed so happy about that. Eliza had been happy, too.

"It's so *gut* to have you back in my kitchen, Eliza," Connie had told her earlier while they prepared the biscuits. "Just like old times."

"It's nice to be back," Eliza replied. "I have special memories here."

Connie gave her a curious glance. "Do you have special memories of my son?"

Eliza couldn't lie. "I do. He told me he explained to you and Linden what happened. It wasn't his fault. It was no one's fault. I . . . I just wasn't ready, even if my heart wanted me to be."

"Nonsense." Connie worked the biscuit dough with a big wooden spoon. "You were young and scared, and our son knew better. He was trying to impress his friends and in doing so, he went too far, too fast, and frightened you. You had every right to turn away from him."

"But he left, and all these years I thought it was because of me."

"*Neh*, that boy left because he had a wanderlust in him that wouldn't go away. Breaking up with you gave him a reason to get on with it. It broke our hearts when he up and decided to leave, but we never blamed you. Not one bit."

Eliza hugged Connie. "I'm so sorry. Sorry that he went away and sorry that I never talked to you about it. I was . . . ashamed."

"There is no shame in loving someone and wanting to be with them," Connie said. "Those terrifying feelings you had as a teen are now tempered because you're all grown-up. Levi and you both know more about life and love, ain't so?"

Eliza nodded and wiped at her eyes. "You're right. It all feels different now. But what if it's too late?"

"Love is never too late," Connie said, handing her a towel. "Love is always in *Gott*'s own time."

Now as she searched for Levi out in the yard, Eliza wondered if their timing would ever be right. She'd begun to enjoy her visits to the stables to watch him work. She liked talking to him and questioning his every move, even if she could see with her own eyes that the man knew what he was doing.

He'd won her over with kindness, not kisses, with respect, not assumptions. He hadn't touched her other than to help her out of buggies and carry her in his arms. But he'd been nearby, just nearby. And that counted for something. Something more powerful than a physical feeling.

Her heart had a yearning that she couldn't stop.

That might scare her more than any kiss in the dark.

Right now, she wanted to talk to Levi. The tables had turned. She wanted him to forgive her for thinking all the wrong things for so many years.

Levi came around the barn and saw Eliza standing on the porch alone, one hand holding the railing. When their eyes met, he hurried to her, his chest heaving, his mind racing. "Are you tired? Do you need to sit?"

She shook her head, her eyes bright with relief. "I was wondering where you were."

She looked so dejected and lost, he couldn't crack the smile that wanted to come out. "So, you missed me?" he asked, keeping his tone solemn while his soul danced.

She straightened, her expression changing into a blank wall. She wouldn't admit to anything, this one. "You said we'd talk later. Well, it's later. We'll be leaving soon."

"You're correct about that," he said. "I was checking on the goats. They were so happy about their mended fence, they were dancing. The baby goats had me in stitches. Would you like to see them? They ran from one side of their pasture to the other." He took a breath. "They jumped from old hay bales to a bench to some rocks I was using to keep them from getting out. They were playing, Lizzie. It was a beautiful thing to see."

Her answering smile took his breath away. He loved her smiles, which had been so rare when he'd first arrived at the inn. "I'd like to see the kids playing. That would be *wunderbar*."

Levi glanced around to see where everyone else had gone. "Should we let someone know?"

She laughed. "I think they've already figured that out, Levi. The other men are on the side porch and the women are inside. The windows are right behind me."

He glanced inside and, sure enough, their two *mamms* were standing at the kitchen window, watching. When they saw him looking, they hurried away so quickly, it reminded him of the playful goats.

"I guess we're okay then," he told Lizzie. Then he offered her his hand. "Lean on me and be mindful of your healing leg."

She gave him a look that showed trust. He could accept trust because he wanted her to trust him, always. He would not dare hurt her again in any way.

But that nagging thought kept popping into his head.

What do you have to offer a woman like Eliza King? She's smart, reads books, knows horses, has opinions, and she comes from a successful, loving family. A family that depends on her to help make their thriving business a success.

What do you have to give?

Only his heart, he thought. And he'd given her that a long time ago.

He should just turn around and take her inside. He should avoid her at all costs. You'd think he would be mature enough to see the truth in front of him. He had nothing to offer a woman like Eliza. Maybe he'd realized that a long time ago but hadn't been able to admit it. Her rejection of him had hurt, no doubt. But deep inside, he had to have seen the differences between them, and he'd used their awkward breakup as the best excuse to run away from what was so obvious. He didn't know back then how to make things right with her, so he'd done the best thing for all. He'd gone out into the world and learned a trade he could bring back home with him.

But would that be enough for them to have a life together?

He couldn't be sure. He wanted to give her everything, but how could he when he had nothing much to give? Trying to imagine her away from the grandeur of the inn, away from her prized stables, made him wince. Made him fear moving forward on his own dreams.

And yet, when she took his hand in hers and let him help her along while she favored her healing leg, Levi knew he'd walk to the ends of the earth to win her heart and make her happy.

"I wanted to talk to you," she said. "I had a nice discussion with your *mamm*."

He gave her a quick glance. "Should I be happy about that?"

Eliza laughed. "She holds no ill will. She is so kind and sweet. You know, I blamed myself for your leaving, but she said you wanted to strike out on your own. I should have been concerned to hear that since we never discussed it. But really, I was relieved. I thought your going was all my fault."

"It was never your fault," he replied, wishing he could wipe away those bad memories. "I didn't know myself that I wanted to try something different until . . . until I made the decision. But Lizzie, I had many reasons."

"I just want you to forgive me," she said. "For all the

assumptions I made back then, and even since you've been home."

"There is nothing to forgive," he said, knowing he'd made the wrong choices then, that he might be the wrong man for her now.

"Then we're even," she said, her eyes bright with hope.

"That we are." But they weren't really even. He'd seen that today.

They walked to the barn, and he showed her the repairs the men had spent most of the day working on. Then they watched the kids playing and chasing each other until they both laughed out loud.

"I can't thank you enough," he said. "I'll never forget what your family did for us."

"You don't mind?" she asked, her gaze moving over the fresh wood and the mended fence. The kids were still hopping here and there, making her smile. "I worried that I'd insulted your pride by mentioning this to Mamm."

Levi wouldn't admit that his pride had been wounded; he'd told himself to get over that pride. Amish helped Amish. Amish helped anyone in need. He'd once worked on a team that traveled to Grand Isle, Louisiana, to help rebuild a church. They'd lifted and moved, then rebuilt a whole staircase and ramp so anyone could get inside that tiny church.

No one there held pride as a shield. The islanders had been thankful and joyous, and they'd all shared a meal together, just like today.

How could he explain this hurt in his chest? This need to provide for the family he'd left here to fend for themselves. His *daed* might be alive today if he'd stayed. Guilt had Levi questioning everything.

"You did a kind thing, Lizzie. Sometimes it's hard for a man to admit he needs help, but you knew how to handle it. Our mothers are back together, laughing and frolicking, my sister is happy to see you again, and what your *daed* did for James today, well, that is why your family is so well-respected around here."

"We only do what anyone would do, Levi. We help each other. People have *kumm* to our aid many times. You're one of those people."

"*Ja*, but I get paid to take care of your horses."

"You could have said no, knowing . . . what happened between us."

"I could never say no to you." And he'd needed the income.

There. It was out. He never wanted to say no to her, but soon, he might have to do that very thing.

"Then stop worrying about pride and accept that you are home. You're back in Shadow Lake and we need you here."

"Do *you* need me?" he asked.

She stared into his eyes, leaned closer, touched a hand to his face. "I want you . . . I want you nearby. You make me feel safe."

Not exactly a declaration, but he'd take it. Then he plunged right in. "You're brave and sure and you've always taken care of yourself and your family. Why would you need me?"

She backed up, her face going pale. "What kind of question is that?"

"One you should ask yourself," he said. "I work for you, Lizzie. Do you see what that means?"

"*Ja*, I pay your salary and you take care of my horses. That's a *gut* plan, isn't it?"

"It's the best plan because, as you can see, I have no money. This farm is small and we're barely able to make ends meet."

She studied him, her frown growing dark with shock and resolve. Her eyebrows lifted like dark wings. "Are you saying I'd hold that over you?"

"*Neh*, I'm not saying that at all. I like working at the inn." He let out a sigh. "But . . . you live there. Your life is there. I . . . I only have this."

"Are you jealous of me? Resentful? Ashamed to work for a woman? You do know I don't own anything myself. The inn was a gift to my family. I only work there, too." Her eyes changed from forest green to a golden-green. "You can't be serious."

"*Neh*, not jealous." He shook his head, wishing he'd kept his worries to himself. "Maybe a bit ashamed that I can't provide more for my family, and I'm worried that . . . that I don't have much to offer a woman like you."

Realization held her there, but she stiffened, her head coming up, her spine straight. "Well, isn't that just like you, Levi Lapp? You've found the perfect excuse. You come home, ask for forgiveness and work your way back into my life, and now you decide who's good enough for me and who's not." Shaking her head, she added, "I only had to forgive you, and I just now asked you to forgive me. I haven't agreed to anything more, so don't flatter yourself so much."

Backing around so quickly, she almost fell, Eliza grabbed for the fence, but Levi tugged her back before she got caught in the barbed wire. "I've got you."

She pulled away. "*Neh*, you have not got me. You, with your kind gestures and sweet words, do not even *get* me. You've just insulted me, and you can't even see it. Do you really think me so shallow, Levi?"

"I didn't mean—"

"I know what you meant. You're just too *dummkopp* to

see the truth that's in front of you." She stepped out of his arms. "Now let me go. I'm tired and I want to go home."

"Lizzie?"

"I have to go."

She hobbled away, no cane, no crutches. Just sheer will and determination.

Well, she was right about one thing. He'd been dumb to admit his fear to her because it had sounded feeble and as if he didn't appreciate working for her or her family. She'd hold that over his head for a long time to come.

But she was too *gut* for him. Best they establish that now. He had hurt her again and he hadn't meant to do that. Acting as if he thought she was better than he should end any plans he might have for them. Plans she apparently had not even considered, no matter how friendly she'd been over the past few days.

But somehow, his heart seemed to think he could run after her and once again ask her to forgive him. Forgive him and love him. Really love him, no matter what.

Only, this time he wouldn't. This time, it really would be better if he didn't try to win her back.

CHAPTER FOURTEEN

"You were quiet on the way home," Abigail said when the sisters gathered for the first time since her accident in Eliza's bedroom upstairs.

Her sweet sisters had cleaned it from top to bottom, put fresh linens and a warm blanket on the bed, and placed nice-smelling herbs in water on the old dresser. It felt homey and comfortable. She'd never take the luxury of a pretty bedroom for granted again. Or the luxury of being able to walk, even if she still wobbled a bit.

She'd finally managed her way up the short staircase, taking care to move just as the therapist had had her do on a small set of stairs in her last session.

Now, worn out and needing to be alone, she couldn't speak.

"What happened?" Colette asked, still basking in the glow of a day with Matthew. "Did I miss something?"

Abigail got out the quilt Eliza had started, then sent Colette a speaking look. "You'll have some nice ideas for your quilt after today, *ja*?"

"I'm done with the quilt," Eliza said, pushing it away, her heart feeling battered again. And this time, it was even worse than when she'd been a teenager.

"*Neh.*" Abigail held her hand up. "Tell us what is wrong. You can't stop working on the quilt. Look at the panels. They're so pretty."

Eliza glanced at the pot of mums, the ice cream cone her sisters and Mamm had helped her cut and shape. The primitive buggy and horse Abigail had sketched and made into a pattern Eliza had pieced with dark red and stark black materials.

"It's not working. I've forgiven Levi. I was ready to move forward today. I even asked for *his* forgiveness. That should have been the end of it. A new beginning."

"But—?" Colette asked, her hands twisted together.

"But now Levi has decided I'm too *gut* for him."

"What?" Abigail's eyes flashed fire. "What does that mean?"

"He's working for us and . . . he thinks he's not right for a woman like me. He says he doesn't resent my being his boss, but I think he does. His pride got to him. It bothers him that we helped his family today and that he . . . he can't give me the life I have here."

"*Lecherich*!" Colette got up to pace around. "That's silly."

"That's how men think," Eliza replied. "He's just found another excuse, and after all the times he asked me to forgive him, told me he wanted to help me, wanted to be my friend. I think he wanted all of that, but today he saw the difference between his world and ours. So that's my fault?"

"*Neh*, that is not your fault or his," Abigail replied. "I can see how our family can be overwhelming at times. Jonah certainly felt that way when we were all together. But Levi knows the Amish way. We believe that no one is better than anyone else. We help when we need to do so, and I can't see that helping Levi and Connie today showed us in any kind of special light. It was the right thing to do since Levi is helping us in our time of need."

"But we pay him," Eliza replied. "He thinks we're treating him as a charity case, or that's the impression I got."

"This is troubling." Colette spread the quilt pieces over the bed. "But you can't stop your work. Mamm says we have to finish what we start. She did ask you to do this."

"I don't know if I can." Grabbing her covers, Eliza burrowed beneath the sheet and blanket. "I want to rest."

Abigail got on one side of the bed and Colette took the other space, ignoring Eliza's need for quiet. "Did you tell him that's ridiculous?"

"I told him he'd insulted me if he thought I'm so shallow, that I'm like some lady of the manor, needing special treatment."

Colette started giggling. Which only infuriated Eliza. "I see nothing funny about this situation."

"I think Levi is intimidated by your power, sister."

"I have no power. I can't make someone care about me when they talk like that. He's pushing me away, and I don't believe any of his pretty talk right now."

"But he does care," Abigail said. "He cares so much that he's offering you a way out. He saw a disparity today, Eliza. His home life is different from ours. We work hard and we don't need much, but we want for nothing. We've been taken care of here because we love this place."

"And because we take care of ourselves and each other," Eliza said. "We've always been close, and none of us will ever leave this old place—"

She stopped, sat up, winced when her leg twinged. "Oh, oh. I . . . I understand now. I see why he's decided he doesn't want me after all."

"Why is that?" Abigail asked as she brushed a hand over Eliza's hair.

"He sees my life here and he's afraid I won't be able to leave the inn, to leave my family. He's ashamed of his home because—look at mine." She waved her hand in the air. "Even this cottage is like a fairy-tale house. Then the inn, massive and full of warmth, always busy. We make a living here. We live here."

"And Levi thinks he doesn't belong. That he can't compete with what you have here," Colette said. "That makes sense, but he's still being ridiculous."

Eliza bobbed her head. "Do men really think that way?"

Abigail nodded. "Jonah wouldn't have dreamed of building a house with Daed's money. He had some saved up and used most of it for our home."

"Did you contribute?" Eliza asked, since they all got a salary of sorts.

"I paid for the decorations, which were few," Abigail admitted. "I buy material for sewing and anything related to running the house. But Jonah pays the mortgage."

"But he's one of us now," Colette said.

"*Ja*, but he has his little nest egg, as he likes to call it. For a rainy day."

Eliza slapped her hands against the covers. "Levi is a hard worker. He went out and learned a trade and he stayed true to his faith and his community by working as an Amish man in the *Englisch* world. My doctor recommended him. That's how *gut* he is at what he does." She let out a big sigh. "He can make a living here. He could set up a blacksmith shop anywhere in Shadow Lake." Staring down at the unfinished quilt, she said, "I wish I could make him see that."

Abigail grabbed Eliza's hand. "You still love him."

Colette grabbed the other hand. "I think she does."

Eliza felt trapped by those sweet touches. She shook her head, and then she got all teary-eyed. She blinked, refusing to cry. "I never stopped loving him. But now, he is refusing to let me love him." Pulling her hands away and crossing them over her stomach, she said, "This is why I've never tried to find a husband. It's too overwhelming and confusing. I'm never getting married."

Colette scoffed at that, then glanced at Abigail. "They are so getting married. I predict next year at this time you will be Mrs. Levi Lapp."

"I will not." Eliza thought that over. "Because I'm never leaving the life I'm living here."

Her sisters looked skeptical, but she couldn't help wondering where she would live if Levi stopped being stubborn and asked her to marry him.

Where would they go? And would he accept her help in any way?

"I need to sleep," she said. "This is too much. Too much."

"Another wedding," Colette said. "When you're feeling better, you'd best get on with that quilt. You'll need one for your home."

"I have a home right here. We're all going to stay here forever. You might want to mention that to Matthew."

"Okay, she's in a real mood," Abigail said. "Let's go."

Colette shot Eliza a hurt stare. "Matthew likes working here. He's never once said to me what Levi said to you today."

"Maybe you should ask him," she suggested, hating how she sounded.

Colette looked unsure, but Abigail stepped between them. "Eliza?"

"I'm sorry," she said. "I told you I'm tired."

Colette shook her head. "I'm going to pretend you didn't say that to me."

But Eliza knew she'd put that seed of doubt in her

sister's head, just as Levi had put it in her head. Abigail and Colette left, closing the door behind them.

Misery loves company, as Aenti Miriam always said.

Right now, Eliza's world felt completely miserable and now she'd hurt her sister, too. "Not a *gut* day, after all."

She slipped under the covers and ignored the unfinished quilt still lying at her feet.

Forgiveness was too hard sometimes.

Levi dropped the rasp and let out a grunt.

"Sorry, Rosebud," he said. Releasing the docile mare's leg, he reached for the tool that he'd used to smooth and shave Rosebud's hoof and shoe, then gently lifted her leg and held it between his knees. "Let's try that again."

Rosebud whickered a soft reply. Levi went back to his work.

He missed Eliza. She'd avoided him for most of the week, but he'd promised he'd take her to her therapy session today, and he never broke a promise.

So he finished, checked Rosebud's gait, gave her an apple to munch on, then cleaned his work area. He'd just washed up and was about to hitch Pickles to the small black family wagon when he heard Eliza's voice.

"I told you, Jonah. Mamm said she'd take me into town."

"And I told you, Levi has already planned to do that to save Sarah the trip. Your mother is being kind because she loves you, but she doesn't like leaving Abe these days."

"She told you that?"

"I heard her talking to Abigail. Abe won't complain, but ever since his heart trouble, she's worried about your *daed*. So it would help all of us if you'd let Levi take you."

"We didn't hire him to cart me around."

"No, but he has offered, and I think you two need to clear the air."

"Nothing to clear."

Levi stepped out of the tack room and strolled toward the spot where they were standing. "I thought this was settled."

Eliza's lips jutted out, her gaze hitting him like a strike of lightning. "I'd rather someone else gave me a ride. Or I can try to drive myself."

Jonah rubbed his nose with his thumb and forefinger. "So you two are back to not liking each other."

"I still like her," Levi said.

"I don't think it's wise for me to be seen with the hired help," Eliza said.

"Eliza?" Jonah's shocked expression mirrored how that cutting remark had zinged against Levi's soul.

"Levi has made it clear that he . . . he wants certain boundaries between us. I'm trying to honor his wishes."

Jonah's blue eyes went black. "Did something happen between you two? You haven't been to the stables all week, and this one"—he pointed to Levi—"has been in a foul mood."

"Nothing," Eliza said stubbornly.

"Nothing." Levi didn't know how to fix the situation, but he refused to ask for forgiveness. He was done with that. He'd tried everything, and they'd come so close to working through their differences. Then he had to go and say the wrong thing when he was only trying to do the right thing.

Jonah didn't speak. But his compelling gaze swept between the two of them while he waited like a hawk to swoop in.

"He thinks—"

"She thinks—"

Jonah held up his hand. "What do you think, Eliza?"

"He thinks," she said on a hiss of breath. "He thinks he's not *gut* enough for a woman like me. He is uncomfortable with me bossing him around."

"That's not what I said—"

Jonah did the hand up thing again.

"What did you say, Levi?"

"At my house the other day, I tried to explain my shame about my lack of income. You gave me work and I appreciate that, but I don't have much to offer anyone, especially—"

"—especially me!" Eliza finished, her green eyes lighting up with bright annoyance. "Me, Jonah. He doesn't think—he doesn't want . . . me." She stopped, running out of steam. "I can't be around a man who thinks I'm a spoiled, shallow princess."

Jonah's frown twitched just a tad. Shaking his head, he stood between the two of them, obviously trying not to laugh.

"Eliza," Jonah said on a quiet drawl, "no one would call you a spoiled, shallow princess. You'd never act that way or be unkind to anyone."

Levi heard the hint of sarcasm in that summary. But thankfully, Eliza missed it completely in her self-righteous frustration. "I know. So I don't understand what Levi's problem is."

Jonah shot Levi a long-suffering eye roll. "Right now, his problem is that he finished his work early because he genuinely wants to escort you to your therapy, so your parents don't have to go to town. So . . . sweet Eliza . . . do everyone a favor and get in the buggy and go to your appointment."

Eliza's head came up, her gaze studying both of them. "Whose side are you on, Jonah?"

"I don't take sides," her brother-in-law said. "I have my reasons. One, I have a headache, and two, I'd like to see my lovely wife, and three, Levi is here and ready and you're wasting time. He's still on salary, even if it means he has to cart you around. Just go and do what needs to be done and think about it this way. Once you're all healed, you can take charge of the stables again. Levi will find plenty of work elsewhere."

Eliza's mouth dropped open, but she didn't argue.

Instead, she did her best to walk with a straight spine to where Pickles and the buggy were waiting. Then with a grimace of pain, she lifted herself up and into the back.

Levi grunted. "Guess she does consider me her chauffeur and nothing more."

"Oh, she considers you," Jonah said. "More than you'll ever see or know. I hope you two work things out. That would make my life so much easier."

Then he slapped Levi on the back, his smile full of mirth. "I wish you the best, friend."

Levi prayed he'd get through the next couple of hours.

But he had a feeling Lizzie wouldn't make it easy for him.

CHAPTER FIFTEEN

Levi pulled the buggy up to the rectangular building that held the doctors' offices, a small emergency room, and the rehab center. Then he hopped down to help Eliza, but she was halfway out before he got there.

She held her mouth tight, bracing herself against the pain. She'd not let him help her down. He'd made it clear about boundaries, so she'd make it clear she intended to put up some new ones of her own.

Levi sighed and shook his head. "Don't mess up your leg trying to make a point with me, Eliza."

He'd called her Eliza. *Gut.* Another boundary. She told herself she was glad about that, ignoring the stinging hurt in her heart and the pain hissing down her leg.

"I'm better. I could have driven myself," she said, her breath shallow from exertion. "I just need a minute."

Then she stumbled on a piece of broken concrete.

And fell right into Levi's arms.

He held her there, his gaze locking on her with a longing that pierced worse than the pain in her leg. "I don't know what to do about you," he said, his voice low, his eyes burning with a heat she could feel in her soul.

"You do not have to do anything about me," she said to

erase that heat. "You really should let me be. I can find a way to my sessions. We do have cabs."

He didn't let go of her. "You have to be the most stubborn woman I've ever known."

"I reckon you knew a lot of them out there in the world."

"Jealous or just curious?" he asked, his eyes still on her.

"Neither." She pulled away and caught her balance. "I'm just surprised you didn't marry and get on with your life."

"I did get on with my life, but I never found the right woman out there. But thank you for wondering."

"I'm not wondering," she said, curiosity making her even more aggravated. "I'm going inside. You can run errands or sit on the buggy or . . . find a shade tree."

"I'll be right here on the bench. And when we're done, I'll get you straight home."

So no ice cream today. *Gut.* She would not eat ice cream with a man who'd insulted her and accused her of being a snob. Spoiled? A princess? Amish girls didn't become princesses, and this was certainly no fairy tale.

She would put something new on her quilt, something to remind her that this man had found yet another reason to put a wall between them.

She'd do that. She'd put a fence on one of the panels and leave it up to the viewer to decide why that fence was there.

But she'd know the reason. She'd remember his words to her every day. And every night. She had not slept well since he'd told her he wasn't *gut* enough for her.

Eliza gave Levi one last glance, then went inside and signed in. She would never, ever get married. Just trying to understand a man's mind was torment enough.

Why had he pulled away? she wondered while Lynsey,

the sweet female therapist, put Eliza through her paces. She stretched, going up and down on her toes at a slow pace, shifting her weight more to the injured leg as each week went by.

"Now try standing on your injured leg," Lynsey told Eliza, her blond ponytail swinging, her sky-blue eyes always happy.

Lynsey was engaged to a pharmacist who lived in Shadow Lake, too. They were building a small house here in town.

Eliza liked hearing about Lynsey's plans, but it hurt to think she might not ever have such plans. How could one man mess up her life in such a profound way?

She tried to stand on her healing leg, but she stumbled and groaned.

"You're off today," Lynsey said. "Is something wrong? Did you hurt your leg?"

"*Neh*," Eliza said, motioning toward the window. "I got flustered earlier when I found out he was bringing me to therapy."

"That handsome man on the bench?" Lynsey asked, craning her neck to get a glimpse of Levi out the big front windows of the building. "Didn't he bring you last week?"

"He did, but I don't want to be around him anymore."

Lynsey glanced at Eliza and then back to Levi. "I see."

"And what do you see?" Eliza asked as she tried to pose like a flamingo again. She'd seen pictures of the pretty birds standing on one leg.

"I see two people who've had a quarrel," Lynsey replied. "A fight, a misunderstanding."

"All of the above," Eliza said through a breath. Then she lowered her leg. "Do you and your fiancé ever argue?"

"Many times," Lynsey admitted. "But we love each other,

so we talk it through. Work, the wedding, the house, life. It all happens. And it causes stress."

"He is my stress," Eliza admitted.

"You love him?"

"*Neh*, I just have a history with him. One I'd like to forget."

"Right," Lynsey said with a knowing smile. "For your sake and the sake of getting this leg well, try to make peace with the man. He looks miserable out there all by himself."

"It's the heat. I told him to find something to do."

"Hey, it's late October. Not that hot, and he is not going to leave you here alone."

"He's stubborn that way."

Lynsey grinned. "Just like you, huh?"

Eliza smiled. "I'm not stubborn. I'm decisive."

Lynsey laughed. "Decisive. I'm gonna use that one."

Then she turned serious. "Don't let being decisive mess with your therapy. You're doing great, but being distracted can cause people to slack off on their exercises."

"I'm not going to do that," Eliza said. "The sooner I'm well, the sooner I'll be done with needing his help."

"That's a shame," Lynsey said. "The way he keeps glancing toward the door means he cares a lot about you."

Eliza looked out the window. Sure enough, Levi was watching the door. Probably because he was ready to go home.

She thanked Lynsey, got her printed instructions for next week's work, and managed to get herself out the door.

Levi jumped up to meet her. "How'd you do?"

"I did great. I'm getting better every week."

"Soon you won't need me anymore."

"That's the plan."

She turned to face him and saw the dejection in his eyes. A hurt that he hadn't meant for her to see. He quickly replaced it with a blank look and let her get into the wagon on her own.

She wanted to tell Levi she had always needed him and would probably always love him. But he'd made it clear he couldn't love a woman who had more material things than he did.

Couldn't he see that she'd give up just about anything to be with him, that she would have done that all along?

Neh, he couldn't see, and she'd never voiced her thoughts to him, so he'd assumed the worst when he compared their lives. She could almost understand how her world made him feel. His parents had struggled their whole lives. But Levi had left them, left her, left Shadow Lake.

Maybe his guilt was holding him back.

Such a mixed-up confusion.

His rejection hurt even worse this time than years ago.

But you rejected him the first time. That fact hit her square in the heart as she silently settled herself into the back of the buggy.

Maybe that had led him to believe he could never prove himself to her. And maybe, just maybe, she needed to come down off her haughty high horse and show him that he was wrong.

Two days later, Eliza did a slow walk from the cottage to the stables. She carried her cane in case she lost her balance, but she was determined to get back to the chores she loved.

She'd helped in the inn's kitchen this morning, under the watchful eye of Edith. The cook ruled the kitchen, but she'd sat Eliza down to peel potatoes and they'd had a nice talk.

"You and Levi—what's going on there?" Edith had said with her hands on her hips.

"Nothing."

Edith huffed. "Something. It's always something when one says nothing."

"It's something that will amount to nothing," Eliza had replied, while she took out her frustrations on the poor potatoes.

Edith turned back to her work but finally returned and put a hand on Eliza's arm. "I think we have enough peeled and sliced potatoes to last for three days, dear."

Working in the kitchen had not gone very well.

"Do us all a favor," Colette had told her. "Go to the stables."

So here she was, out of breath and with one leg throbbing. But she'd made it to her bench. She sank down, wondering what she could do to show Levi she wasn't above him in any way. She wished she could carry a pitcher of lemonade, but she was afraid she'd spill it. And maybe some snickerdoodle cookies since Edith had offered them.

But here she was empty-handed and unable to help anyone in any way.

Then she looked up and saw Abigail coming up the alley between the stalls with . . . a pitcher of lemonade and a basket full of cookies.

"What are you doing?" she asked on a whisper. She didn't want Levi to come around the corner and find her.

"I'm bringing lemonade and cookies. Edith said you wanted to bring some out to our men, but you were afraid you'd drop everything."

"That's true." Eliza felt hot tears burning at her eyes. She never cried, so why was she such a mess these days? "*Denke*."

Jonah and Levi came back from checking the livestock,

laughing and talking until they saw the two sisters waiting for them on the bench near the front of the stables.

"Ah, my lovely wife has brought refreshments," Jonah said, all grins.

"I'm not thirsty," Levi replied. "Or hungry."

Jonah grabbed Levi's shirt, dragging him forward. "It would be rude to turn down fresh lemonade, bro."

Levi frowned. "Bro?"

"Sorry, I revert to the outside world every now and then," Jonah said, and his determined stare caused Levi to nod finally.

"Oh, I guess I am a bit thirsty," Levi said, his tone not a happy one.

"*Gut,*" Abigail said. "Eliza was thoughtful enough to remind me to bring this out to you."

"So thoughtful," Jonah said, taking his glass of the icy drink.

"*Ja,*" Levi said, not even looking at Eliza.

An awkward silence followed as the men chewed their cookies and sipped their lemonade.

Abigail set the huge tray holding the plastic lemonade pitcher, small paper cups, and the cookies down on the bench next to Eliza. "Jonah, we should check the apple orchard. We've had a lot of pickers out there today. I need to go over preparations for the Harvest Festival, too."

Jonah looked confused and then he smiled. "Oh, yes, we should do that. We should check things over."

They walked away, in love and holding hands.

Eliza didn't finish her cookie. She laid it down and stared at the dirt floor.

Levi cleared his throat. "You haven't been out here in a while."

"*Neh.*"

"You are still angry with me, then?"

"What do you think?"

"I think I shouldn't have been so honest with you."

"Well, you were and now we know where we stand."

"I thought we could still be friends."

"I thought you wanted nothing more to do with me."

"That's not what I meant, Lizzie."

"You can't call me that. We are from different worlds. My name is Eliza."

He took off his straw hat and hit it against his leg. "You are a frustrating woman."

"You are a confusing man."

"So, are we going to fight like this every time we're around each other?"

"We won't have to be around each other much longer. I am getting better every day. Hardly a limp at all."

He put down his empty cup. "Well, then, I'd better give you the gift I bought for you when I was in town the other day. I was saving it for a special time, but that might not work."

Eliza finally looked up at Levi. "What are you talking about?"

He walked toward his shop in the back, nudging the horses as he strolled along. Then he returned and handed her a floral-colored tote bag. "It's heavy," he warned.

"What is this?"

"You like books, so I bought you some—they've been approved by your *mamm*, so you can enjoy reading while you're here or when you're resting at home." Then he shrugged. "My *mamm* made the tote bag for you."

Eliza reached in with all the joy of someone finding treasure. A book about horses. Another one about quilting. Then another about the history of Lake Erie and some of the houses along the lake. Finally, a book about flowers and landscaping.

"And one more," he said, pointing to the little wrapped book at the bottom of the bag.

Eliza was speechless as she lifted out the little book. She opened it and stared. "There are no words. Is this a journal?"

"*Ja*, Lizzie. Your journal. You are writing your own story every day. I thought a journal might help you figure things out, in your own words."

"What should I write?" she asked in earnest. "I've never thought of writing about my life."

He leaned down, so close she could smell the mint and rosemary in the soap his mother had shown her when they were visiting. "You could write about us and what's right with us. Or what's wrong with us. Maybe then, we will both understand what went wrong so long ago, and how we could make things right in the future."

Tears pricked at her eyes. "But you don't want a future with me, Levi."

"Lizzie," he said, touching a finger to her cheekbone. "I have always wanted a future with you, but there are so many reasons it won't work."

"Such as your thinking I'm better than you—which you know is not something the Amish believe or use against each other."

He kneeled on one knee and smiled over at her. "I do know that, but I want to give you everything, and I don't have much to give."

"So you'll just . . . leave it at that?"

"I have to, for now."

"What does that mean?"

"It means . . . I will find a way to make things right between us, somehow. We can start all over again."

"And again, and again?" she asked as a tear slipped down her cheek and hit his finger.

"Again and again, until we both know it's right."

He caught the tear and then he leaned in and kissed her other cheek. "Enjoy your books. We will one day have a story to tell. I have to keep believing that."

Then he grabbed a cookie and strolled back to his work.

While Eliza sat there alone with an open, empty book, its pages so white and bright, her tears fell and hit the paper, leaving an imprint of the stain that would always be there.

CHAPTER SIXTEEN

That night, she pulled out the unfinished quilt. Tomorrow, they were having another quilting frolic, and Abigail wanted her to work on her forgiving quilt. She glanced at the books, knowing she'd add a book panel. Then she thought about cookies and lemonade, and how Levi had touched her cheek and caught her tears with his finger. She'd make a cookie panel with a glass of lemonade in the same panel—yellow and bright. And somewhere on the quilt, she'd add a floral pattern for the beautiful tote bag he'd given her. She planned to visit Connie and thank her for making the bag. What a thoughtful gift. That also meant Levi had talked to his *mamm* about Eliza. She hoped Connie could shed some light on him and help her understand the grown man he'd become.

Colette popped into her room and dropped onto the bed. "Have you written in your journal yet?"

Eliza nodded and picked up the pretty little blue book. "I have. I started with falling down the ladder and breaking my leg."

"Why there?"

"Because that was what caused Levi to come back into my life," she told Colette.

"It's like Alice falling down the rabbit hole," Colette replied. "Although Mamm wasn't so keen on me reading that one."

Eliza shook her head. "*Ja*, falling off that ladder started a chain of events that has left me puzzled and confused, but at least I'm almost back to my old self."

Almost.

Abigail came in with her sketch pad and shut the door. "Jonah is with Mamm and Daed, so we have a few moments alone." She leaned close. "Aenti Miriam will be here next week. At least now she can sleep in my old room."

"We are both thankful for that," Colette said. "She snores something fierce."

They all giggled like teenagers. Then Abigail got the update on the forgiving quilt. "I thought you were through with quilting," she said to Eliza.

"She was, but Levi has redeemed himself yet again," Colette said before Eliza could speak.

Eliza explained, one hand on her eager sister's arm. "So here we are." She told Abigail what she wanted to put on the quilt next. Abigail sketched, her lips twisted while she concentrated.

"How would this look?"

Eliza took the small sketch pad and studied the drawings. "That's it—the lemonade glass, a bowl of cookies, and my blue book. Very nice. Then we can find a pretty floral pattern for the middle panel."

"So you'll be at the frolic tomorrow?" Abigail asked, her expression eager.

"*Ja*, but why are you so excited? You know I'm not the best at quilting."

Abigail smiled. "I just want both my sisters there."

"Why?" They both asked, confused but mostly curious.

"I have a surprise."

"You aren't going to hide Levi in that powder room where Jonah heard about your quilt, are you?" Colette asked.

Abigail giggled. "*Neh*, nothing like that. You'll find out tomorrow."

She tried to stand. But her two sisters pulled her back down. "I have to go."

"You can't leave until you tell us. Your eyes are bright, and you've got that dreamy expression on your face," Colette said. "What is going on?"

Eliza studied Abigail. "She's rosy-cheeked and glowing." Then she gasped and grabbed Abigail's hand. "Are you . . . with child?"

Abigail's eyes grew bright with tears as she nodded. "A *bobbeli*. Jonah and I are going to have a *bobbeli*."

"Oh!" Colette let out a yelp so loud, Eliza was sure Mamm and Daed would come running.

Abigail put a hand to her mouth. "Shh. I want to surprise Mamm."

"Does Jonah know?" Eliza asked, in awe.

"*Ja*. I told him on our walk through the apple orchard because when we were falling in love, he promised me we'd walk through there alone one day. And so we did. Again. We walk through there a lot."

"We should tell Mamm and Daed right now," Colette said. "I don't think I can wait until tomorrow."

Abigail sat thinking. "You're right. I can't wait either. Let me warn Jonah when we get downstairs, okay?"

They all hugged, then danced around in a circle. Eliza's happiness for her sister outweighed the envy she felt. She'd never thought she wanted love and marriage, but now her heart seemed to burn for both. And a *bobbeli*.

So much to put in her journal. So much to put on her quilt.

Eliza had never been this conflicted about anything. She

truly did feel like one of the lead characters in her beloved books. Would she find her own happy ending?

They all marched downstairs and out onto the porch where the chill of fall felt crisp and fresh, and the leaves danced a secret waltz across the paths leading to the inn and the big lake.

Abigail whispered to Jonah and smiled. He smiled back, the love in his eyes so precious and so true.

Daed, confused as always, looked around and then looked at Mamm. "What is going on?"

Mamm smiled but didn't say anything. She'd probably already figured this out.

Jonah took Abigail's hand. "We have an announcement. Abby had wanted to tell the ladies at the quilting frolic tomorrow, but I think she's ready now."

Abigail grinned and looked at Mamm and Daed. "Jonah and I are having a *bobbeli*."

Colette and Eliza hugged each other and wiped their eyes. Mamm grabbed Daed's hand and wiped her eyes. Jonah put his arm around Abigail and gave her a sweet kiss on her cheek.

"A *bobbeli*," Daed said, his eyes a bit misty. "Our first grandchild."

Mamm hugged him close. "*Ja*, Abe. Our first. The first of many, I hope."

Then everyone hugged, laughed, and cried, and finally after the sunset drifted through the trees, Eliza and her family waved to Jonah and Abigail as they walked back to their house.

"We'll need more quilts," Mamm said. "And we'll need to help with the nursery. And . . . I can help deliver my first grandchild."

They headed inside, smiling.

Colette turned to Eliza. "We will be *aenties*."

Eliza nodded, her mind on her own quilt and what she needed to do to figure out her life. "A *kinder* to love and spoil."

"Do you think we'll ever be like that, so in love?"

"I thought you were," Eliza replied to her sister.

"I think I am," Colette said. "Matthew has been around me all my life. Why does it feel so *wunderbar* that I finally noticed him?"

Eliza shook her head. "Why did it take Levi returning to show me just how much I missed him?"

"We are a pair," Colette said. "We've always longed for romance and love and now that we have it, we don't quite know what to make of it."

"I reckon that's why we make quilts," Eliza said. "So we can figure it all out."

They walked hand in hand back inside the house and finished cleaning up downstairs before heading back up to their rooms. Later, when Eliza was lying in bed, she thought about Levi and how he'd tried to make her happy in so many ways. Even offering to *not* love her if he wasn't worthy of her.

"Maybe I'm the one who is not worthy," she whispered to the night. Then she held her little blue book and wrote her secrets in it and fell asleep with it tucked beneath her pillow.

No matter, she'd always have the thoughts she put into that book. And she'd have the quilt that showed all of Levi's attempts to be the man she needed him to be.

Could she become the woman she needed to be for him?

Levi arrived the next day to find several women gathering to go into the big meeting room at the inn. Jonah had warned him about avoiding female frolics.

"They laugh and talk . . . about life, food and family—and stuff that can scare a man." Then he told Levi how he'd overheard them once talking about the quilt Abigail had made from his tattered memories. "I was upset at first, but in the end, those quilting sessions brought out the truth about my past and showed the way to my future."

The truth? Levi didn't know what that was anymore. And the future was as vast and unattainable as ever. He didn't know what he wanted anymore, but he did know he'd keep fighting for Eliza. He'd make himself a better man, a more prosperous man, for her.

He grabbed some *kaffe* and a biscuit from Edith. She always kept food for the staff. Then he tried to sneak out the back door, but just as he opened it, Eliza came bursting through with fabric held tightly in her arms.

They ran straight into each other.

"I'm sorry," he said, *kaffe* sloshing, but he managed to hold on to his biscuit.

"Excuse me." She glanced up at him. "Levi."

"It's me. Just grabbing my breakfast. My second breakfast, that is."

She smiled at that. "Does your *mamm* know you sneak biscuits from Edith?"

He stood back, wiped his shirt, and took in the sight of her in a burgundy dress and a fresh apron. "It hasn't *kumm* up in conversation, *neh*."

Eliza's eyes grew wide as she stood so close to him. "I won't tell."

"*Denke*."

They kept standing, staring at each other.

"Are we friends again?" he asked.

She studied him for so long, he was afraid of her answer.

"*Ja*. We are friends."

He could tell she wanted to say more, but she seemed to hesitate. "What have you got there?"

She glanced at the bundle in her arms. "It's a quilt, or the beginnings of a quilt. A mess, really. I'm not very *gut* at sewing."

"But you enjoy spending time with your sisters and *mamm*?"

"Mostly," she said with a saucy smile.

"Better than nagging me in the stables?"

"I don't nag. I instruct."

"Oh, you instruct. I see. As if I don't know what I'm doing."

"I observe, too, of course."

"And what do you observe? The horses? Or me?"

She blushed and blinked, her eyelashes fluttering. "My horses, of course. Soon I'll be riding again."

He bit into his biscuit, the idea of her getting on a horse scaring him. After chewing the buttery dough, he asked, "Are you ready for that?"

"I might not be able to get on by myself, but I think I'm ready to ride."

"I'll help you. Get you up there and watch you so you don't damage your leg again."

"I'd like that."

Surprised she hadn't turned him down, he said, "Later maybe?"

"Maybe. Unless this quilting session makes me tired."

Matthew came walking up. "*Guder mariye.*"

Levi stepped away from Eliza. "*Gut daag*, Matthew."

Eliza nodded to Matthew. "I'll see you later," she said to Levi as she slipped past him.

"The frolic?" Matthew asked, shaking his head.

"*Ja.*" Levi watched as Eliza hurried up the hallway toward the big room. "It scares me to think about it."

Sarah came out of the room and waved to both of them. "Levi, next time we plan a quilting frolic, I'll invite your *mamm*. Connie can spend the day with us."

"She'd like that, I'm sure," he said. "I'd better get on with things."

"Me, too," Matthew said.

They scattered, but Levi glanced back and saw Sarah's amused face. They were all in a great mood this morning.

That made him smile. Eliza was speaking to him again, so he could be in a great mood himself. And she'd said she'd see him later.

He hoped she would visit him at the stables.

Maybe they'd taken another turn in their relationship. A better turn.

CHAPTER SEVENTEEN

Eliza placed her quilt top on the worktable by the wall. She'd sewn the first few panels together on Mamm's sewing machine. The other women would help her place the square panels on the puffy white batting they'd stretch across the quilting table. Right now, she wasn't ready for that. She'd sit at a smaller table with her adjustable wooden frame and hope no one would notice her feeble attempts.

Abigail had shown her how to take the paper patterns they cut out from her sketches and trace them with a pencil or charcoal on a white backing. Then they'd cut the shapes from the different colors of cloth they'd selected and stitch them to different colored panels. Orange and burgundy mums, and a black flowerpot. Yellow for the ice cream cone and creamy white for the ice cream. Blue for her journal and several different colors for the stack of books. They were still working on the buggy ride to the cottage after she'd gotten her cast off.

"What are you thinking over there?" Mamm asked, her hands held together over her apron, her smile serene as always.

Eliza knew she could be honest with Mamm. "I want

this quilt to show what my heart feels, Mamm." She sighed and shrugged. "Except my heart feels too many things."

Mamm touched a hand to her face. "Then put down what you receive from him, the material gifts that show kindness. We Amish aren't *gut* at accepting too many showy gifts, but gifts from the heart are the best kind, Eliza. With each gift Levi gives you, think of the gestures he's shown you. Gifts from the heart mean the world to a woman. We don't need diamonds or fancy clothes, or fancy homes. We need love, assurance, and strength. The kind of strength that cements a union for a lifetime."

Eliza thought about that. "I don't know if I can find a lifetime kind of love. Levi and I hurt each other so much when we were young. For years, I blamed him. Only him."

"*Ach vell*, I understand," Mamm said. "You feel guilt, ain't so?"

Eliza had not realized that until now. "I do, Mamm. I do."

Sarah gave her an indulgent smile. "*Leibling*, you need to find some kind gestures of your own, don't you think?"

Eliza stood there with the pieces of her quilt all around her, realizing she'd been so wrong in so many ways. She couldn't move forward with Levi until she'd resolved all the reasons she'd panicked when they'd kissed that first time. What if she panicked again? And again? What if she wasn't meant to kiss a man or fall in love? What if it wasn't really about the kiss, but about giving up her freedom and independence?

"What are you doing over there, Eliza?"

Aenti Miriam had arrived.

Eliza glanced up from her stitching and forced a smile. She'd hoped to be done before Aenti showed up. Stating the obvious, she said, "I'm making a quilt, Aenti."

Miriam came forward, her hands on her hips, her lips pursed together as tight as a stitch. "I can see that with *meine* own eyes. But what kind of quilt is this?"

"It's a forgiving quilt," Eliza replied without thinking. Aenti would want to know the whole story.

"Who needs forgiving? You or someone else?"

"Both," Colette said from her perch near the big quilting table. Then she glanced up and put a hand to her mouth. "I mean, everyone needs forgiveness, ain't so?"

Aenti Miriam glanced around, her chin up, her eyes slits of disapproval. "I don't like these modern primitives. This is not the Amish way of quilting."

Mamm took over, always protecting her *bobbelis*, even if they were all grown now. "Miriam, the girls like to experiment with new ideas. The *Englisch* like pretty, interesting quilts, and we make all kinds. But for ourselves, we make things that show our creative nature in keeping with our plain ways. Eliza's quilt shows kind gestures, which I'm sure you'll agree makes for a nice quilt."

"I do not condone, nor do I understand why you let these girls do whatever they please. You'll regret that one day, sister."

"I regret that I invited you to stay for two weeks," Mamm said with her sweet smile. "Can you try to enjoy yourself?"

Aenti Miriam had a bad disposition due to a hard life, but she also had feelings. She huffed and sniffed. "I can leave."

Mamm shook her head and hugged her older sister. "I was only teasing you to make you smile. We do not want you to leave. We want you to help us, since your quilts are known far and wide. You are *gut* at this, so let's enjoy that and get some work done."

Miriam glanced from Eliza back to Mamm. "I suppose it doesn't matter what I think, since you allowed Abigail to marry an *Englischer*, and now you are encouraging Eliza with another strange quilt. Makes no difference to me. They are yours to deal with, after all."

"Exactly," Mamm said, still as calm as always. "Jonah is Amish now and . . . he and Abby are having a *bobbeli*. We rejoice in that. And Eliza is maturing into a kind, understanding young woman. Colette is happy with her Matthew. All is well with me."

Aenti Miriam stood quiet as she processed this information. "A *bobbeli*? Abby and Jonah? Sister, why didn't you tell me that sooner?"

"You did not give me an opportunity," Mamm pointed out.

Eliza pasted a smile on her face and went back to stitching as Aenti hugged Abigail and beamed with pride. Eliza found it soothing to hear her *mamm* and Aenti go on and on about the new baby and different quilting patterns.

Eliza became lost in her stitches as she remembered every moment of her time with Levi. She took her time putting the needle to the fabric, her thimble tight on her finger, her mind watching the white threads that would highlight each kindness he'd shown her. She'd find ways to show him she intended to be kind and understanding and forgiving, too, and that she in turn needed his forgiveness.

It was a long process, learning to forgive someone. It was an intricate part of the Amish faith, yet some still held grudges all their lives. Eliza didn't want to be that kind of person.

She didn't want Levi to leave again, thinking he'd been the one in the wrong and taking the blame for it. She prayed that wouldn't happen. And she prayed he'd see the *gut* in himself and not think he was beneath her. That was silly, after all.

She had a lot of prayers poured into her work today, for certain sure. A prayer for each panel she put on her quilt.

This one might take a long time to finish.

Levi went about his work while a family of four watched. The *Englisch*, so fascinated by Amish life, often asked if they could observe him at work. Though he smiled and nodded, he felt like a zoo animal.

Today, Samson gave the couple and their two children a real show. Samson didn't like a lot of people buzzing around him, so he stomped, snorted, and tossed his gray mane.

That brought giggles from the children, who stood in awe of the big animal.

"Does he bite?" the boy asked while Levi held Samson's hoof between his knees and examined the shoe for wear and tear.

"He doesn't bite on purpose," Levi explained. "Only if he's taken by surprise or if someone startles him."

"Why do horses wear shoes?" the girl asked, grinning, her strawberry-blond hair falling down her back.

"They have many jobs," he explained. "So they need *gut* shoes to protect their hooves. They run hard and fast sometimes and carry humans on their backs. That makes for a lot of stress on their hooves."

"Like me when I run barefoot," the little boy said. "I get stickers, and rocks hurt my feet."

"Exactly," Levi patiently agreed. "They are the same. A hurting foot makes for a grumpy horse or boy."

The boy beamed and nodded, while his sister giggled.

Mom and Dad thanked him and turned their children toward the apple orchard. But the little boy ran back. "You have an important job."

"That I do," Levi said. "That I do."

He looked up to find Eliza standing a few feet away, watching him. "Are you done quilting then?" he asked after the boy ran toward his family.

"*Ja.*"

She stepped forward with only a slight limp in her left leg. He knew she still fretted about that limp, but he tried not to ask too many questions about how she was doing.

"How did it go?"

She smiled and did a little twist like a sashay. "It went fine, except for Aenti Miriam disapproving of everything and telling us how to quilt. She is an expert at quilting and making us feel as if we've failed horribly with each stitch."

"There are no perfect quilts," he said, remembering the old saying Amish women used a lot. They always left one mistake in each quilt, because only *Gott* was perfect.

Samson grew impatient so Levi let him go. The big horse headed straight for Eliza and lowered his head.

She gave him the big chunk of sliced apple she had in her hand. "*Neh*, well tell that to my *aenti*."

Samson chewed on his treat while Eliza stroked his head and nose. "I have missed you, my big *bobbeli*."

Levi finished his work and washed up at the old pump behind the stables. After running his hands through his hair and making sure he'd cleared off any dirt, he turned back to Eliza.

"Did you need to talk to me?"

She blinked, looked confused. "Oh, you mean what am I doing here?"

He nodded, glad she was here but afraid to make any assumptions.

"I thought I'd check on the horses and . . . I wanted to see you."

"Oh, and why is that?" he asked, stepping closer to her.

Eliza's eyes flared with awareness, going dark green like a reflection of fresh leaves on a pond. "I've been grumpy lately and I wanted to make up for that."

"We did decide we were on speaking terms again," he reminded her. "So . . . you missed me?"

"How can I do that when you're right here?"

He moved an inch closer. "But you came here looking for me, *ja*?"

She blushed and glanced around. "I suppose I did, at that."

He stood, enjoying seeing Eliza unsure and flustered. Enjoying seeing her, period.

"I have an idea," he said as he stood in front of her. "Why don't we take a walk through the apple orchard, and then I'll walk with you to the cottage."

"That's taking the long way home," she said.

"Exactly." He held out his hand.

Eliza took it. Her hand felt soft and warm against his rough skin. Fragile, delicate, but with an underlying strength.

They walked slowly down to the apple orchard, leaves chasing their footsteps and falling across their path. The air breathed hope, the wind felt crisp, fresh, and new as it pushed the scents of water and earth around them.

"Fall is like a grace period before winter," he said, enjoying being with Eliza. "Just right. The harvest is here, and we can rest a bit before the growing season starts all over again in the spring."

"When did you become so philosophical?" she asked, her eyes skimming over him and back to the leaves.

"I want to be a poet for some reason when I'm around you."

She giggled. "Now you are being silly."

"You don't think I could write a poem?"

"Have you ever tried?"

"I will now."

They laughed. Together.

Just be near her.

Levi was beginning to see the wisdom of that advice.

He reached up and picked a pretty apple for her. "I love apple pie," he said.

She held the fruit and studied it, her eyes widening.

"Eliza?"

"*Ja?*"

"Are you . . . ? Is something wrong?"

"*Neh.*" She rubbed the apple against her apron. "This is a perfect apple."

Every time he thought he had her figured out, Levi was surprised by Eliza all over again. "I never knew you wanted your apples to be perfect."

She held up her apron and said, "I'd like enough to make a pie, please."

"That's a *gut* idea." Then he leaned down and asked, "Can I have a slice of that pie?"

"I'm baking the pie for you and your family, Levi. So you can have more than a slice."

Levi grinned and started filling her apron with apples.

The *Englisch* family of four came walking by.

The little girl ran up to them. "Whatcha doing with all those apples?"

"She's going to bake me an apple pie," Levi explained.

"Are you married?" the *kinder* asked, so innocent and so blunt.

"*Neh,*" Eliza said rather quickly.

"Not yet," Levi said with firm assurance. "But one day."

"When you have your wedding, can I come?"

Eliza's mouth dropped open. "Uh . . . I'm not sure if your parents would allow that." Then she handed the girl a pretty apple. "You will have your own wedding one day, I'm sure."

"I like your hat," the girl said. "Can I wear one of those at my wedding?"

The girl's dad ran up to them. "Sorry, she's inquisitive. C'mon, Laurel, let's go pay for our apples. Then we'll go into town for dinner."

He dragged his daughter away with a playfulness that had her giggling.

After they were gone, Eliza glanced up at Levi. "What did you mean by that?"

He stopped picking apples. "Oh, you mean about us being married one day?"

"*Ja.*"

"I meant we are not married yet. But I hope one day we might be."

She nodded and held her apron high so the apples wouldn't fall out. "I haven't decided if I want to get married."

"Oh, I see. This is news to me."

"I know we talked of it when we were young."

"But now we are fully grown, and you obviously value your independence."

"I do," she said. "And you think you don't have anything to offer."

"I do," he replied. "I mean I do think that."

She stopped as they left the shelter of the orchard and turned to him. "Before we can somehow fit those two notions together, Levi, I'm going to have to cook you a lot of pies."

He nodded, accepted that they had a long way to go. "*Gut* thing I like apple pie then."

CHAPTER EIGHTEEN

The big event would be in two weeks, and everyone was in an uproar planning this year's Harvest Festival. The kitchen staff moved chaotically through the hallways and the restaurant, setting up extra tables on the deep front porch of the inn. They'd also put tables out on the lawn. The official Shadow Lake Harvest Festival was celebrated all over the township, but tourists knew the way to the Shadow Lake Inn, so it had become tradition to be ready with extra food, a pumpkin patch, and a craft show. Part of the proceeds went to the local community—the fire department, the clinic, and several other organizations.

Which meant everyone had to pitch in and help.

Aenti Miriam had made herself the supervisor of all things.

"I want this place spic-and-span," she'd announced this morning.

"My kitchen is always sparkling clean," Edith had retorted with a stiff smile as she flounced back to the pantry.

Edith ran a tight kitchen and today, even Eliza got involved in the cooking and cleaning. Jonah and Levi had the stables under control, so she had no excuse to hide away out there. They'd get Peaches ready for the pony rides that the *kinder* loved so much. Eliza didn't mind hard work; she just preferred being outside in the cool air and warm sunshine.

So here she sat, peeling apples and crimping crust. They always sold pies at the festival. The whole town turned out with food booths, arts and crafts, and all kinds of jams, jellies, and preserves. And the quilts—the inn displayed them in the main lobby, and people came from all around to buy them.

Of course, Eliza's quilt would not be on display. She'd have to explain it, and she wasn't ready to shout her story to the world. Aenti Miriam was already wondering if she'd found a man with no memory as Abigail had. But Eliza's man had a *gut* memory. Too good.

"Why do you stare at him?" Aenti Miriam had asked several times.

"Because he's there, in my staring range," Eliza finally told her.

"You girls, always with the boys on your mind."

"He's not on my mind; he's in my way."

Her *aenti*, who liked to huff, huffed her way straight to Mamm to warn her of her daughter's callous ways.

Mamm had nodded and gone to work on anything she could find.

"What are you dreaming about?" Colette asked as she sank down on the stool next to Eliza. "If I see another apple pie, I might throw up."

"I'm thinking about how I wish I could be in the stables," Eliza admitted. "And please, don't throw up. Edith might banish you from the kitchen forever."

"And you'd rather be banished than have me go, ain't so?"

"I'd rather be with my horses and books."

"And Levi," her sister replied. "You two have been walking out a lot."

"So I hear, especially from Aenti," Eliza replied. "We are not walking out. We walk . . . together."

"Is there a difference?" Colette asked with eyebrows raised.

"I need the exercise," Eliza explained. "And yes, there is a difference for us."

"Right. And Levi needs to move around more, too, I suppose."

"Stop spluttering," Eliza replied, a flush warming her skin. "We have agreed to be friends."

"*Ach vell*, that is something."

"It's a little thing. Just two friends. I'm going to send his *mamm* an apple pie."

"Well, you'd better do it soon," Colette replied. "I heard him earlier telling Jonah he has to go out of town."

"Out of town?" This was news to Eliza. "Why wouldn't he tell me that?"

"Maybe your *friend* forgot," Colette said. "Or maybe he didn't want you to know."

Vexed, Eliza stood so quickly, she dropped apple peelings all over the floor. "I will find out what's going on."

Colette watched her with wide eyes. "And I suppose I will clean up these apple peels before Edith or Aenti Miriam get out a wooden spoon and use it on us."

Eliza didn't care about the peels right now. She walked too fast to the stable, stumbling over a jutting rock, her sneakers no protection. So now one of her toes was throbbing along with her leg. When she reached the stables and glanced down the long alleyway, she could see that Levi had cleaned out his equipment.

"He left again?"

Jonah came out of the tack room just as she plunged forward. "Whoa," he said. "Where's the fire?"

"Why did Levi leave?" she asked. They'd been getting along so well. They'd become close—friends close. They had a comfortable, pleasant bond between them now.

"Why?"

Jonah stood in front of her. "Breathe," he said. "Levi got called away on an emergency. A horse he used to take care of needed new shoes. The animal is a handful and no one else will work with him. Levi went to Spartansburg for a few days."

"Why didn't he tell me?" she asked, an odd burn inside her heart. Maybe she shouldn't have eaten that meatball sandwich for lunch. "He should have told me."

"Eliza," Jonah said, "Levi works for us as needed on a part-time basis. He has other work, too."

Then she understood. He could have turned down the other job, but he wanted to make a better living, for his family, and for her.

"I see. I mean I understand. I overreacted."

"A bit," Jonah said, his dark eyes full of sympathy and mirth. "He will return."

"I thought that the last time he left," she said, realizing her feelings for Levi extended far beyond friendship.

"Oh, he did leave something for you," Jonah said, hurrying to the empty shelf where Levi kept his tools. He came back and handed her a small package.

"*Denke*," she managed to squeak out. "I shouldn't have gone on like that."

Jonah chuckled. "When have you not gone on like that?"

She blinked and stared at her brother-in-law. "Where is Abigail? She told me to peel apples, but I haven't seen her in a while."

Jonah glanced toward the open doors. "She's resting. The baby. She overdid things yesterday."

"But she's—"

"Everyone is fine. The *bobbeli* and my wife are both fine."

Eliza leaned against the wall, thinking he didn't seem so sure. "I talked to her earlier, but she didn't mention feeling sick."

"She got a little faint when she came out to show us where to set up the tents and tables," Jonah explained. He perched against the worktable. "I have to say, it scared me. Really scared me." He glanced toward the big rock where he and Abigail had been married. "The festival last year— the day I remembered who I was—I think it's weighing heavily on both of us. What we went through to get here."

Feeling for him, Eliza forgot her own problems as she remembered how terrified Abigail had been that day. "I will go and check on her. You know she's strong. Everything will be fine. Mamm will see to that." Then she touched his shirtsleeve. "Jonah, you're both safe now. Abby is safe because she has you."

Jonah looked up at her, and for a moment she remembered how lost he'd been when he'd showed up here with no memory and no hope. She saw the fear in his courageous eyes.

"Jonah, do you need to go? I can handle the rest of this. I'm better now and I could use the time alone to think and to pray."

He gave her a look full of gratitude. "I have been worried. I'll be back to shut everything down."

"I can do that," she said. "You stay with Abby. She will be worried, and you are the one who can calm her."

He nodded and got up. "Are you sure?"

"I'm sure," she said. "I'll finish and get back to the kitchen. But I'll stop in to see Abby first."

"*Denke*," he said, his smile unsure. He loved her sister so much.

"Go," she said, shooing him away. Eliza said a silent prayer. Abigail wanted children so much.

He washed up and hurried out the open back doors, his anxiety showing. It took a lot for a strong, fierce man like Jonah to be worried.

Eliza shook her head. She'd been in such a panic over Levi going away without telling her or even saying good-bye, she'd forgotten everyone around her. Mamm would be tired if she'd been sitting with Abby. Her near-fainting spell must have scared both of them, since they hadn't even mentioned it to anyone else. She should hurry with her chores and alert Edith that she'd need to leave the inn kitchen to put supper on the table at home.

But first she had to open the little plain-wrapped package Jonah had given her. From Levi.

Tearing the paper away, she found a note and a small wooden carving. A carving of a horse that looked a lot like Samson. He'd carved her a horse from gray driftwood. And he'd left her a note:

> *Eliza, I got called away. I don't know when I'll*
> *be back, but I will be back. Could you check on*
> *Mamm and my siblings for me? I'd appreciate that.*
> *I hope you like the miniature Samson. For you*
> *to keep.*

She rubbed the smooth gray wood and marveled at the cuts that looked like Samson's mane. Another treasure to show her he wanted—no, needed—forgiveness. Another reminder that she wanted and needed forgiveness in return.

Eliza went about her business, her limp hardly bothering her now. Maybe it was time for her to return to the stables a few hours a day at least.

But that would mean Levi wouldn't be needed as much. Of course, they could keep him on as a farrier. He did a much better job than the man they'd had to fire a few months ago.

She pondered all these things as she checked on the animals and made sure the stables were tidy. Then she washed up, grabbed her tiny horse, and hurried to look in on her sister.

Eliza had many things to be grateful for, but most of all, she wanted to be an *aenti*. She'd be a much nicer one than Aenti Miriam, that was for certain sure.

Levi hadn't wanted to leave. But the money Mr. Whitman had offered him to make this special trip was enticing. He could save up more and, hopefully, have something to offer Eliza.

But would she understand?

He'd been a coward, not telling her outright. Maybe the little wooden horse he'd carved would help remedy that. He'd worked on the little carving for weeks, thinking he'd give it to Laura. But somehow, he knew he'd made it with Eliza in mind.

"I'll be back in time for the festival," he'd told Jonah after he'd explained and loaded up his tools. "Mr. Whitman is a wealthy man who breeds horses. He has to have the best of everything. I've worked for him, off and on, for years."

"Shouldn't shoeing the horse be easy?" Jonah had asked. "You could be back tomorrow, right?"

"Maybe. It depends. Starburst is a mean stallion with an

important job. I think he has a big head, knowing he's needed to breed champions."

Jonah had grinned. "Explain no more. When do you think you'll be back?"

"Maybe three days or so. Mr. Whitman is sending one of his workers in a truck so I can load and use my own tools. I'll leave Rudolph here if that's all right."

Jonah laughed. "Rudolph thinks he owns the place, but don't tell Samson. He'll be fine."

Three days or so.

Would Eliza think of it that way?

The truck had pulled up by the stables, and Levi and the ranch hand loaded up what he'd need. Then he'd used the man's phone to get a message to the phone booth near his *mamm*'s house. The neighbors would pass the word.

Now he was in a bunkroom at Mr. Whitman's place. It was outside Spartansburg, near a big Amish community. Levi knew the back roads almost as well as the hired hands, some of them Amish like him. He'd had supper with several of the men he knew here. Some had gone home to their own Amish farms and homes. Some were batching it like him. He thought about that—being a bachelor all his life. Not what he wanted.

This trip would give him time to think about a lot of things. Things such as making more money and not just working piecemeal and part-time. Once he'd reached his goal, he'd work hard on winning Eliza back.

Until then, he might have to make a lot of trips like this one. He'd go where he was needed and pray that Eliza would wait for him—a little longer. Because even though they'd denied it to each other and themselves, they needed to address the strong pull that tugged them together. They were more than friends. Much more.

CHAPTER NINETEEN

"I have never liked waiting."

"We know," Colette said, her tone both amused and aggravated as she stared at Eliza. "Sit down. Your pacing is upsetting Abby."

Abigail sat up against several pillows. "I am fine and you two should go home now."

"*Neh*, Mamm told us to sit with you until Jonah is done helping with the tents. And you know how Mamm expects us to follow her orders."

Abigail's gaze moved from Colette to Eliza. "Levi said he'd be back soon. Why are you so worried?"

"Because there is nothing holding him here. He only came home for his family, but he works away from their home most days. Here and there, and I know he's been out to Dr. Merrill's place several times. Then he goes home to do chores and try to take care of everything. I don't know how he does it."

"He's working toward a future," Abigail said, her hands twisting the blanket falling across her lap. "That's what men do."

"I think Eliza wants to be part of that future," Colette

said. "She is pining, and the man has only been gone one day."

"I am not pining. I plan to visit Connie tomorrow and spend the day with her."

"We need you here," Colette said. "Aenti Miriam is trying to take over the kitchen."

Eliza's frown scrunched her forehead. "I don't often work in the kitchen. Besides, Levi asked me to check on his *mamm*. So that's what I will do. I can take something with me—make pies there if I need to."

"Let her go, Colette," Abigail said. "I am fine. I rested all afternoon yesterday, and most of today. I'm feeling much better. Dehydration, Mamm said. I'm to drink more water."

"And rest more. This is a crucial time—the first trimester." Colette shrugged. "I read Mamm's medical books."

"I'm almost past that," Abigail said, her eyes full of worry even if she said she was feeling better. "I'm at ten weeks." She held a hand over her tummy. "I don't like the morning sickness, but it has gotten somewhat better."

"How does it feel?" Eliza asked. "Having a baby growing in your body? I mean throwing up, fainting, growing big, is it worth it?"

Abigail gave her a surprised misty-eyed stare. "So worth it. Don't you believe that?"

"I want to believe it," she admitted. "But . . . I find it all confusing and frightening at times."

Abigail studied her, then reached for her hand. "Eliza, are you afraid of marriage?"

"*Ja*, but not for the reasons you might think."

"Then what reason could there be?" Colette asked as she handed Abigail some soothing tea. "We all want to be married, don't we?"

Eliza knew she could tell her sisters anything. But this?

She tried. "The night Levi and I kissed, and I mean really kissed in a deep and intimate way, I got so scared. At first, I thought it was about the physical closeness."

"So you didn't like it and you let him know."

"But I did like it. Very much. It was exciting. I panicked because of my own feelings. Feelings that left me feeling out of control."

"You wanted to keep kissing Levi?" Abigail asked, understanding in her eyes.

"*Ja*, and more." Eliza hung her head. "The kind of more that obviously comes with marriage." She glanced at Abigail's stomach. "I mean—*bobbelis*."

"You are so confusing," Colette said, dropping her hands onto her lap. "One minute, you like Levi and his kisses. The next, you are pushing him away and saying you don't like any of it."

Abigail held up a hand, so like Mamm, to hush Colette.

"Maybe what Eliza is afraid of is giving up her independence. A husband and children can be a big burden, a burden we lovingly take on once we find the right person to spend our lives with."

Colette nodded. "Hmm. Eliza, do you think Levi is your right person?"

Eliza bobbed her head. "*Ja*, I do. But he thinks he has to work all the time to prove himself. He feels guilty about leaving his *daed* with the farm. Leaving and then coming home only to watch his father die."

"So he has concerns about marriage, too?" Abigail asked.

"He does. He thinks he needs to be better—so he works as much as possible, for his family and . . . for me."

"As I said, men do that," Abigail replied, putting a hand on her belly. "I have to admit I have some fears about being a mother, but I can't wait."

"You are going to have a fine *bobbeli*," Eliza reminded her. "Mamm says so." Then she shifted on the bed. "Enough about me. I will figure out Levi and my future. It's overwhelming and confusing, but I miss him. I missed him before, but with time, that feeling became a dull ache. Now that I've been back with him, the longing is sharp and continuous."

"That's called love," Abigail told her. "Jonah makes me ache with love, with longing, with hope. I don't want to disappoint him."

"You are fine," Eliza said, wishing she could make sense of this love business. "You will be the best *mamm* ever."

Abigail shifted and slapped her hands against the covers. "Jonah says so, too. So I have to believe we will be fine. Now, tell me about your quilt. Did you bring it?"

"*Neh.*" Eliza grabbed her bag and pulled out the little carved horse. "Levi left this for me."

Colette took it and rubbed her fingers over it. "Samson?"

"*Ja.*" Eliza beamed. "He left me a note, too. The note I mentioned yesterday. But . . . I wanted to keep this carving to myself for a while. I will put a likeness on the quilt, of course."

"Of course," Abigail said. "Even Jonah is interested in this quilt. It's coming along very well, sister."

"I can't believe I'm making my own quilt," Eliza said. "I now understand why you kept yours hidden, Abby. Mine tells a story of love, as did yours. It truly is helping me to be still and know *Gott* is in charge."

"Should I write that down?" Colette asked. "Or have you already written it in your journal?"

Eliza grinned. "My journal is private, but you know one day I might pen a novel—a love story based on Amish women and the quilts they make."

"Oh, that's a *gut* idea." Colette clapped and then she dropped her hands. "I don't know if I'll ever have such a quilt. Matthew is so . . . distant and shy."

"Well, you can be intimidating," Abigail pointed out.

"Me?" Colette looked as if a bug had bitten her. "I am not intimidating at all. I am pleasant, nice, and determined and . . . demanding. I suppose I am demanding."

Her sisters laughed at that. "You try to run Edith's kitchen almost as much as Aenti does."

"Well, I don't get away with it."

"But you do get away with leading Matthew along like we lead Peaches and the *kinder*."

"Your quilt might have a lot of frowning figures on it," Eliza said. "You frowning over a bowl of apples, peeling away."

"Why are we discussing me?" Colette said. "You're the one holding out on Levi. You need to grab hold of him, Eliza. He's a *gut* man."

Eliza wished she hadn't told her sisters about the doubts that plagued her mind. Did she want to marry? Could she be the kind of wife Abby and her *mamm* seemed to be? They made it all look so easy. But was marriage easy? Once a woman got past that first passionate kiss, would that be the end of love and the beginning of being ordinary, even stuck? Maybe she had a fear of that—being stuck. But didn't marriage mean being settled and sure, not stuck and uncertain?

"I don't know."

"You aren't sure?" Abigail asked, concern and understanding evident in her voice.

"I am trying to decide."

Her sisters shared a speaking glance, then turned back to her.

Abigail took her hand. "One day, you will know. That's how it works, Eliza."

Eliza already knew, but she was afraid to share the realization and all the fears that came with it. Especially with Levi. How could she tell the man she loved that she might not be marrying material?

"You want me to stay longer?"

Levi waited for Sam Whitman's response. They'd been talking about some additional jobs that needed Levi's attention.

"I'm offering you first choice," Mr. Whitman said. "You're the best farrier I know, Levi. My horses are bred to sell and sell well. That's how I make money. I'm willing to pay double."

Levi hated to turn down that kind of offer. "I have another big job coming up at the Shadow Lake Inn," he said. "They need me to help with the Harvest Festival."

"You shouldn't just be standing around at an event," his client said, his tone gruff. "I'd think you'd rather be working with horses."

"*Neh*, I won't be standing around much. I can get a lot of work on the horses that will be passing through during the outdoor event. I'd planned to have an open booth, just like everyone else. To advertise my services and help the local Amish with their horses." He gave Mr. Whitman the festival date. "A week from now."

"That's a good plan," Mr. Whitman finally said. "Can you stay two more days instead of the week I suggested?"

Levi nodded. "I need to get word to my *mamm*." His mother hadn't been feeling well, but she kept telling him her muscles and bones were getting old. He worried it could be more.

"You can use the office phone," Mr. Whitman said, nodding. "I appreciate your staying. You won't regret it when you see your check."

"*Denke*," Levi replied. Then he headed to the office, wondering whom to call. Jonah didn't carry a phone, but there was an emergency phone in the stables.

He had Eliza's cell number. The King sisters carried business cell phones because they made their jobs easier. He could break the rules this once since it was important that the Kings and his family know when he'd be back.

He dialed the number Eliza had given him when he'd driven her to therapy sessions, wondering what she'd be doing this late in the day.

"Hello?" she answered, sounding hesitant.

"Lizzie, it's me. Levi."

"Are you all right? Why are you calling? Did something happen? Is your family okay?"

"Slow down," he said, grinning. "I'm fine. I just wanted to let you and your family know I'll be here two more days."

"Oh. I see." He imagined her unhappy look. "You like that place better than here?"

"*Neh*, but I'm needed here."

"You're also needed at home."

Home. That word had a nice ring coming from her lips.

"I'll be home soon." He wondered if she wanted him there because she cared, or because she needed his help with one of the inn's busiest days.

"What about the festival?"

Ach, there it was then. She needed him to work.

Disappointment hit him like soft arrows. Eliza was

industrious and practical. Her family would need a lot of help during the big event.

"I'll be there in time, and I'll work double time helping out."

"Why did you call me? You could have sent word to Jonah."

"Do I need a reason?"

"*Neh*, I suppose not."

"I miss you," he admitted. "How are you?"

He heard what might have been a sigh. "I'm fine. My leg hurts because Abby wasn't feeling well and I sent Jonah home yesterday, so I did a lot of the heavy work. But it's *gut* to be back in my stables."

"You need me there, don't you?"

"Only when you're finished. I know you can't work for us every day. Unless we hired you on permanently, of course."

"Are you considering that?"

"Maybe. I don't know yet."

He couldn't find any more words. Talking on the phone was still foreign to him, even after all the years of being out amongst the *Englisch*. "I will be back soon, Lizzie. You know that, right?"

She didn't speak for a few breaths. "That is up to you, Levi. I'm going to visit your *mamm* later. Do you want me to tell her you'll be gone a while longer?"

"*Ja*, please." Then he added, "And would you check on Laura and James for me? Make sure they're doing their chores and helping Mamm?"

"I will," she replied. "Stay safe, Levi."

"Lizzie?" He wanted to tell her he missed her a lot. More-than-friends a lot. "It's *gut* to hear your voice."

"I'm glad you are finding work," she replied. "*Denke* for the note and the carving. I must go."

Then she was gone.

Would he ever understand this woman? Did she want him back in her life? Did she want the same things he wanted? Could he ever do enough, be enough, to please her?

Or was he just chasing a dream that would never come true?

CHAPTER TWENTY

"Eliza, it's so *gut* to see you."

Connie Lapp's smile showed more tiredness than joy. Troubled, Eliza hugged the older woman, surprised to find she felt thin as a rail. After talking to Levi earlier and finding herself suddenly tongue-tied, she felt a bit awkward visiting his gentle mother. But she'd been looking forward to this visit. Maybe the news that Levi would be away a bit longer had rattled Eliza. Her sisters had been shocked when she'd told them she'd run out of words and ended the call.

"Don't do that with his *mamm*," Abigail had cautioned. "Connie needs someone to talk to, and you need to get to know her better."

"It's *gut* to see you, too, Connie," she said now, determined to enjoy her time with Levi's *mamm*. She drew back to look at the older woman. Connie didn't look as if she felt well. Maybe some news from her son would help. "I have news from Levi."

Connie sank down onto a chair, her eyes brightening. "*Ach vell*, tell me."

Eliza placed the pie she'd baked, along with the other food she'd brought, on the table and sat next to Connie.

"He will be away a bit longer. His boss there needed him to work two more days."

Connie nodded, her eyes misty. "My son is a *gut* man. He's trying so hard to save this place and . . . do his own work, too."

Eliza felt guilty for being slightly angry that Levi hadn't hurried home. But then she'd told herself he was doing the best he could. She missed him.

"He is a diligent worker. We like having him at the inn a few days a week."

"He does what he can," Connie said, admiring the pie. "You didn't need to bring anything."

"Of course, I did," Eliza said. "We have apples everywhere. And Mamm sent you some jellies and some freshly baked bread."

"You are too kind," Connie replied, tears in her eyes.

"Connie, is something wrong?" Eliza asked, worried. "Do you miss Levi?"

Connie wiped at her eyes. "I miss him, but I miss my husband at times like this, too."

"Do you need anything?" Eliza asked. "What can I do to help?"

Connie glanced around. "James and Laura are at a frolic down the road. I need to explain something before they return."

Connie took her hand, and again Eliza noticed the fragility of Connie's worn fingers, the veins in her hands, the pallor of her skin. "I'm listening," she said, dread in her heart. She'd seen such signs before when she went with Mamm to visit the sick.

"I've been ill," Connie said. "But I haven't told Levi or his siblings yet."

Eliza tried to stay calm in the way she'd seen Mamm

be calm, but her heart sputtered, plunged, and bumped. "What is wrong?"

"I've had spells," Connie explained. "Not my heart or anything like that. Sometimes my hands shake, and I drop things."

"Have you seen a doctor?"

"Once, before Levi returned." She looked into Eliza's eyes. "They call it Parkinson's disease."

Eliza couldn't hide the gasp she let out. But she recovered by nodding and holding Connie's hand tightly. "I have heard of it. Mamm has seen it in patients." She knew what the diagnosis meant, but she didn't say anything to Connie. "I can have Mamm *kumm* and visit you, see if you're wrong. Doctors can be wrong."

Connie shook her head. "They are not wrong. Dr. Merrill gave me some information to read. He wants me to go to a specialist, but—"

Connie stopped, her head down.

Eliza guessed. "You have no insurance and it is expensive, *ja*?"

Connie bobbed her head and wiped her eyes with her apron. "Levi is working so hard to save this place. I can't burden him with expensive doctor bills. Linden did the best he could, but the cancer took him so suddenly. My disease will be different. You must know how it will end when my time comes."

Eliza nodded. "I've traveled with Mamm sometimes. She sees things, hears things, being a midwife."

Connie placed her hands on the table. "Then you know I can't stay here alone when that time comes. I need someone I can trust to find a place for me to go as my time draws near."

"But that could be a while, Connie," Eliza said, wishing

she could do something besides try to be reassuring. "The disease can progress slowly."

"It can, but it's so hard to think about what might happen to James and Laura." Connie stared into Eliza's eyes. "Levi loves you. He will always love you. I need to know now, before things get too bad, that he and Laura and James will be taken care of. I don't mean moneywise. Levi will see to that. I mean if he marries, his siblings will need to be part of the deal. Can you live with that, Eliza? I need to know, so I can be at peace in the future."

Eliza sat there and realized love wasn't just about a romantic moment, or a waltz across a fancy room; it wasn't such as she read in the novels she sneaked from the library, although those moments of grand gestures and romance could happen sometimes in real life. It was more like the books Levi had given her, about home, family, and hope. About chickens, goats, and horses. Gardens, and kitchens, and wash day, and working hard all your life. All the things she'd watched her parents do day in and day out. How did they manage? Could she do that and take on a ready-made family, too?

"Eliza?"

She turned back to Connie and knew in her heart she would do whatever it took to protect Levi and his siblings, to help them, to love them, to guide them. If she could just let go and live, instead of fretting about whether she wanted to be married or not.

She looked at Connie, took her hands, and said, "I promise I'll do whatever it takes to make sure they are all cared for."

Connie nodded. "But will you love them?"

"More than ever," she said, meaning it, but thinking loving someone could happen even without marriage. She could be like a nice *aenti* to Levi's siblings and still be friends with Levi.

Couldn't she?

Before she could question the promise she'd just made to Connie, James and Laura came running in.

"Eliza," Laura called, hurrying to hug Eliza. "I'm so glad you're here. Mamm, we had such a *gut* time. We played baseball and rode on a pony. Do you like ponies, Eliza?"

James nodded and shyly kept walking toward his room. "Laura almost fell off the pony, but I helped her."

"Did not."

"Did too."

"Hush up," Connie said. "Give Eliza room to breathe. She brought pie and what looks like macaroni and cheese for supper."

Eliza could only nod and take deep breaths. She couldn't do this. She couldn't. She'd just made a promise she knew she'd regret. What if she messed things up and ruined these precious children and their lives? What if Levi didn't want to marry her? They'd been doing great as friends. Why mess with that?

Putting her worries aside, she helped Connie set the table and then they heated up the food she'd brought. While they ate, she listened to Laura and James telling their *mamm* about their day. Then she told them she wanted all of them to be a part of the festival.

"I don't know about that," Connie said, her eyes wide with fear and uncertainty.

"Levi can bring you and you will be Mamm's guest. You and she can sit on the front porch and watch the fun. And these two can help with pony rides—Peaches will love you both."

The *kinder* giggled at that and started discussing who'd get to lead Peaches.

"May we go to the festival, Mamm?" Laura asked. "We didn't get to go last year."

James bobbed his head. "I'll help, Eliza. I'd like to see Peaches and ride her, too."

"Please?" Laura asked Connie.

"I will consider it," Connie said. Then she turned to Eliza. "I don't want to be a burden."

"You could never be that. My *mamm* will be so happy if you *kumm*. She and Daed have to take it easy, so you can join them."

Laura hugged Eliza and clapped. James nodded and stood stoic and quiet, a soft smile sneaking across his face.

Connie sent them to do their evening chores. "I'd like that, Eliza. But I tire so easy."

"That won't be a problem. You can take a nap or rest inside anytime you want. I'll make sure of that. Meantime, you and Mamm can talk privately. She knows a lot of doctors and she has ways of finding out important information. Of course, the only doctoring she does is birthing babies, but she is inquisitive about medicine. Always has been."

"I think her daughters have that inquisitive trait, too," Connie said, smiling a real smile. "I can't tell you how much I appreciate your coming to spend time with us, Eliza. And I'm so glad I can count on you for the future." Then Connie leaned close. "This needs to stay between you and me. Levi can't know."

Eliza nodded, her heart reaching toward that future. But her head was still balking and wanting to keep her freedom and independence. She wouldn't let Levi's family down, and she didn't want to let him down. Now she had to carry this secret and have that between them. But she would keep the secret, to protect him, to help him, to do what needed to be done.

Did that mean she was truly in love? Or just honoring a promise?

She had a lot more to put on her forgiveness quilt, that was for certain sure.

Two days later, Levi thanked his driver and waved good-bye to Mr. Whitman's foreman, then headed to the inn's stables to hitch up Rudolph. He had to go home and check on Mamm and the kinder before he did anything else. And maybe sleep a bit. Bone-tired and weary, he was glad to be back here.

He moved at a swift pace up the alley of the stables, checking on horses as he went. Finding Rudolph in the last stall, he greeted his constant companion and gave him a handful of oats. "Sorry you didn't get to go with me this time, Rudolph. I had a lot of work to do while you stayed here being spoiled."

Rudolph's dark eyes opened wide; then the big roan shifted and waited for a nose rub.

After a quick visit, Levi glanced around the barn. "Where is everyone?"

When he missed Samson, he turned toward the big corral where the horse often grazed during the day. It sloped away from the stables and ended near the apple orchard. Glancing around, he didn't see the big horse inside the fenced area of the property.

Then he looked toward the orchard, and his breath caught in his throat. He spotted Samson and saw the woman on the Percheron's back, trotting the horse through the apple trees, leaves dancing up as Samson kicked at the dirt.

Eliza. She was riding again.

Levi gulped in air and stood watching her. She moved as one with the big animal, her long blue skirt flying out around her legs, her bright pink sneakers showing the spirit in her that he loved. He thought of her hair, how long and flowing it must be, and imagined it flying freely behind her.

Levi knew in that moment that no matter his income or his status, he loved Eliza King. But he couldn't confess that love completely, not when he had nothing to give her.

Except his heart.

What was he to do about that?

A slap on his back brought him out of his musings.

Jonah grinned at him. "She couldn't wait. I had to help her on, but you should be the one to help her off. You did a lot to get her walking again."

"I mostly annoyed her into doing her exercises and forced her to take slow, painful baby steps."

"It worked. She is nothing if not determined."

"*Ach*, we can agree on that."

"Go," Jonah said. "The stables are in *gut* shape and the big tents go up tomorrow. I'll pay you extra to help with that."

"You don't need to pay me more," Levi said, shame burning his skin. "I'm already behind on my work here."

"It's not charity, Levi," Jonah replied. "I really need a strong man to help me with the heavy stuff. And I'm willing to pay someone. Even you."

Levi shook his head and grinned. "When you put it that way, it's hard to say no."

"Okay, then go and get Eliza off that horse before she decides to really give him a run."

Levi adjusted his hat and hurried toward Eliza. She'd turned Samson around and was trotting him back toward the stables. When she looked up and saw Levi, she urged the horse to go faster.

Stopping Samson near Levi, she said, "You're back."

Not that she seemed thrilled to see him.

"I am." He rubbed Samson's head and ran his hand over the horse's haunches. "Big boy, what you been up to?"

The horse nudged at Levi and gave a soft whinny. Then he tossed his mane and stared back at Eliza.

"I'm riding again," Eliza said proudly. She'd done this on purpose. To show she didn't need him. To get even with him for leaving.

The woman would drive him to drink.

"So I see." He walked alongside as she eased Samson forward. "I'm glad you are able to ride Samson. I'm sure he missed your rides together."

She looked down at Levi, her expression bordering on haughty. "I'm almost completely well."

"I have noticed that."

"Did you get all your work done?"

"I did. But I have to admit it's nice to be back here."

"Back home, or back here at Shadow Lake Inn?"

"Both."

They'd reached the paddock, so he opened the gate and let horse and rider through. Then he stood waiting.

"Do you want me to help you down?"

She glanced around, saw no one about. "Would you?"

"I will."

He went to her. Samson stood still and waited, too. Levi saw her wince. "You overdid it?"

"I might have." Then she pointed a finger at him. "Do not tell anyone."

"Oh, so we're keeping secrets now?"

She looked surprised, her blush deepening, her eyes turning a deep hazel. "I don't know what you mean."

"I mean, you and I will have a secret—that you overdid it a bit."

"Will you just help me down?"

He lifted her with one quick movement, his hands around her waist, his eyes on her as he gently dropped her to the ground and held her steady.

Eliza's lips opened in a gentle gasp as she stared up at him. A moment, then two, passed. Levi didn't want to let her go.

She finally tugged away. "I have things to do."

He watched as she tried to walk. When he saw her stumble, he caught her up in his arms. "You need to rest that leg."

"I should."

He lifted her, carried her into the stables, and found her favorite bench. Then he grabbed a horse blanket and folded it so she could prop up her leg.

Standing back, he asked, "Why did you go and hurt yourself again?"

Her eyes were misty, and when she spoke her voice cracked. "I just wanted to ride again."

Levi sank down on his knees and pulled her into his arms, the feel of her so close both comforting and confusing. "You will. You did. But you have to be gentle and not push so hard."

"I missed you," she admitted as she buried her nose against his shirt and left teardrops on the fabric. "I'm so glad you're home, is all."

"Home." He loved that word. "I'm sorry I had to go away but . . . it's my job."

She pulled away and wiped her eyes. "I understand, better than you will ever know."

And he had to wonder what had happened while he was away.

CHAPTER TWENTY-ONE

Eliza wrote it all in her journal; then she read part of what she'd written:

Connie Lapp is sick, and she wants me to take care of Levi and his siblings if something happens to her. It will happen. Parkinson's is a bad disease. I studied up on it. She will suffer in so many ways. I promised her I'd . . . do everything to help Levi, James, and Laura. But I did not promise marriage. She wants us to marry. She wants to die in peace.

How can I make that promise when I'm not even sure I want to be married? How can I accept such a change in my life? I don't know if I can do that. But I promised Connie.

Eliza saw the words she'd written, which made what Connie had asked even harder to accept. If she married Levi because of this request, would the marriage be real? Or would she resent the decision she'd be forced into making?

Too tired to figure it out, she wrote a bit more about riding Samson and then finding Levi waiting for her. If she were wise, she'd tell him the truth. But she'd promised Connie she wouldn't do that. Torn between wanting to do the right thing and wondering what the right thing was, she stayed in her room during supper, saying she'd overdone things today and her leg hurt.

Colette came into her room and flopped onto the bed. "I'm bushed. So bushed, I actually let Aenti Miriam clean up the kitchen."

Eliza made a *hmm* sound and then read over her notes.

"What are you writing in that journal?" Colette asked, trying to take it away.

"None of your business." Eliza held it tight against her stomach. Then she looked up at her sister. "I do need to tell you and Abby something. Is she staying to talk tonight?"

Colette's eyes became two curious orbs. "I'll find her. She's very tired these days, but she was sitting on the porch with Mamm and Jonah, watching Daed clip and prune the roses."

"Don't make a production of it," Eliza said. "Tell her I need help with my quilt patterns."

"What if Mamm comes up and brings Aenti Miriam with her?"

Eliza shuddered. "Then I will have to tell you what I want to talk about later."

Colette left, probably scheming to make sure she got to hear whatever Eliza had to say. Should she confide in her sisters? Colette was known for blurting out secrets. Abby would be more discreet. She was *gut* at keeping secrets.

I have to talk to someone. She couldn't tell her mother about this yet. She had to ponder her dilemma and see what her sisters thought. Then she'd tell Mamm, because her mother did know a little bit about certain diseases.

She sat silent, looking at the words in her journal, a journal Levi had given her. A gift that now held the secret she had to keep from him. What a twisted mess.

Her door flashed open as both of her sisters entered in a flurry. "What's going on?" Abby asked, breathless. "Colette cornered me in the kitchen and dragged me up here."

"I told you to be careful," Eliza said to Colette.

"I was careful. Everyone is out walking around the garden. So Abby called out that she'd be up here with us."

"I have to go soon," Abby said. "It's late and my feet are swollen."

"Pregnancy is so strange," Colette said.

Eliza hitched a breath, adding that tidbit to her fears about being a married woman. Who liked swollen ankles and throwing up every morning?

"It's not strange," Abby admonished. "It's natural and my body is acting naturally, even though it does feel foreign and unreal at times." Then she smiled. "And yet, it is a blessing. A true blessing."

Colette and Eliza smiled.

Abigail blinked and laughed. "What do you need to tell us, sister?"

Eliza took a breath, said a prayer, and then decided she had to talk to someone, or she'd be in a big mess.

After she'd explained, her sisters sat back and remained silent for a few moments. A first.

"Well?" she asked, wondering if she'd finally managed to shock them.

Abby spoke first. "That is a tall order, but you have to understand Connie is concerned for her children. She knows Levi will do his duty by them and take care of them. And she also knows that you and Levi have a past, so she believes you can have a future. She's arranging things before it gets too late."

"That's what she said," Eliza replied, her heart hurting for everyone involved. "A ready-made marriage."

"One that Levi has to agree to," Colette said on a pragmatic note. "Wait? Does he even know about her illness?"

Eliza shook her head. "She made me promise not to tell him. For all I know, he might not want to marry me or anyone."

"Exactly," Abby added. Then she amended her response. "But if he were to marry, it would be you."

"So you think he won't agree?" Eliza hadn't given that possibility any thought. "What if he doesn't want to marry me? I'm not sure what to do."

"You don't want this then?" Colette asked, shock in her eyes.

"I have concerns."

Abby and Colette glanced at each other.

"What?" she asked, already knowing what.

"We thought you were just unsure, and you'd get over that."

"I'm still unsure," she admitted. "And now, I have this promise to consider and fret about. And I can't tell Levi any of it."

Abby studied her. "You're in a pickle."

"*Ja*, a big one."

Colette stood and paced. "Let's consider all the pros and cons. Pro—you know the groom well and seem inclined to be around him a lot. Con—you hated him for a few years, but that's over now, for certain sure. Pro—he's nice and not bad looking, he is employed, and he seems to want to be around you a lot. That's about as close to love as two people can get. But con—if you were to marry him, you'd have two siblings to take care of and his *mother*. Siblings that are already growing up, so that's a pro, but the con here is still—you'd be expected to take care of them and nurture them and love them, too."

"I care about all of them," she put in.

"*Ja*, but do you want to take on all of them?" Abby asked. "That's the important question, the question only you can answer."

"I don't know," she said on a wobbly whisper. "I just don't know."

Abby stood. "I must go, but sister, you have some time to figure this out. It's *gut* that you and Levi have become close again. Start from there and see how things go with him. The situation could take care of itself."

Eliza lifted her chin. "Meaning?"

"Meaning that love has a way of overcoming all obstacles. And I am certainly proof of that."

"*Ja*," Colette added. "Proof and pregnant."

They all laughed at her quip.

After her sisters left, Eliza curled up and held her journal tight to her chest, her thoughts on the quilt she'd been making. What else could she add? Maybe two siblings laughing as they did their chores? Or maybe a woman riding a gray horse through the apple orchard, a man waiting for her near the corral?

Is this what love feels like? she wondered.

* * *

Levi couldn't figure it out. He'd thought he and Eliza had made progress, but now she seemed to run away any time she saw him. Not literally run, but hobble, walk as fast as possible, hide in the tack room, or have an excuse to leave the stables.

Of course, everyone had been busy this week. The festival was the only thing on anyone's mind. He'd helped put up tents, cleaned the stables, set out pumpkins and hay bales, and set up tables all over the property. Food trucks would be here this weekend and people would be milling around. The café would have an outdoor booth offering sandwiches and mini-casseroles, baked goods, and their latest offering—tart cherry jam.

He hurried into the kitchen to see what needed to be done in the café. Jonah had told him they'd put out more tables and chairs along the big front porch.

Colette spotted him first. "*Gut*, you're here."

"That I am. What needs to be done?"

She put her hands on her hips and glanced around. "So much, but let's start in the dining room. We'll dress more tables, and you can put the fold-up bistro tables and chairs out on the porch. If the weather is mild, folks can sit out there and eat."

"It might be chilly, but I'll do as you ask."

Colette stared at him, her eyes wide. "How's your family?"

Confused, he said, "They're fine. Laura and James are excellent scholars and Mamm is taking it easy, as she should. But she likes to do her chores and bake every day."

"Glad to hear it. We try to get our *mamm* to do the same."

"Uh-huh." He waited a beat. "The chairs and tables?"

"Oh, *ja*. I'm so busy I can't keep up with myself."

She took him to a large closet behind the kitchen. "All here. They might need dusting, but I'll send someone to help."

Levi nodded and got a flat metal cart, so he could carry more in one trip. Once he had it loaded, he moved through the café and out onto the front porch, stopping for a moment to admire the view.

"What are you doing?"

He turned to find Eliza sitting in a chair, folding napkins. "I'm going to set up these tables."

"But you aren't supposed to work here at the inn."

Why did she seem so shocked? They'd discussed his jobs at the employee meeting just yesterday.

"I'm helping as needed, per Abigail's instructions."

"I don't understand why you aren't helping as needed in the stables."

"Do you want me to leave, Lizzie?"

"*Neh.*"

She'd said that too fast. "So, you *do* want me to leave?"

She let out a sigh that lifted on the wind. "I just didn't expect to see you here." She twisted her foot. "I was doing my foot exercises while I fold napkins. My *aenti* fussed at me for not doing them more, but I feel silly doing them in front of people."

"Well, I'm not people. I'm me—the one who made you do your exercises in the first place."

"You didn't make me do them. I wanted to get well, so I did what I needed to do. You just supervised."

"Which exercise are you working on?"

She moved her ankle from side to side. "This one is the easiest and it does make my leg feel better."

Levi walked over to sit down across from her. "Are you still in pain?"

"Not as much," she said. "The muscles just get tight

when I sit for too long, but then everyone tells me to sit and take a load off."

He smiled at that. "A problem, for certain sure."

Then he leaned in. "Why are you avoiding me?"

"I'm not."

Again, she spoke too fast. Something was up with her, but then something was always up with his Lizzie. "You can't wait to get away from me, and I want to know why. I thought . . . I thought we'd cleared the air between us, but you've been acting strange since I got back from working with Mr. Whitman. Are you still angry about that?"

She looked away.

"I see. Lizzie, I have to take work when I can find it. Why does that bother you? Or is it that I need the work, that you know I'm not a rich man?"

"I've always known that," she blurted. Then she covered her mouth with her hand. "Levi, I didn't mean it that way."

He stood, pride hiding his anger and embarrassment. "I believe you did. I'm sorry I'm not *gut* enough for you, but I tried to tell you that from the beginning."

"I don't care about that, and if you really knew me, you'd realize how insulting that comment is."

He shook his head. "You've only known a safe, comfortable life here, Lizzie. You work hard, but you don't have to worry about paying the bills or hoping you can feed your family. I have to think about that every day. The farm, my clients, this place, keeping everyone happy, and sometimes that means I have to take jobs away from here. Away from you."

"But you went away for years and didn't seem that worried about returning."

He stepped back, the zing of her remark hitting the center of his heart. "You still resent me for leaving even though we broke up? You wanted nothing to do with me, and I wanted to see the world. So I did. I have. I'm home now. You need to understand that about me."

He turned to get to work but felt her hand on his arm.

"Levi, this isn't about me, and it's not about you leaving. You make me sound like a spoiled child, demanding too much." Her eyes were a golden green. "I told you I missed you. That was the truth. But I have a lot on my mind. I do worry about the future. My folks are getting older and my *daed* has to take it easy. He had a heart attack last year. He's older than our *mamm*, but she's worked so hard all her life, she hurts all the time. So it's up to my sisters and me to keep this place running. As you can see, it's an ongoing, everyday operation and an expensive one at that."

She stopped and sank back down on her chair. "I want to be well, Levi. Well, so I can prepare for whatever the future brings."

Levi felt like the worst kind of human. "I'm sorry," he said. "I shouldn't have said all those things. You're right. This place is big and always needing something fixed, and you never really get to slow down."

She put her head in her hands, her elbows on the table. "No, and Mamm and Daed can't do as much these days. You know how it is. I'm sure your *mamm* gets more tired now than she did before."

He thought about that. "She does take naps more. But the *kinder* do a lot of the chores now. I take care of things when I get home every afternoon."

"You have a lot to fret about," Eliza said. "So do we, even though we are blessed to have this beautiful place. But you know that saying—'With great things comes great responsibility.' We both are responsible for others."

She was right. "*Ja*, we are. But we're adults now, and that brings responsibility."

She shook her head. "We have to be diligent and serious

about those responsibilities. That means you take your work when you can, and I'm stuck here working wherever I'm needed—the stables, the gardens, the kitchen, the orchards. There is always something to do. It takes a toll.

"We have to consider everything, especially personal relationships." She stood and glanced out at the lake down below the bluffs. A sailboat slipped by, and a blue heron lifted out of a tree and took flight. "We have beauty all around us, and yet here inside"—she pointed to her heart—"we have turmoil. How do we keep the beauty and get rid of the turmoil? That is what I'm trying to figure out as an adult."

Then she turned and went inside.

And Levi realized he still didn't know the real reason she was avoiding him.

CHAPTER TWENTY-TWO

Two days before the festival, Eliza and her sisters cleaned out the room in the inn they used for quilting, leaving the quilting tables and an unfinished quilt for display. They'd hold quick lessons throughout the day for anyone who wanted to watch or join in. Visitors had to sign up for sessions, since this was one of the highlights of the festival and they could only accommodate about six or eight people in the room.

"I think that's it," Abby said. "The place is sparkling, it smells fresh, and we have samples and plenty of needles and thread to give everyone a finished panel to take home."

"I'll take the morning shift," Colette said. "That will keep me close to the kitchen."

"And I'll take the midafternoon," Abby replied. "Eliza, you can handle late-afternoon classes."

Eliza stared at the quilting table, remembering her conversation with Levi yesterday. Had she let anything slip? Did he suspect his mother was ill?

"Eliza?"

She pivoted to find Colette and Abby watching her like two prim hawks. "What?"

"You've been quiet all day," Abigail said. "Are you feeling poorly?"

"Neh, I'm fine. Just . . . worried."

"If you're worried about me or Jonah, don't be," Abigail said. "I know last year was horrible when we were almost shot, but that's over. This year is so much better." She touched the tiny mound of her stomach. "Who would have believed what could happen in a year?"

"Is Jonah doing well?" she asked, to keep Abby talking. She wouldn't explain that she'd been worried about Connie and how Levi would react if he found out the truth. "He's not having flashbacks or nightmares?"

Jonah had been a police detective in his other life and some bad guys had found him here and tried to kill him. But he was so different now from the man who'd washed up on their shore. After he and the authorities had taken care of the people after him, he'd gone through all the steps to become Amish, including going before the church and confessing, and committing himself to the Amish way. The family had even been teaching him Pennsylvania *Deitsch*.

"*Neh*, we are both healthy and happy," Abigail said. "Make that all three of us." Again, she touched her tummy. "Jonah's nightmares and fears have calmed, and he has done everything to prove he wants to be here. I'm so happy that he has accepted *Gott*'s love."

"And your love," Colette added, her eyes dreamy. "He loved you from the start."

Abigail smiled and blushed. "He did."

"*Gut*," Eliza said, glad they'd talked through that worry, instead of her having to explain all her concerns. She missed the days when her life seemed so simple. "Let's hope nothing goes wrong this year."

"Well, what could go wrong?" Colette asked, shrugging. Then she gasped. "Never mind. I don't want anything to happen so let's change the subject."

Eliza let out a sigh. So many things could go wrong. Levi and she had briefly spoken this morning. Clueless, he'd told her he planned to bring his mother and siblings to the festival. Well, they had been invited, so that made sense. She prayed there would be no problems.

Saturday came and with it, a chill in the air. No rain or snow but a crispness that made everyone dig out sweaters and jackets. Levi loaded up the family buggy, making sure his *mamm* was covered and warm. He'd noticed how pale she looked sitting in the bright sunshine. Other than church and going to the market now and then, she didn't get out much. He hoped she'd enjoy the activities and visiting with Eliza's family. Sarah had sent word that Mamm could sit with her and watch people walk by.

Laura and James, however, could not contain themselves. "We haven't been to the festival in forever," Laura had told him while they packed up. "I'm going to eat pastries and cupcakes for lunch."

He laughed at that. "You'll be so sweet, the goats will chase you."

His sister had laughed. "Silly, the goats won't see me eating all that."

"They know such things," he said, clicking the reins as Rudolph started trotting up the road toward town and then turned off toward the inn. "But you must mind your manners and stay close to Mamm unless you're with another adult."

"We're too old for that," James insisted. "I like to wander around."

"Me too," Laura added, her curls trying to escape her black winter *kapp*.

Mamm smiled and glanced back at them. "I'll probably stay on the cottage porch with Sarah and Miriam. I'll have a good view from there, so you can check in now and then."

"Why can't you walk with us?" Laura asked.

Mamm shot Levi a glance, then shrugged. "I enjoy visiting with Sarah. She is a joy to talk with. She's smart and we discuss recipes and quilting. She will give me new knitting ideas, for sure. Besides, I am older now, so walking becomes tiring."

"She might give you some *gut* food," James said. "Then you'll have more energy."

"Yes, so that is why I'll be with her most of the day," Mamm repeated. "I will trust both of you to behave and find some youngies to play with."

That ended that conversation, but Levi thought he'd heard a tremor in his mother's words. Was she nervous about the crowds, or like him, ashamed she had nothing much to offer? He wanted to tell her she had more than enough to contribute wherever she went. Sarah wouldn't be unkind to Mamm. They liked each other. He couldn't ask in front of his siblings, so he let the matter go for now.

But he'd make sure to buy his *mamm* and the youngies some nice gifts today. They deserved that, didn't they?

Eliza had been right about one thing. He was responsible for his family now. If he'd been here helping Daed, things might have been different. But he'd been away. Away from the family that needed him, and away from the woman he'd hurt.

He prayed he could push all his angst aside, just for today, and enjoy this celebration to benefit those in need. He also prayed his family would never need such assistance. He'd make sure of that, and if that meant he'd always be working here and there, he could accept the new challenges. Eliza had hinted at certain obstacles the other day. Did that mean they could never work out their differences and be together? They lived in the same community, but they were of two different worlds.

Neither of them was ready for marriage, or a family.

Eliza managed to get Peaches hitched to the new pony wheel and ready to give the *kinder* rides. She only had to watch and guide Peaches because the wheel rotated like a carousel. She would be a spotter for the little children, and she had to make sure no older children tried to sneak a ride. Peaches was docile and compliant as long as there were carrots and apples involved.

A metal pole hitched to the pony guided it around. Praying she wouldn't tire, trip, or limp, Eliza hoped her leg would behave. It had been weeks since the cast came off, and she'd finished therapy but still did her own exercises as often as possible. Would she ever be completely back to normal?

Levi came walking toward her and normal went up into the clouds. Maybe it wasn't her leg that hurt the most. Her heart seemed to ache constantly these days. She turned around to face Peaches and pretended she didn't see him.

"I came to help," he said. He walked around to face her and carefully checked the carousal to make sure the pole was secured, and the cylinders would turn correctly. "This is a nice size—about twenty-five feet in diameter. Small enough for one or two ponies."

"I hope to get a Shetland mare one day," she replied. "They are better for the *kinder*. Peaches will get too big soon."

Levi studied the red metal that surrounded the pony carousel. "And enclosed. That's a great safety measure." He turned to her. "I can find a mounting block for the tiny people."

"I've already done that," she said, her tone sounding petulant in her ears. Pointing to the big wooden block by a tree, she asked, "Aren't you needed elsewhere?"

"I thought you needed two people for this."

"We usually ask a parent to walk beside the pony," she explained. "We are careful."

He glanced back toward the inn. Already cars and buggies were filling the parking lot and the grassy field next to it.

"I wanted to help you today. I've done all I can setting up and marking parking spaces and such. Jonah thinks I need to hang around the stables and answer questions about horses and how I keep their hooves happy. That is my work, after all."

She pivoted and put her hand on her hip. "You're right. You are *gut* at explaining your job to people. So get busy. I've handled the pony rides for years, by myself."

"We don't have any people yet," he said, waving his hand in the air. "They'll be here though. I heard we might have our largest crowd ever."

"That would be *wunderbar*."

"Did I just see a smile on your pretty face?"

She smiled again. Maybe they could be nice to each other during this busy time. After all, he hadn't done anything to justify her being so mean to him. Fretting about his *mamm* and her request had Eliza all tense and agitated.

Could she marry Levi and take care of his family? Did

Gott want that for her? Was it His will? She didn't know which signs to look for in this situation.

She would behave and be kind. She owed Levi that at least. He'd need a friend when his mother's illness progressed. Eliza thought about talking to Mamm, but Mamm would want to go to Connie and help her. Eliza wanted to help, too.

That gave her an idea. What if she practiced being domestic and wifely? She'd visit with Connie and the youngies and see how it felt. See if it helped her decide about the request Connie had made. Having made that plan, she gave Levi another smile.

"*Denke*," she said. "I will probably need to take a break now and then. Youngies can wear you out."

She regretted saying that. Why didn't she think before she spoke?

Disappointment colored his eyes before he nodded. "My two sure do—I mean my brother and sister. I have to try to guide them on everything. Another responsibility."

She watched him, her question earnest. "Do you miss the days when we only had after-school chores? When we ran along the roads and sang at frolics?"

"And walked out together," he added, his tone soft with memories.

Memories that had become bittersweet. "We're not young anymore, Levi."

He nodded. "*Neh*, so you'd think we could be more honest with each other."

"I've tried to be honest," she said, her heart flipping. Had his *mamm* said something to him? Or could he see what Eliza was trying to hide?

"I know. And I've tried to do the same with you."

When they heard laughter and voices, he turned. "Looks like people are arriving. I'll be in the back of the stables if you need me. And I'll relieve you every hour, so you can take care of that leg."

"*Denke*," she said. "If you get hungry, I can get sandwiches from the kitchen."

"Sandwiches? Is that your way of saying you want to eat a meal with me, Lizzie?"

She slanted her head to one side and smiled. "Maybe. And I'll steal some cookies."

"That sounds like a *gut* idea." He nodded and hurried toward the stables.

"Probably not a *gut* idea at all," she told Peaches. The little golden pony neighed and shook her mane. "You did not have to agree with that," she whispered. "Now behave. You're about to go around in circles all day."

Which was exactly how she felt, too.

CHAPTER TWENTY-THREE

The day went by fast and soon it was past noon. While she'd enjoyed all the *kinder* wanting to ride Peaches, Eliza felt the pain of standing on her healing leg for too long. She was relieved when Matthew showed up, coming from the inn's busy kitchen.

"How are things going up there?" she asked.

"*Gut*. The café has been packed all morning. Edith is being even more snappish, and your *aenti* is ordering all of us around."

"So, normal," she said on a laugh.

"*Ja*, but I need a break. I'm here to relieve you," he told her, his brown eyes full of mirth. "Orders from your *mamm* and your *Aenti* Miriam. She sure watches out for people even when they're out of sight."

"My *mamm*?" Eliza glanced toward the cottage on the hill. Her mother and Connie waved to her. Which made her nervous. What were they discussing?

"Where is Aenti Miriam now?" she asked, thinking she did not want her *aenti* to hear anything more about her and Levi. Aenti Miriam liked to gossip and stir up trouble. Widowed now, she'd halfway admitted that her marriage had not been as happy as most people thought.

"She's driving Edith to the brink," Matthew said. "I can see where Colette gets her bossiness."

"*Ja*, maybe," Eliza said, more concerned with the happenings on the porch right now. "She has *gut* intentions, but a bad way of expressing herself, as Jonah likes to say."

"Well, I'm glad to be away from her for a while," Matthew replied. "So go and eat and rest."

She'd like to go sit on the porch with her *mamm* and Connie, but she wasn't sure she'd make it that far, and she'd feel awkward, knowing Connie's secret. But no need. She saw Levi coming toward her with food. Matthew smiled and patted Peaches on her nose, then gave the pony a carrot.

Levi nodded and grinned. "Are you hungry?"

"*Ja*," she said, limping toward him. "But I had planned to bring you lunch."

"I beat you to it," he said. "You need to rest that leg."

She glanced around. "The bench in the stables?"

"That's a *gut* spot. Private."

Did he want private? Did she want private?

Her stomach didn't care. "You brought sandwiches?"

"I did. And Colette gave me two huge coconut-oatmeal cookies. Said they are your favorite."

"She is correct on that," Eliza replied as they walked into the coolness of the stables. "Have you been busy back here?"

"*Ja*, but I'm going to help you for the rest of the day. Jonah said he could handle any stable visitors."

"Then where is he?"

"He's helping all around, but he'll be back soon. I'll keep an eye on things until he's done. He might be grabbing a bite, too."

She settled sideways on the bench so she could prop her leg up. "Where will you sit?"

Levi looked around and found an old barrel, then tilted it into a stool. "This'll do just fine for me."

He unwrapped two roast beef sandwiches centered on paper plates and handed her one. "I brought napkins."

"So you did. How kind."

Soon they were nibbling away. Eliza relaxed and took a deep breath. "This is the best sandwich," she said between bites. "I was hungry and tired."

"Maybe you should rest this afternoon."

"I can't. I always take care of the pony rides."

"I'll bring you a chair and a crate to prop your leg on. You don't want to set back your healing."

Eliza smiled at him. "*Denke*."

He handed her a bottle of water. "Stay hydrated."

"You are taking *gut* care of me."

"And you are being so agreeable. You must have been starving. Or maybe too tired to fuss at me."

"Why wouldn't I be agreeable? You brought me food, water, and dessert. I can't wait to eat that cookie."

They laughed and talked about all the people they'd seen today. *Englisch* and Amish families from all over the county and township, and some coming in from New York and other nearby states.

"People love a fall festival," she said. "It's like a big picnic for the whole area."

The sunshine and fresh air brought out even more people than usual. Some walked along the lakeshore, watching for herons and gulls, and some wanted to walk through the apple orchard and pick enough apples to make a pie. The inn workers always included their apple pie recipe in the braided baskets they offered each guest.

Eliza enjoyed Levi's company as long as she didn't stop to think about the burden she carried. How could she tell him what Connie had asked of her? He might get angry and confront his mother, or he'd blame Eliza for keeping such a big secret. His *mamm* was sick. She'd want to know if her own mother was ill.

But she had promised Connie.

"How's your *mamm* getting along? I saw Mamm and her on the porch."

"She's enjoying herself, but I'm worried about her."

"Why?" Eliza asked so quickly that Levi gave her a puzzled glance.

"She seems tired and shaky these days. She rarely eats much and sometimes she'd not able to cook, so the *kinder* are taking over while she instructs them."

"Maybe she's just teaching them, allowing them to cook on their own. That's how we all learned."

"*Ja*, but I still worry. I hope she'll talk to Sarah if there is anything wrong."

"Do you think there's something wrong?"

"I think she's tired and still grieving," he said. "I hate that I wasn't here to help more."

"You're here now, Levi. That's the important thing to remember."

Eliza wanted to say more, but she was caught in a promise she wasn't sure she could keep. So she stayed silent and let Levi tell her about the many people he'd talked to that day.

She loved watching his eyes light up and his smile turn mischievous. A happy Levi was much better than a worried, sad Levi. Maybe after the festival was over . . .

They finished their meal and just in time. A family came walking through the stables wanting to visit the horses. Levi told the family to go ahead and stroll. "But please respect the animals and don't pet them until I'm with you."

He took their empty plates to a nearby trash barrel, then nodded to her. "You need to rest. I'll be back in a bit."

Eliza obliged and sat still for a while, her cookie half-eaten. She'd missed the perfect moment to tell Levi what she knew about Connie. To soothe her frazzled mind, she listened as he patiently told the *Englisch* couple and their two children all about Samson.

"He's a Percheron. A draft horse and so strong he can pull a wagon without any problem. He weighs about nineteen hundred pounds and stands about seventeen hands."

"I don't see any hands," the little boy said, giggling.

"That's a term we use to measure how tall a horse is," Levi said. "He's about sixty-eight inches tall. Let's see, you look to be about three and a half feet tall, so you'd be around seven or eight hands high, I'm guessing."

"I don't have enough hands either," the boy said, clearly confused. His father explained further while his sister gave Samson some apple slices.

"Does he like apple pie?" the girl asked, her tone shy.

"He might, but he has a special diet that does not include apple pie or ice cream, two of my favorite things."

"Mine too," the girl said. "We bought a whole pie."

"Then you will enjoy it because I know all the piemakers around here and they are the best."

"Why do you talk so funny?" the boy asked.

Levi laughed even while the child's mother moaned in embarrassment. "I speak two different languages," he explained. "*Englisch* like you, but I also speak Pennsylvania *Deitsch*—Dutch, which is really more German than Dutch."

"So how do you say horse in Dutch?" the girl asked.

"*Gaul*," he replied, spelling out the letters. "And you have a *bruder* who likes *gauls*."

He pointed to her brother and then he pointed to Samson.

The girl beamed a smile. "You're funny."

Samson snorted and they all laughed.

Eliza loved the gentle way Levi handled the *kinder*. He had a lot of patience, and she for certain sure knew that firsthand.

He would make a fine father one day.

Realizing where her thoughts were going, she got up and snuck out the front of the stables to go watch Matthew and Peaches. Matty was doing a fine job, so she found a seat and rested awhile longer.

And wished Levi could come and sit with her. Why did her heart have to be so torn when it came to Levi Lapp?

Eliza took over again so Matthew could go help clean the kitchen and dining room and spend time with Colette. Those two, so cute with their crushes. But she wasn't sure if Colette would ever commit to a man. Would she herself?

But it was the way of life. People got married, especially in the Amish world. It was expected, assumed, necessary.

All her romantic thoughts seemed to taunt her now. She'd read books with happy endings, and she'd seen happiness blossom between Jonah and Abigail. Why couldn't she let that happen in her own life?

But if she married Levi, would she have to leave the inn and her stables? Would Levi be willing to live here? But he'd still need to take care of his family. If she married him, she'd help with that. It wouldn't be a burden because she liked his brother and sister and *mamm*.

So what was holding her back?

A couple came up with a cute little girl. Taking their money to pay for the ride, she helped the girl up onto

Peaches, then coached her father on how to walk beside her. Little Charlotte appeared to be around eight or nine, and wore jeans and a cute sweater, her smile captivating.

"Have you ever ridden a pony before?" Eliza asked.

"No," Charlotte said. "But my daddy promised me I could today."

"Well, then, we need to honor that promise," Eliza said, thinking she had promises to keep, too.

"Hold tight to the horn," she said, showing the girl the firm leather handle over the pommel.

"Is this a real horn?" Charlotte asked, giggling. "Can I honk it?"

"No, that's just the name it's called because this is a Western saddle. Some don't have a horn to hold onto, just the pommel which is slanted up to help keep you on the horse. Now hold tight and Peaches and I will do the rest."

They'd made it around twice when Eliza heard her *mamm* calling. "Levi? Levi, *kumm* quick."

Mamm never called out that loudly. Something had happened.

Eliza saw Levi coming around the barn and heading toward the cottage. Had something happened to Connie?

She guided Peaches around a turn, then glanced at the cottage and saw her mother talking to Levi. He ran inside the house. Eliza's heart hit against her ribs in a fast beat of fear and apprehension. Glancing around, she searched for someone to help. When she spotted Jonah, she called out to him.

The couple watching her with their daughter gave her an odd stare. "Hey, are you all right?" the father asked.

Eliza tried to speak. "I need to check on my mother," she said.

Jonah came over. "Eliza?"

She leaned close. "I think Mamm needs me. She called for Levi and . . . it could be Connie."

Jonah's confused frown told her she was babbling. "Go. I'll take over for you here." Then he turned and smiled at the family. "It's becoming a tradition around here that something big happens on festival day." Then he nodded to the little girl. "But you, little lady, get an extra trip on the pony ride."

Eliza loved her brother-in-law at that moment. She hurried past the parents. "I'm sorry but I have to see what's going on at my house."

The woman gave her an understanding nod. "Of course. That's your family."

Eliza mumbled, "*Denke*." Then she took off running. If something bad had happened to Connie, Levi would never forgive her for keeping his *mamm*'s sad secret. And she'd never forgive herself either.

She ran up the steps and into the house. "Mamm? Connie?"

"Connie, are you all right?"

She whirled around and then heard them in the mudroom.

"He'll need some stitches," Mamm said when Eliza got there. Levi was holding James by the arm while Mamm cleaned a deep gash near his elbow. Connie sat on a stool with bandages and a wet cloth.

"Oh, what happened?" Eliza said, out of breath. James had dirt and mud on his pants and shirt.

"What are you doing here?" Levi asked, surprise bright in his eyes.

"I heard Mamm calling out for you. I . . . I was afraid something had happened to . . . *Daed* or . . . someone else."

Aenti Miriam came into the already crowded room. "The pig is fine," she said, her hands on her wide hips. "I don't condone pig chasing. All that mud and other unspeakable things. It's not sanitary. We should find this boy some clean clothes."

Mamm nodded. "I have a few leftover shirts and pants here."

Eliza glanced from her aunt to Levi. "Pig chasing? When did we add that?"

"Jonah's idea," Mamm said. "It seems to be a hit." She glanced at her sister. "And yet another thing Miriam disapproves of."

"It's just too messy and smelly," Aenti Miriam said. Then she turned and headed toward the kitchen. "I'll find the clean clothes."

"My *bruder* decided to chase a pig and the pig won," Levi replied, shaking his head. "He'll need to see a doctor. He hit the fence and got caught in some wire."

"He might need a tetanus shot," Mamm said, her focus on the nasty gash on James's right arm.

"I thought I told you two to stick together," Connie said, "and to stay where I could see you."

"We *were* together," Laura said from the corner. "He had to run after the pig. I only watched."

Connie let out a sigh. Eliza noticed how pale she looked and how her right hand trembled. "Connie, would you like to walk a bit with me?"

Connie gave her a warning glance. "*Neh*, right now I need to find one of those paramedic people to check James's wound."

Levi pivoted for the door. "I know where their booth is set up."

"I'll walk with you," Eliza said. "Jonah is tending the pony rides until I get back."

Levi absently lifted his chin. When they got out the door, he turned to her. "You called out to my *mamm*. Why would you ask her if she's all right?"

Eliza hoped the blush burning her skin wouldn't show. "I panicked. I was afraid for Mamm and Connie and . . . last year my *daed* had a heart attack, not on festival day but still, when Mamm calls, everyone comes running."

"Your *daed* is strolling around and your *mamm* is fine. It's nice of you to worry about my mother, but as you saw, she's okay. It's just James I'm worried about. He's trying too hard to be a man, and he still has a lot of boy in him."

Eliza relaxed and laughed. "Well, he's growing up and I guess he wants to prove that. You did much the same, ain't so?"

"That is so," he said, giving her an embarrassed glance. "There's the paramedic booth. Let me see if one of them will go and check on James." Then he grinned. "I'm sure your *aenti* has him in a tub of hot water by now."

"She always has someone in hot water." Eliza let out a breath. "It's been an exciting day. I'm just glad everyone is okay."

Levi glanced up toward the cottage. "Jamie had fun even if he got hurt. I'm glad Mamm and the youngies got to come today."

"I'm glad, too. Mamm has enjoyed the company."

But still, she worried about Connie. Levi needed to know the truth, but how could she tell him about his mom's sickness without telling him his mom's plan for their lives?

CHAPTER TWENTY-FOUR

The paramedic cleaned the wound all over again and gave James some antibiotic ointment, then wrapped his arm in gauze. "You should see a doctor as soon as possible to make sure no infection sets in."

Levi assured the man they'd get it checked first thing on Monday.

James frowned and studied the clean shirt and pants he now had on. The pants were big, and the shirt was small. He looked uncomfortable. "I'm fine. I want to go back out."

"*Neh*," Connie said. "You need to sit and keep those borrowed clothes clean, and we'll have some cookies and fresh apple cider. Sarah has made a whole batch of pumpkin cookies."

"May we sit on the porch?" Laura asked as she held her apron up and twirled herself around like a ballet dancer. "I don't want to miss anything."

"If you promise to sit still and behave," Connie replied. "It's been an eventful day and I heard you sampled a lot of different foods. Only one or two cookies, understand?"

Laura gave her brother a stern stare. "Did you tell on me, James?"

"*Neh*," James said, shaking his head. "The stains on your apron told on you."

Laura glanced down. "I had a corn dog and the ketchup dripped." Then she put her hands on her hips. "At least I don't smell like a pig."

Connie smiled and shook her head. "I'm glad you both had fun, but no more chasing pigs, James."

Mamm shot Eliza a perplexed glance. Nothing got past Sarah King, so Eliza might have some explaining to do later. Maybe Connie had told Mamm about her illness and her hope for the future of her family. A future that would include Sarah's middle daughter.

Then Mamm suggested, "Eliza, you don't mind sitting with the youngies, do you? I'm sure you need to rest your leg. And I need to check on Miriam. She might have gotten into a food fight with Edith."

Eliza couldn't say no. "Of course. We can watch the activities from here, and if you two see something you want to do, I'll walk with you and stay until you're finished."

"*Gut*," Mamm said, smiling. "I'll bring out the refreshments." Then she glanced at Levi. "Would you like to stay, too?"

"I should get back to the stables," he said. "Jonah for sure will need some help." He gave Eliza a reassuring smile. "I'll look after Peaches, too. But she is *gut* at her job."

"Don't let her get too many treats. We don't want her digestive system to get all out of whack."

"I'll make sure she is taken care of."

He took off, probably glad to be away from women and children for a while. Levi worked here and other places all day then had to go home to take care of the farm and his mother and siblings. He was doing the best he could with the time he had. She needed to stop pestering him, since the man had a lot on his mind.

If she became his wife, she could ease some of that burden.

More and more, Eliza was learning the true meaning of grace and serving the Lord. Levi tried so hard to do that, to help anyone in need, to make a good salary, to care for his family, and to spend time with her.

And yet, he rarely spoke a cross word to anyone.

Mamm came out onto the porch, a huge tray balanced in her hands. Eliza immediately helped her set it down on the table by the rocking chairs. "Sit, Mamm, and I'll serve."

"Well, how nice of you," Mamm replied. "Now that the excitement has died down, you can tell us how your morning has gone."

Eliza smiled and handed out cookies. "Not much to tell. Just a lot of pony rides. Levi brought me lunch, and Matty supervised the rides for a while so I could rest my leg. I haven't had a chance to check on Abby or Colette."

When she mentioned having lunch with Levi, both *mamms* looked at her and then at each other, secretive smiles on their faces.

Eliza had to wonder what else these two had cooked up for her and Levi.

Eliza rested her leg for a while and then offered to take James and Laura up to the inn. Sitting on the cottage porch was boring when so many interesting things were going on. "I'll show you the lake from the inn's front porch. That porch is famous because of the *wunderbar* view of Lake Erie. And our little inlet is very pretty, especially this time of year."

James pushed his glasses up. "Maybe I can spot some migrating geese or other birds."

"*Ja*, and you'll enjoy the boats that come by. They are huge at times. Often if we wave, they'll blow their horns or whistle at us."

Laura wanted to collect leaves. "We'll take a bucket for leaves or anything else you might find. We can walk the beach if we take it slow. We might find some sea glass or other treasures there."

"How did the glass get there?" Laura asked.

"Well, it's said that thousands of ships went down in these waters, and they all carried things like dishes, fine china, and glasses. Also, we can search for marbles that might have come from ballast or from a marble factory near the lake.

"What's a ballast?" James asked, his glasses slipping down again.

"From what I've read," Eliza explained, "it's the part of a ship that stores a lot of heavy cargo to keep the ship balanced. The story goes that some captains put marbles deep inside the ballast as weights, and that they sometimes threw the marbles overboard or the marbles washed up after a shipwreck. That has not been proven, but I think it's romantic to read about. If we find one of those, it will be a rare treasure. Want to look a bit?"

They both liked that idea.

As they walked and she showed them different spots of interest, she asked, "Do you both enjoy school?"

James bobbed his head. "I love to read."

"I do, too," Eliza replied. "I used to get in trouble for reading when I was supposed to be doing chores."

"He does, too," Laura declared. "I like to sew and play with dolls."

"That is a fun thing to do," Eliza replied as they watched all kinds of people milling around. "Do you both enjoy going to frolics?"

"We don't get to go often," Laura said. "Mamm is too tired to take us, and Levi is always working."

James looked around. "It's hard to make friends when we don't see anyone much." Then he lowered his head. "I get teased about my glasses, so I mostly stay home."

"But you have friends from school and church, of course."

"Not many," Laura said. "I get invited to their houses but no one *kumms* to see us. Except you and your *mamm*. We like having you both."

Eliza's heart did a strange little tilt. She'd always had friends around and still attended frolics and youth get-togethers. Connie must be worse than she'd let on. These children needed to be around others, but their *mamm* might not be able to take them and Levi worked all the time.

Just another thing she'd have to put on her list if she married Levi. If he even asked her to marry him.

Everyone around here assumed they belonged together, but how could anyone be sure when neither of them knew what they wanted? They'd been close growing up, but they'd parted in a bad way. Then he tried to win her back but decided he wasn't good enough for her, and now, she'd been asked to marry him and take care of his siblings. Could two confused people be forced together and then find love?

It seemed doubtful. But she could help his family as a kind gesture, whether they got married or not.

Having made that decision, she took the children for a walk along the shore. They found some sea glass and some pretty leaves, but no marbles.

Tired and aching, Eliza managed to get them back to the inn. She was about to tell them to go along to the cottage without her, since she needed to rest. But she didn't want them walking alone. She'd find someone in the kitchen to walk with them.

"Oh, great," James said, glaring at a young Amish woman walking through the crowd.

"Not her again," Laura added.

Eliza watched the pretty girl with the dark hair and a beautiful garnet-colored dress and black apron waving to someone in the crowd, her smile dazzling.

But when she saw the smiling man headed toward the girl, she felt sick to her stomach.

"Who is she?" Eliza asked.

Laura snorted. "That's Rebecca Speicher. She likes Levi a lot, and she thinks she's going to marry him."

Eliza almost stumbled.

What was this? Levi had been walking out with someone else while he'd practically offered his heart to Eliza?

"How long have they been together?" she asked, hoping the question sounded casual.

"They aren't really together," James replied. "Rebecca thinks they are, but Levi explained to me that they aren't."

"I'd like to hear the explanation," Eliza said with a false grin and several glances to where Levi stood talking to the flirtatious woman.

"She likes Levi, a lot," James said. "He did some work for her *oncle*, and she showed up to visit her relatives while he was working at their place—that's how they met. But Mamm told us Levi doesn't prefer Rebecca. She comes by our house with casseroles and pies, but they ain't as good as the ones we've had here."

"I see," Eliza said, finding it hard to relax. Levi seemed to be enjoying Rebecca right now. "Does she visit often?"

"She *kumms* to see her *oncle* several times a year."

Eliza tried again. "And does she visit your home a lot?"

"Not much, since Levi's never there," Laura said, a

scowl on her face. "She doesn't like sitting with Mamm, so Mamm is kind to her but sends her on her way."

Eliza had to smile at that. "Your mother is a kind woman."

"And patient," James said. "Mamm says she has to show patience with that one, but that one day, Levi will marry the woman *Gott* has chosen for him."

"But we sure don't know who that is," Laura added. Then she took Eliza's hand. "I think Mamm wants it to be you, and so do we."

Eliza's heart melted in a puddle at her feet. "That is so sweet and kind of all of you. I love you both, you know. So we will just have to see, won't we?"

They both grinned. "And let *Gott* work it out?" Laura said, her face all scrunched.

"*Ja*, that is what we must do," Eliza said, feeling lighter by the minute. "I have an idea."

"What?" they both asked.

She took them to a picnic table, so she could rest her leg. She'd taken the easiest way to the beach, but it had also been the longest way.

After they'd all sat down, she said, "Let's give Levi and Rebecca a few more minutes together, and then we'll go and drag him away."

They both snickered at that idea. "He'll be relieved," James said. "I don't plan on walking out with any girls. They'd probably just laugh at my glasses."

Eliza wanted to tell the boy that any girl would be blessed to have such a sweet person in her life. Instead, she said, "One day, *Gott* will find someone for you, too, James. Remember that."

He beamed her a thankful smile.

Then Laura chimed in. "I want to be married and have babies, because they will be like dolls, only better."

"*Ja*, only better," Eliza replied, not wanting to dampen the girl's dreams with the reality of being a mother. "But take your time on that and be sure."

"*Gott* will be sure," Laura replied with confidence.

"*Ja*, that is for certain and sure." Eliza smiled at both of them. She was just about to take them to their brother when she glanced up and saw him walking toward them. Without his friend Rebecca.

I wonder where she went, Eliza thought. And she wondered when Rebecca would be back.

CHAPTER TWENTY-FIVE

Levi spotted Eliza and his siblings, which gave him a good excuse to extract himself from the pretty but talkative Rebecca. She'd hinted way too often about seeing him at church next week, where they could visit more. Or maybe having supper with her family one night soon.

He liked Rebecca, but he didn't want to be near her, not in the same way he wanted to be near Eliza. Eliza was pretty, smart, funny, interesting, and independent. She didn't cling to him like growing moss. She didn't drop hints all the time or bat her eyes at him like she had something stuck in her eyeball.

Now Eliza was smiling at him in a daring way that meant she'd seen him with another woman. Could she be a tad jealous? Or was he asking for too much?

"We saw you with Rebecca," Laura blurted, her frown cute rather than ferocious. "Did you tell her to scat?"

"I did not tell her that, *neh*." He ruffled his sister's hair and then nudged his studious brother. "I had to be polite."

"Why?" James asked, clueless.

"Because our *mamm* taught us to be that way."

"But if you don't like her—"

"I didn't say I don't like her," Levi replied, teasing. "She's a pretty girl and available and eager to find a husband. She can cook and she dresses clean and nice. But she does prattle on about so many things."

He heard what could have been a cough or a scoff. He took a glance at Eliza. Her ears were a burning red, and her expression was fiery.

"Are you feeling ill?" he asked, trying not to laugh.

"*Ja*, a bit sick. You . . . failed to mention your Rebecca."

"He don't like her," James said with scorn.

"He seems to like her very much," Eliza replied, her eyes flashing fire toward Levi.

"I like a lot of people," he said, grinning. "But what I like right now is seeing how the one person I like being around most in the world seems to be jealous of poor Rebecca. Ain't so?"

Eliza stood and stumbled.

He was there to help her.

Their eyes met and a slow, sweet burn fizzed through Levi. This woman—she had his heart.

Eliza dropped her gaze and pulled away. "I . . . I have to check on Peaches, and then I'm going to take my shift in the quilt room."

"We'll walk with you."

She gave him a glare and a pout. "You are mean, Levi Lapp."

"Mean? Just because I like to see that you are a wee bit jealous of Rebecca? And just because you care about me more than you're willing to admit?"

Lowering her gaze, she watched her feet as she started walking away. "I don't know what you mean."

He followed. "*Ja,* you do, and now I know you care about me."

"You tried to hurt my feelings and, well, it worked. But

you are a free man, and you can talk to any woman you want. I encourage it."

"You encourage it?"

She bobbed her head weakly.

"Then I guess I'll take Rebecca up on going to supper at her house."

Eliza gave him a green-eyed glare. "Why don't you go at that?"

"Maybe I will."

He gave up and motioned to his siblings. "Let's get Eliza back to her Peaches. Then I'll take you two and Mamm home. I think she's tired."

Eliza's anger dissipated like fog. "Is Connie feeling sick?"

"She's just ready to go. This is more activity than she's used to."

"For sure."

He glanced over at Eliza, touched that she cared about his mother's welfare. He had to get used to Eliza's sudden mood changes. One moment she was spitting nails at him and now she was demure and concerned. Perhaps she liked his family better than she liked him.

No, he'd seen the jealousy in her eyes. This sudden turn back to sweetness had to be caused by something else. He was just too thick-headed to figure it all out. But he would and soon.

Now he knew she liked him a whole lot more than either of them had realized.

Eliza hurried into the inn's long back hallway, where the hub of waiters and waitresses and cooks and dishwashers moved like a choreographed ballet before her eyes. The noise of sizzling food merged with the clatter of pots and pans. The place smelled like a Sunday dinner and made her feel loved and secure.

"You look like you could use a piece of sweet potato pie," Abby said as she whirled by. "Aenti has been asking when you'd be here to take your shift."

"In the quilting room?" Eliza asked. "She's not in charge there, is she?"

"She's helping," Abby said, emphasizing the word *helping*.

"Let me get this food out and then we'll go check on things together. Colette had seven people in her session."

"And you?"

"I had five, I think. We had a nice time. Some of them were seasoned quilters and some not so much. Aenti was actually a big help."

"That's something to be thankful for," Eliza said. She wanted to tell Abby about her day, but someone called her sister's name and Abby took off.

Making her way to the quilt room, she spotted Rebecca Speicher sitting at a table in the café. With another man. Hmm. Maybe a brother, or another possible bridegroom. The woman was pretty and obviously flirtatious, but how did she get to know Levi so well and so fast? The man worked all the time. Not that it was any of her concern. Not at all.

"Did you swallow a lemon?" Colette asked as she dashed by.

"I kinda did," Eliza replied, staring at Rebecca. "Do you know her?"

Colette squinted across the pass-through window. "Rebecca Speicher, niece of Elsie and Paul Speicher, *kumm* from Ohio to visit through the holidays. They live on the outskirts of town but have no children. She is precious to them and . . . they hope she'll settle down and find a *gut* man."

Eliza studied her sister. "You should be a reporter. Who told you all that?"

Colette sent a soft glare toward the woman now eating coconut pie. "Matthew," she said with disdain, "after I caught him laughing it up with her earlier."

Surprised, Eliza dragged her sister aside. "She did the same thing with Levi."

"Ah, so she's testing the waters of the Shadow Lake Inn. We do seem to attract handsome men. I mean the inn, not us. Although we are both fine catches."

"Maybe someone should tell precious Rebecca Speicher that."

Colette and Eliza stood there staring so long, Aenti Miriam came hustling out of the quilt room. "Land's sake, why are you both dawdling there as if you don't have things to do?"

"Coming," Eliza said. "I haven't seen my sister all day long. I wanted to catch up."

"And I'd like to catch my breath," Miriam huffed. "I've done a lot of the work around here, whether anyone's noticed or not."

Eliza gave Colette an eye roll. "We did notice, Aenti. Mamm said you should go to the cottage and rest. You are free to leave for the rest of the day."

Miriam looked perplexed, and then she looked pleased. "*Gut*. Glad to know my sister has noticed my hard work."

"We've all noticed, trust me," Colette said as she hurried away.

Eliza rushed past her *aenti*. "She has pumpkin cookies waiting."

Aenti Miriam took off faster than a jackrabbit. One

thing their *aenti* loved more than bossing everyone around was snack time.

After she'd pranced down the hallway and out the door, Colette came running back. "Did Mamm really say that?"

"Neh. But I'm guessing she's thinking it."

"You are so bad at times," Colette said.

"They'll be fine. Mamm will know someone sent Aenti home. She can handle Aenti just fine."

"I'll send your quilters back," Colette said. "Oh, and by the way, one of the women who just signed up is our new friend, Rebecca Speicher. Have a nice time."

Eliza couldn't believe this was happening. She wasn't the best of quilters and now here she stood with Rebecca Speicher smiling at her with such intensity, she had to blink.

Two other women came in—one a young *Englischer* with a pretty bob haircut and her mother, almost an exact replica of her, except older. They were Audrey and Sheila, the mom told Eliza. Then an elderly woman sat down at the long table, her eyes gleaming with delight.

That left Rebecca.

She approached Eliza with swishing skirts and a darting smile. "I'm Rebecca. I've heard so much about the quilts at the Shadow Lake Inn. My *aenti* told me all about the memory quilt one of you made last year. What a story behind that!"

"I'm Eliza," Eliza replied, her smile tight. "My sister designed that beautiful, meaningful quilt, *ja*."

Rebecca's giggle sounded like pebbles hitting glass. "I love a *gut* romantic story, don't you?"

"I do, indeed," Eliza said. "Now if you'll get seated, we can get on with our hour."

Rebecca turned to sit but whirled back around. "I've learned so many interesting things today. One being that Levi Lapp works here part-time. He's such a delight, don't you think?"

Eliza was thinking things she couldn't speak at the moment. But two could play this game. "He is a delight. We love his work, and he often stays for dinner. But then, we have a lot of people who stay for dinner around here."

"Well, you do all go out of your way to welcome folks to the inn."

"Especially staff," Eliza replied. "We only hire the best."

Then she clapped her hands together, picked up a needle and thread, and said, "Ladies, let's talk about quilting."

She wanted to jab the needle at Rebecca's knowing smirk, but Eliza reminded herself the Amish did not condone violence. Peaceful. They were peaceful, kind people. But right now, glancing at Rebecca, Eliza felt anything but.

She needed to pray about this streak of jealousy that had come over her today.

"Will you show us how to get started?" mom Sheila asked.

"We start with squares," Eliza said, regaining her poise and confidence. She held up a deep burgundy twelve-inch square. "We sew the cut squares to make a background for our quilt top, which will have a design on it."

"Is that where we put the appliqués?" daughter Audrey asked.

"*Ja*, that's how it starts. Today, you will work on one square that you can keep and take home with you."

Nancy, the elderly woman, smiled. "I used to help my mama with her quilting. I don't know why I came today except to experience that feeling again. I studied Amish quilts and I find the symmetry fascinating."

"What kind of feeling?" Rebecca asked primly. "What is there to feel about making a quilt?"

"I know what you're saying," Eliza replied to the woman. "That feeling of creating something with people you love, a lasting item that captures memories or events or emotions in vivid color. Usually, Amish quilt patterns are practical and simple—a star, a wedding ring, a pinwheel, or maybe a nine patch. We use geometric patterns, squares, rectangles, and diamonds mostly, and lots of colors, mauves, greens, blues, deep colors."

Rebecca nodded as if she knew all of this. Amish girls learned to sew and quilt at an early age.

"So tell us about the memory quilt," Rebecca said, all smiles. "Did it really hold someone's memories?"

Eliza didn't know how to respond. "I don't think we have time for that story. I will say my sister Abigail is a great quilter. She did a memory quilt last year, and it does tell a story. But that's not my tale to tell."

Rebecca smiled again. "What is your story? Have you made a special quilt?"

Eliza wanted to throw wads of fabric scraps in this woman's face. "We all have a special quilt," she replied. "And they each tell a story. Maybe you will figure out what your story is today, *ja*?"

Rebecca nodded, her eyes slanting with shrewd awareness. But she shut up, thankfully, and let Eliza conduct her workshop. One twelve-inch square. They each had one square and one pattern to make. She had to wonder which of the sample patterns Rebecca would choose.

Of course, the other woman decided on the wedding ring pattern.

CHAPTER TWENTY-SIX

That evening after everyone had gone home, Eliza stumbled toward the cottage. But a strong hand reached out to guide her.

Levi.

"What are you doing?" she asked, aggravated and grumpy. Her quilting session would have been great without all the unnecessary questions from Rebecca Speicher.

"Escorting you home."

She glared at him. "Wouldn't you rather be escorting Rebecca?"

"Are you still smarting from that?"

"From what? Me? *Neh.* I just don't want you to waste time with hopeless little me when you could have spunky, chatty Rebecca."

"Spunky? Hmm. Chatty, true. Seems I know a woman who is twice as spunky as what's-her-name." He nudged her arm. "And three times as pretty." Then he chuckled. "Although when this woman gets going, she can give anyone a *gut* talking-to."

"You expect me to believe that?" Eliza said, sweet warmth filling her heart.

"You don't know who I was talking about."

When she saw his mischievous grin, she slapped his hand. "You are trying my patience."

"Oh, me, trying your patience? Woman, you give patience a new meaning, and I'm sure the Lord has heard me wailing about that in my prayers."

She stopped and glanced up at him. "Do you think of me in your prayers?"

"*Ja*, and most every other hour, too."

"But we're just friends. You don't think you're *gut* enough for me, remember?"

"I'm remembering and wishing I'd never brought that up," he said, shaking his head. "I'm also remembering the past and how we felt about each other, and remembering how I missed you all the time I was away. And now, along with my memories, I'm having these daydreams where we are walking just like this, together, and smiling, and laughing, and—"

"And—?"

He whirled her around. "And kissing."

Then he kissed her, a soft, sweet, slow touch of his lips to hers with a featherlight brush of need and understanding.

After a sigh from her, he pulled back and stared into her eyes. "How was that kiss, Lizzie? Was it bad and horrible, or good and plenty?"

Eliza caught her breath, her hands pressing against his chest. His solid chest. "It was—" She stopped and savored the feeling. "*Wunderbar gut,* Levi. And plenty."

He touched his finger to a strand of hair escaping her *kapp*. "I hope it can be even better, between us, I mean."

For a few brief moments, Eliza had forgotten all that stood between them—his feelings of unworthiness, her uncertainty, and that one big thing—his *mamm*'s request that Eliza marry Levi and take care of him and the youngies.

She pulled away. "Aenti Miriam will tell my *mamm* if she sees us kissing."

He laughed. "That might be the only way I can get you to marry me."

That stopped her cold. "Don't joke about that, Levi. No person wants to be forced to marry someone. I have to go."

"Eliza?"

She turned and headed to the cottage, leaving him standing there.

And leaving her heart behind with him.

Levi brought the buggy to a halt in front of his home, the rich gold and orange sunset behind the modest little house only reminding him of the how the same sun shined on both him and Eliza.

But she had a big cottage to go home to, and a thriving property to take care of. He hadn't had much time to fix up his own home, but this place could shine if he just worked harder. He could make this a proper home if he added on a few rooms and worked with the land. He'd buy livestock and grow vegetables and fruits. He'd plant trees and flowers to please his *mamm* and maybe even a new wife. But how to start? And would such improvements work in his favor with Lizzie?

"You are quiet," Mamm said, as she watched him. "Are you tired, too?"

"I am weary," he admitted, taking his hat off to run a hand through his disheveled hair. "Seems I can't catch up."

"You do work day and night," Mamm replied, her hand patting his arm. "We rarely get to talk much at all."

He wanted to pour his heart out, but Mamm had too much to deal with already.

Besides, he couldn't talk about the bone-weary ache in

his heart. Eliza cared about him, but she wasn't ready to marry him. Would she ever be? She'd implied they could be forced to get married if her persnickety *aenti* caught them kissing. That wouldn't be a problem for him, but it would for Eliza. She'd be embarrassed and she'd feel forced. *Forced.* That word haunted him. He'd forced a kiss on her long ago and that hadn't gone so well. Today, he'd tried to be gentle and respectful, and she'd kissed him back. Really kissed him in a way that showed she cared.

Did she still feel forced?

"Levi, *was der schinner is letz*?"

"I can't explain, Mamm," he said as he helped her down. Telling James and Laura to do their chores, he turned to his mother. "I don't know exactly what's wrong. Sometimes everything, sometimes nothing. I'm confused."

"Levi, you have always taken on problems."

"Problems? What problems? Isn't this just the way life is?"

"*Neh*, that shouldn't be the way your life is, son."

"But how do I figure it all out?" he said as they walked up the steps to the porch. "I'm working to build a future, and I'm trying to win back the girl I have loved all my life."

Mamm turned and touched his cheek. "*Mer muss uff sich selwer achtgewwe.*"

"Take care of myself?" He grinned, trying to lighten the moment. "What does that even mean?"

Mamm laughed. "It means you need to take that girl you've loved all your life and do something fun with her—a ride or a picnic or a nice supper. Something she would love. Continue your gifts to Eliza as you have started. Don't give up on love and hope, Levi. *Gott* has given us these gifts—grace, sharing, forgiving, loving. Go and enjoy them."

Levi looked at his sweet mother and realized she was right. "So instead of fretting over what I can't control, I should rejoice over the things I can make happen?"

"See how smart you are?" Mamm said, patting his cheek again. "I always knew you'd become a *gut* man, Levi. And you are—don't forget that."

He opened the door and they walked into the dark house. He lit the propane lamps and guided her to her room. "Do you need anything?"

She shook her head and lifted a shaky hand. "I just need to rest, *denke*."

Levi nodded and called out to James and Laura to clean up and get to bed.

Then he sat in the chair where his father used to sit, wishing he could fill his father's shoes. After a few minutes of silent prayer, he knew what he had to do.

He'd walk in his own shoes, and he'd tell Eliza King that he loved her, and he wanted to marry her, if she'd have him. Then he'd let *Gott* work out the rest.

Before Levi could plan his next grand gesture for Eliza, she and her *mamm* showed up at his house. It had been a few days since the festival, and he'd helped clear away the tents and booths, tables and trash.

Eliza had gone back to avoiding him. He needed to stop kissing her. Every time he did, she withdrew. Was he that distasteful to her?

Neh, he reminded himself. He had not gone around kissing other women, but he had dated a few. Never worked out. But he knew when a woman returned his feelings, and his instincts told him Eliza King liked his kisses. Maybe that was the problem. She liked being with him too much, and she was trying to avoid temptation. As if he'd do anything to dishonor her.

He'd waited this long. He'd make plans to win her heart for sure and certain.

Right now, he had to find out what had brought Eliza and her *mamm* to see his mother so early in the morning.

Mamm greeted them with a clap of her hands and a feeble smile. Did he see tears in her eyes? It pained him to think how she must miss Daed.

"*Wilkom*," she said, motioning them to the porch. "I did not expect you to *kumm* so soon after the festival."

Sarah huffed at that. "We promised we'd check on you and visit more often, so here we are. Abigail and Jonah picked too many apples yesterday, so we thought we'd help you make applesauce for the youngies."

"And me?" Levi asked, his gaze moving over Eliza. She looked proper and pretty as always, but he could sense tension radiating from her. Did she want to be here?

"Of course, you," Sarah replied when Eliza didn't answer. "I think we have enough to make apple bread or another pie, too. Eliza tells me you love apple pie."

"I could eat it for every meal," he admitted. "I used to steal apples on my way home from school."

"Levi!" Mamm gave him a mock frown. "I'm shocked."

"They were on the ground," he said with a shrug.

Mamm and Sarah shook their heads and laughed while he grabbed the basket at Eliza's feet. "How are you today?"

"Fine," she said, her eyes on their mothers. "Those two are getting so close."

"Is that a bad thing?" he asked. "Mamm needs a close friend."

"I can agree with that," Connie said with a smile.

"*Neh*, it's not bad at all. It's a *wunderbar* thing," she amended, her green eyes bright. "My *mamm* needs a friend, too. I have my *schwesters*, of course. We three meet up a lot in one of our rooms and talk."

Mamm heard and chuckled. "And they think Abe and I don't know that, even though they've been doing it since they could first speak."

She went on inside with Connie.

"What do you talk about with Abby and Colette?" Levi asked Eliza after their mothers were out of hearing. He imagined his name came up now and then.

"That's private." She busied herself unpacking a casserole and what looked like freshly baked oatmeal bread.

"I get it. Girl talk."

"Women talk."

She was back to prickly. "My mistake. You are certainly a grown woman."

"You noticed?"

"Several times over."

"Heard from Rebecca lately?"

"*Neh.*"

She gave him a look full of disbelief.

Levi helped her place the food on the big table in the kitchen. He could hear Sarah and Mamm chattering away in the sewing room. A small one compared to the huge quilting room at the inn. He needed to stop comparing things.

"Eliza, are you ever going to forgive me?" he asked.

She whirled around. "For what?"

"Everything," he said with a shrug. "I know you care about me, but I don't think you can truly love me until you forgive me."

"I thought we'd had this conversation," she replied, her expression bordering on displeasure. "All is forgiven."

"I don't think so. You keep pulling away just as I think we're making progress."

"That is not true. I write in my journal, Levi. The journal you gave me. I quilt with my sisters and that is soothing, surprisingly. I admire the pretty mums you gave me, and I've enjoyed our outings together. I help out in the stables now that my leg is better, and I see you there. We talk, we tease, we laugh. What more can I do?"

"You can start by being honest with me," he said. "But not here. I want us to have a real day together—no doctors, no sisters, no festivals, and no mothers or siblings. Just you and me, talking."

"I'm busy."

"All the time?"

"Most of the time."

"Too busy for some fun time?"

"I'm not sure."

"Think about it then," he said, throwing up his hands in defeat. "You know I'll be around."

He turned and left the house, hoping he had the courage to keep walking. He had work to do out in the barn, where he planned to stay all day if need be.

CHAPTER TWENTY-SEVEN

Eliza wanted the earth to swallow her. She was hurting Levi at every turn, and she had not meant to do that. But her secret was eating away at her. Levi said he cared, and he'd hinted—no—said he wanted to marry her.

It had been a throwaway line—*that might be the only way I can get you to marry me*—but it had stayed with her. She didn't want him to feel forced to marry her, and she sure didn't want a wedding demanded by everyone else because someone had caught her and Levi kissing. Many a marriage had started that way and many a man had been tricked that way. Some women, too. Levi would think she'd felt obligated to marry him, and that would not be a *gut* start for them. Nor would he agree to marry her just because his *mamm* had asked Eliza to take care of his family. He'd resent the arrangement and never believe they had a real love. Did love always end in marriage?

This day had not gone the way she'd planned. Mamm had surprised her first thing by announcing this visit to Connie. She loved Connie, and Levi's siblings, but she'd had plans today to work in the stables with Jonah and . . . maybe Levi. To talk to him about certain things and drop hints so he'd ask Connie the questions he needed to ask.

Then when Mamm had told her he'd be working here at home, she understood why her mother had insisted she come along. Levi would be here all day.

Now she'd said the wrong thing and he was questioning her motives and she'd seen the deep pain in his expression. Had she pushed him too far? If she'd done that, he would stop trying to make things right between them, Connie would be disappointed and . . . Eliza might lose Levi forever.

"Why do you look so down?" Laura asked as she strolled into the room.

"Why aren't you in school?" Eliza countered.

Laura glanced around. "Don't say anything, but Mamm didn't feel *gut* this morning, so she asked me to stay home in case she needed me."

"Oh." Eliza put a finger to her lips. "Is there anything I can do?"

Laura shrugged. "I don't know. She rested so she'd feel better, but she wasn't expecting company. I'm glad I cleaned up for her."

"You did a great job on that," Eliza replied. "I love the smell of lemon wax. That's the sign of a clean house."

Laura beamed with pride. "*Denke*. I'm glad you're here, Eliza. You make things fun and . . . it's nice to have someone to talk to. Someone other than my *bruders* or Mamm."

"Me too." Eliza felt humbled by Laura's sweet words and the girl's efforts to help her *mamm*. But Laura shouldn't be missing school. Eliza would have to visit more often.

Denke, Lord, for making me see I am needed here.

Someone had to help this family. Had *Gott* put her here to do just that?

Only one way to find out.

"Let's surprise your *mamm* and make her a *gut* dinner. I brought a chicken casserole. My *mamm* helped me make it this morning. And we have oatmeal bread. Then you and

I will make applesauce, so she won't have to do all the work. I hear you love it almost as much as Levi."

"We all enjoy applesauce. Mamm just hasn't made much this year." Laura shrugged. "It's hard for her to turn the crank on the food mill. She always lets me help."

Eliza nodded her understanding. "Then you and I will do it for her. And my *mamm* will help." Chuckling, she said, "Your *bruders* should learn how to do this, too. Since they'll be the ones to eat most of it."

"That would be *wunderbar gut*," Laura said, her dark hair shining underneath her *kapp*. "We can surprise her, except she'll smell the apples simmering. But she will still be touched. I can't wait to eat all the things you've brought for us."

Eliza leaned close. "I also brought books for you and James. Reading is the best way to learn about life, and also to learn about yourself."

Laura giggled. "I know myself and I love my life."

"Then you are a blessed young *maedel*."

They worked to get the casserole heated up and the bread sliced. Then Laura showed her where the V-shaped manual food mill was tucked away in a large cabinet. Once the apples were peeled, seasoned with sugar and cinnamon, then cooked to mush, they'd strain the apples into a puree by hand turning the crank.

"We have jars for the applesauce," Laura told Eliza. "And seals. Mamm taught me to wipe everything clean or the jars won't seal properly."

"You are a quick learner, for certain sure," Eliza told her. "I'll go and talk to my *mamm* and tell her our plans." She hurried down the hallway and found Mamm and Connie quietly working on some mending. Connie glanced up, her eyes wide. "Is Laura being a bother?"

"*Neh*, we are going to get dinner ready, and then we

plan to make applesauce. You must act surprised. She is excited to do this for you, Connie."

Connie's left hand trembled but she carefully slid it down against her apron. "You are a *gut* influence on her, Eliza. She thinks the world of you."

Eliza blinked and smiled. "I feel the same."

Connie's expression held a plea and a reminder. "I will be very surprised to see what you two cook up."

Eliza saw Mamm watching her, but she pivoted and went back into the kitchen. "I told them we will be busy cooking. They can *kumm* and watch when we make our special applesauce and give us advice. *Mamms* love to do that, ain't so?"

"For sure." Laura grinned. "*Denke*, Eliza."

The smile on Laura's face brought tears to Eliza's eyes. How could she resist that sweet face? It wouldn't be difficult to take care of this family. She glanced around. She could spruce up this place and keep it clean, and there was plenty of space to add on rooms if needed.

It would be different from living with Mamm and Daed, but she needed to become independent. She didn't want to be stuck working at the inn, or in the stables, all her life. Could they have stables here? There was a barn at least. So much to consider, but so many reasons to do what would be right.

And . . . to do what would finally bring her and Levi together.

Show me the way, Lord. Lead me on the right path.

She'd be a married woman. Married to Levi Lapp and the head of this household. She'd be here for Connie and Laura and James. Or maybe even her own child. She'd be here for Levi.

She let out a sigh, thinking of that. A husband, a baby, a new home, ready-made with siblings. It was the way life went. Jonah and Abby seemed to love being married. They were older than she, but Eliza wasn't getting any younger. She'd always dreamed of these things, but now she realized she wanted more than the dream. She wanted the life. Why didn't she just go to Levi and tell him? He'd never have to know his *mamm* had forced Eliza's hand.

"Are you ill, too?" Laura asked, her dark eyes so like Levi's. "You look pale. Are you worried about all these apples?"

"*Neh*," Eliza said. "I'm just dreaming of being a wife one day. It's an important job and brings a lot of responsibility. I don't know if I'll be *gut* at it."

"You'd be the best," Laura assured her. "And Levi wants you to be his wife."

A deep voice spoke. "That's for certain sure."

They both whirled and saw him standing in the small living room, his gaze on Eliza.

Laura let out a gasp. "I'm sorry, Levi."

Levi looked at his sister, wishing he could be the one to have announced what she'd said. But then, Eliza knew how he felt. Or did she really?

"You've only stated the truth, Laura." He gave Eliza a questioning glance.

Her eyes met his and she smiled. "I was telling your sister I'm not sure I'd be a *gut* wife."

"Is that your way of saying you won't ever marry me?"

Laura's eyes moved from one to the other.

"That's my way of having a conversation with your sister. She stayed home today to help your *mamm*, but she and I have dinner ready and we're going to make applesauce after we eat."

So she was avoiding the question. Well, it wasn't exactly

a marriage proposal. More like asking her to tell him her true feelings. He'd keep at it, and he'd plan a big gesture, as Jonah called it, to woo her. He wanted the happiness he witnessed in Jonah and Abigail's marriage. But he was beginning to wonder if he shouldn't just walk away. Forget it. Forget Eliza. Seemed he'd been wooing this woman all his life. Even when he'd been away, she was never far from his mind.

Deciding he'd speak with her later when they were alone, Levi sniffed. "Smells *gut*. I'm starving."

Eliza gave him another smile. "Then go wash up and . . . will you tell Mamm and Connie that dinner is ready?"

"*Ja*." He gave her one last look, then went into the mudroom by the back door.

Maybe Eliza wasn't so scared of marriage. Maybe she just couldn't decide if she wanted to marry him. That thought threw him back a few paces, but he would not give up.

How could he when she looked so sweet standing there with Laura? As if she was right at home in his kitchen.

She'd want a stable, too, of course.

After washing his hands and arms, he ran his wet fingers through his hair. When he turned back toward the kitchen, Eliza glanced up at him, her eyes going wide. He saw it there, the trace of love that flittered away like a butterfly, to be replaced with a determined nod and something he couldn't identify. An evasive shadow of doubt.

Eliza was being secretive with him. And here he'd thought they had no secrets. Could this be part of why she was hesitant when he kissed her, and why she'd been avoiding him at every turn?

Avoiding, ja, he told himself. *But she is here in your home helping out today.* That meant a lot to Levi and showed him many things they'd left unspoken.

He turned toward the short hallway and heard Mamm whispering to Sarah. When they saw him enter, their talk stopped, but he could tell it had been serious.

And Mamm's eyes were red-rimmed and swollen.

"Mamm?"

"I'm fine, Levi. Just remembering your daed. He's safe and healed in heaven, but I miss him a lot."

Sarah patted Mamm's hand. "We women hold these feelings close at times. But a friend can listen and understand. I am Connie's friend. I'm worried about my Abe, and she has comforted me, even through her tears. I appreciate your kindness, Connie."

Levi relaxed a little. "I'm glad you two have each other then. And I have instructions to bring you to the kitchen for dinner."

"I am a bit hungry," Sarah said, rising off her chair. "We have done the mending and even managed some quilting. Connie's star quilt is quite lovely."

Mamm beamed a smile. "I'm hoping I can give it to Levi one day—for his wife."

Sarah sent Levi a knowing smile. "Mothers love to dream about such things."

"So I've noticed," he said. "Could you two be any more obvious?"

"I don't know what you mean," Sarah said on a chuckle. "Let's go and eat. What a joy to have a meal with such *wunderbar* friends."

Mamm stood and wobbled, her eyes going wide. Then she grabbed the back of the chair. "Oh, I'm sorry. I lost my footing for a moment."

Levi rushed to her. "Do you need to sit back down?"

"*Neh*," Mamm said. "I just stood too quickly. It happens when you're getting on in years."

"Mamm, you're not that old." His mother wasn't even

fifty yet, but she did look pale and tired. "Have you been overdoing with the housework around here? Laura told me she didn't feel like going to school today, but maybe you're the one she was worried about."

"I'm fine," Mamm said, shooting Sarah a quick glance. "Let's go to dinner. Food will help, I'm sure."

Sarah took Connie's arm. "We've worked so hard, we have a *gut* appetite. Levi, I believe my chattering has worn Connie out. But we rarely get to visit."

Levi guided his mother and Sarah to the kitchen. When Eliza glanced up from pouring their drinks, she gasped. "Connie, are you all right?"

She laughed. "I'm fine. My son is being overprotective."

Again, Levi watched as his *mamm* sent Eliza a speaking glance. Something was going on here.

And he was obviously the only one who hadn't been clued in.

Too many secrets in this kitchen.

CHAPTER TWENTY-EIGHT

After lunch, Levi left the kitchen.

Eliza had noticed his tension during the meal. Mamm kept the pleasantries going, but each time Eliza glanced up at Levi, he gave her a long stare, as if he were trying to read her thoughts. Connie barely touched her food, but she kept a smile on her face. Every now and then, she'd glanced at Eliza, a soft beseeching look in her eyes.

Eliza felt the weight of that gentle stare.

Now Eliza and Laura were getting the jars ready for the applesauce, while Mamm and Connie sat peeling apples. She longed to ask Connie how she felt, but Mamm had already sent Eliza several worried glances. Did she know? Or did she just suspect something was off with her friend?

Eliza couldn't discuss this with Laura and Connie in the room, so she busied herself with the task at hand. Normally, when she was fretting or had a problem, she'd go for a ride on Samson or Rosebud. Without that outlet, she'd have to make do with applesauce. At least this work required her attention.

"How are you two doing over there?" she asked Mamm. "Did we surprise you?"

Mamm chuckled, playing along. "Laura sure did. What

a great thing to do—stay home and help with making the applesauce and possibly a pie, too. No wonder Connie brags on you so much, Laura."

Laura turned from wiping down the jar lids. "*Denke*. I like staying home with Mamm. We get things done."

Connie's chuckle was weak. "Laura is a big help to me. James does his chores, but that boy keeps his nose in a book whenever possible. Used to upset his *daed* to no end."

"Now James does as he wants," Laura added. "But he loves Mamm so much, he doesn't make trouble."

"*Neh*," Connie said. "But I fear my James will never be a farmer. I'm not sure what will become of him, but Levi is here to guide him now."

Eliza felt the stab of that innocent statement. Connie had a right to worry about her children. She wouldn't be able to take care of them if her condition got worse. Levi needed to know this, to hear it from his mother. Eliza was so focused on this dilemma, she almost knocked the food mill off the table. It wobbled precariously on the corner, but she grabbed it in time.

"Eliza!" Mamm stood and came to her. "Is that too heavy?"

"*Neh*, I just pushed it too close to the edge," Eliza replied. "I'm glad I caught it, or I'd have a broken toe or two."

Mamm gave her a stark glance. "You're not yourself today. Is your leg bothering you?"

Eliza shook her head. "It's much better. Almost back to normal. My elbow hit the food mill, is all. I'll be more careful."

Mamm nodded, meaning they'd get to the bottom of this later. And her mother would. She'd insist. Sarah King could always tell when something was up with one of her girls. They never could hide anything from her.

"Well, let's get going on this," Mamm suggested. "We want to help Laura so she can have applesauce anytime she wants."

"And Mamm, too," Laura said, beaming.

Connie's eyes brightened with tears. "I'm thrilled you decided to be the head cook this year, Laura. I can sit and enjoy my friend's company."

Eliza found her own eyes tearing up. She wanted to finish the applesauce and hurry home to write in her journal. Then she'd ask Abigail to help her with another square for her quilt—a young girl holding a jar of applesauce.

She had too many emotions warring inside her head. This house, Connie's illness, Laura's innocent comments, Levi's constant presence, and her own confused thoughts each time she was around the man. Now her *mamm* suspected something. How could she keep Connie's secret? She wouldn't lie to her mother.

Two hours later, they'd finished the sauce and had a pie in the oven. Eliza packed up her basket and went to take it out to the buggy. She saw Levi there, checking on Rosebud.

"You spoil her," Eliza said, trying to load the basket quickly.

When she almost dropped the whole thing, Levi took it from her. "You've been fidgety all day."

"I'm fine."

"You don't want to be here, do you?"

She stopped to stare at him. "Is that what you think?"

"It's not hard to see. You don't even try to hide it."

Eliza gulped in a breath. "Hide what?"

"You don't want to be around me, you avoid me all the time, and you were forced to come here by our mothers. Am I right so far?"

Anger curled inside Eliza like an ugly bug. "So far, you've assumed too much, and you've insulted me. I like being around you and your family, Levi. I'm not trying to avoid you, and no one forced me to come here. Mamm and Connie have grown close lately, so Mamm asked me if I'd like to come and bring some apples to Connie. I immediately said yes."

She couldn't tell him she'd dreaded the visit, but not for the reasons he'd stated.

"Immediately? You said you'd come right away?"

"I thought about it and agreed."

"But you didn't really want to come here. I can see it in your eyes. And when I try to talk to you, I can see you want to avoid me. You're hiding something, not speaking something, trying to decide on . . . something. And my guess is it's marrying me. You don't want to hear about that, do you? You like me—maybe care about me—but you're not ready to take that next step. Will you ever be ready?"

Eliza wanted to scream. Why did everyone demand an answer to that question? She was about to tell him everything, to show him the truth he couldn't see. But before she could form the words, Laura came running out the door.

"Levi, something is bad wrong with Mamm. We must get help."

Eliza pulled out her phone, her fingers trembling. "Go, Levi. I'll call nine-one-one."

How she managed to tell the first responders the address Eliza would never know. She shook so hard, she almost dropped the phone. When she hung up, she said a prayer for all of them. Because now, unfortunately, Levi would finally learn the truth.

* * *

Levi sat by his mother's bed, his hands pressed against his head as he silently asked the Lord to help him understand.

Mamm—sick with some horrible disease he'd never heard of, a disease no one had told him about. Not even Eliza.

She'd grabbed him while the paramedics checked over his *mamm*. "Levi, I need to explain."

"What?" He'd been too concerned to listen.

"Levi, I know what's wrong with Connie."

Eliza had explained the diagnosis Mamm had gotten just before he came home. How her condition had worsened. And she'd told Eliza all of this? But why tell her and not him?

He glanced up now and saw Eliza standing in the doorway, her face tear-streaked, her eyes on him. He turned back to his mother. She'd refused to go to the hospital, and now she slept in peace. He'd promised the EMTs he'd get her to a proper doctor first thing tomorrow. Eliza turned and went back to the other room.

Sarah came in and touched his arm. "Levi, get a bite of supper. I'll sit with Connie. I've made arrangements to spend the night here. Jonah is coming to take Eliza home. Go."

Her expression meant business. She wanted him to talk to Eliza.

He touched his mother's warm forehead and then left the room, but he didn't plan on talking to Eliza. She'd had every opportunity to tell him about this, but instead, she'd fluttered and flittered and avoided him, and kissed him, and then pretended everything was fine.

Biting back his emotions, he headed toward the front door, but Laura and James both ran after him.

"Levi, is Mamm going to die?" Laura asked, tears in

her eyes. "She was ill this morning and she asked me to stay home. I didn't know she was so sick. She made me promise not to tell you."

James bobbed his head. "I heard them talking. Mamm told me to go on to school. Laura promised everything was okay, Levi. Now Mamm is worse."

He didn't know how to handle this. Eliza walked to where they stood. "Laura, you didn't cause this. You were obeying your mother. And James, you didn't do anything wrong."

Levi studied her face, saw the pain there, the hurt, the fear. Turning to his siblings, he pulled both of them close.

"Mamm will be okay. She's resting. If you're quiet, you can go and sit with her and Sarah. I love you both and I'm not angry at you."

He kissed Laura's head then ruffled James's hair.

They held hands and walked slowly down the hallway and into their mother's room.

Levi turned back to Eliza.

"I'm so sorry," she said, dropping her hands. "But I made a promise to her that I wouldn't tell anyone about her illness, not even Mamm. I only told my sisters, to get advice. Connie especially didn't want me to tell you."

"But why? Why would she tell you and nobody else?"

Eliza looked away. "I . . . I don't know. She had her reasons, and I have to honor my promise."

"Do you know her reasons?"

"I know she loves her family, and she wants the best for all of you."

"But you know more, don't you?"

She didn't answer. Which was the answer he expected.

"So . . . that's the way of it then."

He walked out the front door and headed to the barn. The broken, worn, old barn where his *mamm* had found his father ill. Daed had not wanted to burden anyone with his illness, and because they didn't have enough money to get the help he needed. Or . . . he was too proud to accept any help that might have been available.

Now the same thing had happened with his *mamm*.

Levi sank down on an old stool and held his hands together. He tried to form the words to pray.

What do I do, Lord? How can I help my mamm*? How can I go on thinking I know what's best, that I want Eliza to be my wife?*

He'd been so sure that they could work things out, but this was a new kind of hurt—a betrayal that could cost his mother her life.

I made a promise to her.

Eliza's words echoed in his mind.

A promise. To his mother.

Why hadn't Mamm told him, trusted him? He'd do anything for her, for James and Laura. He sat, his eyes burning with shame and anger. Shock. He was shocked.

A shadow moved toward him.

Jonah.

"Levi?"

He nodded, unable to speak.

Jonah sat down across from him, silent and steady.

"I'm okay, Jonah."

"I can see that."

"It's just hard to accept."

"You want to talk about it?"

"My *mamm* is sick and no one told me."

"And you're angry."

"*Ja*, wouldn't you be?"

Jonah nodded. "I would, indeed."

Levi sat there for a while. "I feel helpless, Jonah. A failure. I should have noticed."

"Levi, I just talked with your mother. She told me it was her choice to keep her illness a secret for as long as possible. She is scared, she is worried. She wants her family to be okay."

Levi stood. "Why didn't she tell me? Is it already too late?"

"I don't know," Jonah said. "Parkinson's is a strange disease. I do know from my former life she will need the kind of help we can't give her. Medication, therapy, a healthy diet, rest, doctors to give her advice. This disease will progress and get worse, but no one can predict how fast it will go. Some patients end up in assisted living."

Levi scrubbed his hand down his face. At least someone around here was being honest with him. "I don't know how we can pay for all of that."

"There are people who can help, you know. You've been all around the country, so you must know about insurance and medical plans that can help."

"Charity?"

"Not so much charity as protection against such calamities."

"But we are not protected. I know about the cost of insurance, and I know about saving money. I've saved up most of my earnings, but that won't cover this."

Jonah stood and put a hand on Levi's shoulder. "Then we will—your community will help in any way we can. And don't say you can't accept our help. That is what family is for, Levi. That is one of the things I love about giving my life over to *Gott* and becoming a member of this community. We help each other."

"And you think my pride will get in the way of that?"

"I think you are a *gut* man who's had a lot of hard knocks in his life. I've been that man, too, out to seek vengeance when I needed to seek justice. Let us help. And

Levi, show Eliza the same grace she has tried to show you. She only acted as your *mamm* wanted her to. Connie wanted her to understand. Connie made that clear—she asked Eliza to keep her illness a secret. She told Sarah that and Sarah explained to me."

"When was I supposed to understand or get an explanation?"

Jonah sighed. "That's the whole point. Connie wanted Eliza to be there with you—to be a comfort to you."

Levi let that information soak in. Then he wiped at his eyes and nodded. "*Denke*. You can take Eliza home. Sarah knows what needs to be done, and she will stay the night. I won't be able to work tomorrow. I must get Mamm to the doctor so we can discuss her illness and find out what we need to do about it."

Jonah waited at the barn door. "I understand. You take all the time you need. But think on what I've said. People do strange things in the name of love and *gut* intentions."

Levi nodded. He had a lot to think on. More than his tired brain could handle. He walked out with Jonah and found Eliza sitting on the buggy seat, her head down, the sun beginning to set behind her. His heart warred with his pain. She looked so alone and frightened, he wanted to go to her and comfort her.

She looked up when she saw him with Jonah, hope in her eyes. Levi gave her a quick nod, then headed into the house to comfort his brother and sister. And to talk with his *mamm* about what must come next.

He could feel Eliza's gaze on him as he walked up the porch steps, but he did not glance back.

CHAPTER TWENTY-NINE

Eliza sat in her room, trying to write her thoughts in her journal. Mamm had come home early this morning, stating that Levi would be taking Connie to the medical center for all the necessary steps. Connie was weak, but in good spirts, and Laura and James were going to school. A neighbor would take them to her house after school since Levi didn't know when they'd get home. Mamm stressed that his siblings wanted to do their part, but Levi thought they should be with someone else while they waited.

Eliza had prayed all morning for Levi and Connie. She wanted to do more, but Levi didn't want her around now. Reading over the words she'd written last night, she cringed at the thought of hurting Levi.

Today, I went with Mamm to visit Connie. Laura had stayed home to help, because Connie was having a bad day. Then she got worse, and I had to tell Levi part of the truth. About her illness. I left out the part about her asking me to marry him and take care of

Laura and James. I can't tell him that. Then he'd never be sure of our love, same as I feel right now. I'm not sure about anything. Should I agree to Connie's request and just marry the man? Or should I wait to be sure he loves me, and I love him? This is so hard, and now I've hurt Levi. I never wanted to do that, but I made a promise.

She slammed the journal shut when she heard a soft knock. Her sisters usually just barged on in, but last night everyone had left her alone. Why would they be here before the workday began?

Panic filled her heart. Had something happened?

"*Kumm* in," she called out, fear making her voice shaky.

Mamm entered, followed by Colette and Abby.

"What is this?" Eliza asked, thinking they were going to tell her more bad news. It was still early morning, but anything was possible these days.

"We need to talk," Mamm said in her usual to-the-point way.

Abigail and Colette sent speaking looks to Eliza, trying to convey what was about to take place. She figured it out right away.

Eliza glanced at her sisters. "Which one of you blabbed?"

"They didn't need to blab," Mamm continued as she found a seat in the cream-colored slipper chair Eliza had bought at a garage sale. "Yesterday, I could tell something was wrong with the Lapp family, and I could see that you'd been holding a secret close to your heart. And now we know Connie asked you to keep that secret—regarding her illness, ain't so?"

"*Ja*, Mamm," Eliza said, holding her head down. "I couldn't tell Levi, and now he is angry and hurt. It's all so horrible." She glanced out the window, knowing Levi wouldn't be coming here today. "I've never had to keep such a secret. Connie is ill and . . . Levi should have been the first to know."

"You left out the best part," Colette blurted. Then she put a hand over her mouth.

Mamm looked from Colette to Abigail. Her older daughter just shook her head and turned toward Eliza.

"Is there more?" Mamm asked Eliza.

Eliza stood and glared at her sister. "Can't *you* ever keep a secret?"

"I'm sorry." Colette didn't seem all that sorry, but she did put on a pensive face.

"Tell me everything now," Mamm said, her hands hitting her apron in a way that showed she'd had enough for one day.

Remembering that Mamm had been away and was probably tired, Eliza swallowed and took a breath. "Connie told me about her illness . . . because . . . she wants me to marry Levi and take care of Laura and James and run the house and . . . be his wife."

She sank down on her chair. "I'm so confused and over-whelmed, I don't know what to do."

Mamm sat stunned for a few moments; then she pulled her chair close to where Eliza sat and took her hand. "Eliza, why didn't you tell me this right away?"

"I promised I wouldn't tell anyone," Eliza replied, tears in her eyes. "I promised Connie, and I couldn't tell Levi that she wants me to marry him. Because if I did it for those reasons, he might think I don't really love him. I don't know if I really love him, and I'm not sure I want an arranged marriage."

Mamm patted her hand. "You don't need an arranged marriage, Eliza. Levi is so in love with you, I think the man would walk through fire to be with you. And you love him. I know that. But you are afraid to take that next step. Marriage is joyful and *wunderbar*, but it is also overwhelming, and it demands a lot of work and a lot of understanding between husband and wife. You must be sure, but this is not an arranged marriage; it is a *gut* way to bring you and Levi together, if it is *Gott*'s will."

Eliza glanced from her *mamm* to her sisters. "Are you all in agreement on this? Do you both feel as Mamm does?"

Abby nodded. "It's not a bad position to be in. Some marriages are forced, and the couple does not love each other, but you and Levi, that is a very different thing. You can work through this misunderstanding and have a happy life."

Colette bobbed her head. "You should be glad a nice man is after you, Eliza."

"After me?" Eliza paced back and forth. "As if I'm some varmint he has to chase and capture."

"It's not like that," Mamm said, a twitch in her crooked smile.

Colette shuddered. "That is not a *gut* image."

"It feels like that," Eliza retorted. "Are you all trying to get rid of me? Will Daed force me to do this?"

"Your *daed* has no clue. Yet," Mamm said, leaving the word floating in the air.

Eliza couldn't breathe. "I'm shocked that you are all ganging up on me this way." She felt betrayed by her sisters, and worried that her parents would make her marry. "It's hard enough to figure out without this intervention."

"We are not ganging up," Abby said. "Mamm came to us and expressed concern about you and about Connie. She had already figured most of this out, so we told her part of your promise."

"And now I know the rest," Mamm said. "Which explains the tension I felt yesterday. I'm sorry I talked you into going to the Lapp house with me, Eliza. That must have been agony for you."

"It was," Eliza admitted. "I do not like keeping secrets from Levi or you, but I thought I had to work this out myself." She held her hand to her heart. "In here."

Mamm stood. "It will work out, Eliza. You will discover the right thing to do, for yourself, and for Levi. You will know the moment it becomes clear to you, because *Gott* will place it on your heart."

Eliza bobbed her head. "But what if I'm too late, Mamm? What if Levi can't forgive me for keeping this secret? Then what?"

Mamm hugged her and drew back, a hand on Eliza's arm. "Then we will abide by *Gott*'s will."

Levi pulled the buggy up to the front door.

"Mamm, wait there and I'll come around and help you down."

Connie nodded, her skin as pale as linen and her eyes filled with tired resolve. She could barely speak, she was so exhausted.

Rudolph must have sensed what was going on. The big horse pushed at Levi's jacket when he came around the front of the buggy.

"*Denke*, old friend," he said to Rudolph. The horse shook out his mane and gave Levi a quiet stare.

Mamm did her best to get out of the buggy, but Levi

caught her before she hit the ground. "You'll need to be careful from now on. You could fall and break a bone."

"I'll be cautious," Mamm said. "I heard what the doctors told me, and I have all the written instructions."

Levi had listened, too. A tremor would eventually lead to impaired movement, dementia, speech changes, and a whole list of other symptoms. They had paperwork to read and paperwork to fill out, not to mention tests to get done at the hospital a few miles outside of town. In the late stages of the disease, Mamm would need full-time care. But the doctors couldn't predict when that would happen. First, they had to get her on medication and give her therapy. She'd have diet changes and they'd need to do some things around the house to make it easier for her. If she followed the proper protocols, the doctors had told them, she could be comfortable and live at home for a long time, depending on the progression of the illness.

Exhaustion weighed heavy on Levi's shoulders. He had two big jobs this week. One a few miles out of town and the other for Dr. Merrill. They would take all week or longer.

The only *gut* thing—he wouldn't be at the Shadow Lake Inn for a while. He would have time to sort all of this out. Working would be his excuse to avoid seeing Eliza.

His anger simmered like a pot of all-day stew, but he couldn't get the memory of Eliza sitting alone on the buggy seat out of his head. She had been hurt by what had happened. He needed to ask Mamm why she'd told Eliza about her illness instead of him, but he didn't want to upset her.

After he got her inside and onto the couch, he hurried out to the barn. Laura and James were just coming home from the neighbor's house. Thankful that the Scoggins lived just down the road, he waved to his siblings. They'd want news on Mamm.

Laura ran to him. "Did Mamm have to stay at the hospital?"

"*Neh*, not yet," he said while he fed the cows. "She can rest at home, and later this week, we'll take her to the big hospital for some tests."

They followed him to check on the goats.

"Will they hurt her?" James asked, his glasses sliding down his nose, his arms full of books.

"They will do what they need to do to find out how to treat her condition. Some of the tests might be uncomfortable but they won't hurt her."

"Will she feel better soon?" Laura asked, her hand patting Rudolph's nose as they moved past his stall.

"I hope so. But we need to understand she won't get well. This can't be fixed. We will make sure she has all the help she needs, and we will be with her for as long as she needs us."

"Then she is gonna die," his sister wailed. "Just like Daed."

Levi almost bit his tongue to keep from wailing himself. He pulled Laura close. "I know this is hard to understand, but people get sick. *Gott* knows why, but I don't, so I have no answers. But we love Mamm, and she loves us. You both need to remember that. And also remember, I will be here with you."

"What if you have to leave again?" James asked, looking younger than his fourteen years. "I would miss you. What would we do then?"

Levi let out a sigh. His brother had legitimate concerns. The same kind he had. "I will not take long trips anymore, I promise. I will only work around these parts. Within a day's ride."

James considered his words carefully, then nodded and stood up straight. "You need to show me everything you do here, so I can help."

Laura bobbed her head. "I can cook and clean and I know how to feed and milk the animals. I will help, too."

Levi looked from one to the other. He hadn't realized how little attention they'd been receiving with Mamm being sick. They'd had no one to guide them, even though she had tried her best. "You are both going to be a big help. I could not ask for a better brother or sister."

They all walked hand in hand toward the house.

Levi felt better, knowing his siblings would be brave and do their part. He would guide them and teach them. There was just one more person he wished could be in this picture.

Eliza. But yet more obstacles stood in their way. Even if he could hope to win her over, he still couldn't get past her keeping this secret from him. Nor would he burden a wife with this challenge. That meant he must lose her all over again, but what else could he do? He'd abandoned his family once, and he would not do it again.

Not even for the only person in the world who could be a solace to all of them. The one person who'd known about his mother's declining health, and yet had kept it from him.

CHAPTER THIRTY

Eliza moped around, wondering if Levi was gone for good. Jonah gave her busywork in the barn and stables, and she did her chores with gusto to keep her mind off Levi.

"If you don't smile, I'll send you to the chicken coop," Jonah said. "Abe put me there early on to test my mettle."

"I don't need my mettle tested," she retorted. "I know what it's like in the chicken yard. I'm sorry, Jonah. I just don't have the same pep I used to have."

Jonah nodded while he brushed down Samson's light gray coat. "Levi is working elsewhere this week. That's all."

"The week after he finds out his *mamm* is sick and I knew about it?"

"Coincidence."

"Or avoidance. He's angry with me, and I don't blame him."

"You made a promise," Jonah pointed out. "That's an honorable thing."

"But I knew I should have told him. I just got so confused, and I was afraid for Connie."

Jonah did the Jonah stare, which meant he was carefully weighing his words. "Well, now she has the help she needs. She is the one who has been sick, and she will be the one who has to deal with her illness—and her request to you. I have a feeling she'll tell Levi the truth once he's finished with his week's work. I know he had to take a day to get her back to the hospital for tests, too."

"You see, I could have helped with that if he wasn't so proud and stubborn."

Jonah's eyebrows winged up. "Who around here would know about pride and stubbornness? Oh, is it you, Samson? Or maybe me—yes, me. Or maybe everyone has that malady at times."

"You're not helping," she told her brother-in-law.

"I have an idea," Jonah said. "Why don't you take a break and go visit Abigail? She's not feeling well and your *mamm* went to check on one of her patients. She left early so she doesn't know Abigail is resting."

"I'll go check on her," Eliza said. "But you've done this before, you know. Scared me into checking on my very capable sister."

"I admit to that," he said. "But she's getting further along, and even though I know how to deliver a baby, I'd be a mess trying to help with my own. I depend on you and your sister to help me. Abby can be stubborn at times, too. I think it must run in the family."

Eliza lifted a hand. "I get it. I'm annoying you and making Samson sad. I'll go and fix Abby some soup and . . . talk with her about hardheaded men who can't see what's in front of them."

"Oh, she is an expert on that subject," Jonah replied with a chuckle. "But she sure opened my eyes."

Eliza finally smiled. "She did, for certain sure. She'll be fine, Jonah. Our Abby is tough underneath that sweet veneer. But I will sit with her."

Jonah seemed relieved. "*Gut*, because Aenti Miriam is

there with her now and . . . I'm sure your aunt needs a break."

"*Neh*, Abby will need the break . . . and *denke* for saving that for last. So thoughtful of you."

"At least it got your mind off Levi."

She shot Jonah a mock-frown. "I'm leaving now. Samson, kick him in the shin for me."

Samson neighed low and ignored her. Had her favorite horse turned on her, too?

She walked across the yard to the pretty four-square white house Jonah and Abigail had built on a hill past the cottage. They had a long front porch with rockers, and plenty of privacy with a nice backyard that faced the waterfall where Jonah had finally told Abigail the truth he'd remembered about his past.

That day had changed everything for her sister. This *bobbeli* was important—a symbol of the deep love Jonah and Abigail had for each other. A sacrificing love.

The kind of love she had for . . . Levi.

She stopped near the jutting rock where they all loved to have picnics. She loved Levi. That took the wind out of her. She grabbed at a nearby sapling and then sank down on the smooth rock.

"I love him."

Her heart filled with a warm heat, her eyes misted over, and tears fell down her face. So this was the moment Mamm had mentioned a few days ago. The moment when she realized *Gott*'s plan for her life, a plan that Eliza suddenly wanted to follow with all her heart.

Sacrifice. Despite all the teachings and sermons and schooling she'd had, she'd somehow let the true meaning of sacrifice slip right by her. But she and Levi had always loved each other. Even when they'd parted. And that was what had caused such fear the first time they kissed—that overwhelming, reckless warmth racing through her system, curling in her stomach, igniting a feeling that enticed her and frightened her.

Now that feeling felt right, felt *wunderbar gut*. Now the feeling that had overwhelmed her so often had become a part of her. She touched her heart, feeling its strong beat.

"In here," she whispered. "In my heart, I love Levi."

And she would sacrifice anything to show him that love. She'd gladly help with his siblings because that love expanded to them, too. His *mamm,* sweet Connie, had known this all along. She had just prepared the way for what might come—a test? Or a hope that she'd be able to see them together and happy.

Eliza wiped her eyes and stood. Then she saw Colette coming up the hill with a basket. When her sister saw her, she waved.

Colette hurried to her. "Are you ill?"

"*Neh*." Eliza grabbed Colette's arm. "On my way to see Abigail and I just . . . I'll explain when we get inside."

"I'm bringing her dinner," Colette said. "And I'm to take the place of Aenti."

"Same here," Eliza said. "We will make her feel much better."

Just as Eliza felt much better now. Everything had become crystal clear in her mind. She'd find Levi and she'd tell him what her heart had revealed today. She'd tell him she loved him, completely and forever. She'd tell him she would be his helpmate, his wife, and she'd help him build his farm, and she would take care of his home. She'd find a way to make it work. She was smart and she could study up on things. They would build a good life together.

She'd be there with him, through good times and bad.

She beamed a smile, causing Colette to stare at her. "You're scaring me. What is wrong with you?"

"Nothing to be scared about," Eliza said. "Just . . . I'm happy."

Colette nodded, still unsure. "Or you have a fever and are out of your mind."

"Could be," Eliza said. "But it's not a bad fever."

"So what is going on with you?" Colette asked as they sat by Abby's bed, munching on hefty ham sandwiches and fried squash, compliments of Edith. The food was *gut*, but Eliza was bursting to tell her news. She'd put it all on her quilt, too.

"Shhh," she said, pointing to the stairs. "Aenti."

"I heard that," Aenti Miriam said as she stomped into the room with a tray of hot tea and gingerbread. "I know you all have secrets from your *mamm*, and while that is wrong, you can confide in me. I will listen and understand."

"Aenti, how kind of you," Abby said from her spot on the pillows. "But you've done enough. You should go and rest now."

"Trying to get rid of me?" Miriam ignored Abby's suggestion and served tea like a queen's lady-in-waiting. "I'm not going anywhere. These two came running into your house like a racoon was chasing them. They have something to say. I can see it on their faces."

"It's me," Eliza finally replied, not even caring what Aenti would say. "I have decided I love Levi."

Aenti Miriam almost stumbled. "Well, is that all? We knew that. Tell me something really worth hearing."

"Isn't love worth hearing about?" Abby asked.

Aenti sat down with a thump in a nearby chair. "I knew love once, and I lost it. Turned me into a bitter old woman. That's my confession."

Colette snorted. "As if we didn't know that already, too."

Then when she saw her *aenti*'s harsh stare, she amended, "I mean, that's a tragic story, Aenti. Want to tell us the rest of it?"

Aenti sniffed. "Nothing to tell. He left me and . . . I was forced to marry Joseph. We nearly killed each other, many times over."

Eliza put a hand to her mouth. "But you abhor violence of any kind."

"We weren't violent," Miriam said. "Words. We used harsh words with each other. Probably why my sons turned out so sad and sorry. We weren't the best example."

"I'm truly sorry, Aenti," Abby said, her hand on her growing stomach. "I will do my best to use the right words with this one."

"That is a *gut* plan," Aenti said. Then she turned to Eliza. "You say you love Levi, but he comes with a family you will be expected to care for, ain't so?"

"*Ja*," Eliza said, wondering if her *aenti* had been reading her diary. "I will accept that, all of it."

"And his *mamm* is ill," Aenti said. "I have a suggestion."

Colette whispered, "I cannot wait to hear this."

"Me either," Eliza replied, wondering what else could possibly happen to her love life.

Aenti sat prim in the hickory rocking chair Daed and Jonah had made for Abigail. "I am not returning to my house. I've decided I want to live closer to my sister."

"You're moving in with Mamm and Daed?" Eliza asked, a bad feeling settling in her stomach.

Her sisters sent each other speaking glances.

"*Neh*," Aenti replied with a *tsk-tsk*. "I have found a nice little *grossmammi* house a few miles from here. In fact, it's close to Connie's house."

Eliza's ears buzzed at that revelation. "Really now?"

"Really," Aenti said, leaning in. "I haven't told your *mamm* yet. I know she'll be disappointed I didn't ask to stay here at the inn where my help is sorely needed."

"So sorely," Colette mumbled before adding, "for certain sure."

"Why are you moving from your home out in the country, where you're near your boys?" Abby asked, emphasizing the *near your boys* part.

Miriam shook her head. "My boys are scattered to the wind, and I rarely see my grandchildren. They move here and there and can't seem to settle on a place or their work. They are considering Ohio again, so I told them to go. I found a place to rent that is private and perfect for me. The couple who own the *grossmammi* house are a bit younger than I am, and they said they will not bother me. I plan to not bother them either."

"Did you put that in writing?" Again, Colette. "So they understand this is a *gut* rental contract, I mean?"

"We have a handshake deal," Aenti explained with a smug smile. "I will cook and clean for them twice a week while they work outside the home. They never had *kinder*, so they work at steady jobs. And I get paid. Imagine that."

"Aenti, that all sounds great," Eliza said, "but why haven't you told Mamm? And what does this have to do with Connie?"

Aenti gave Eliza a firm stare. "I wanted to talk to you before I explain this to Sarah. I can help you, Eliza."

"Help me how?" Eliza asked, thinking of all the ways this could go wrong.

"I will sit with Connie," Miriam said. "Look at me— I'm a hefty woman who can lift bushel bags of feed. I can help her up and down, and I'll bathe her and read to her. I'll cook what she needs when she needs it. I will do that."

There was a stunned silence.

"Well?" Aenti said. "Is that so bad?"

Colette touched Miriam's arm. "Are you feeling well or is there something else going on? You love your home. It's such a beautiful place."

"I did love my home," Miriam said, blinking. "But it's a lonely, beautiful home. I have to make up for what Joseph and I did to our boys—we let them run wild and do what they wanted—and that has not been *gut*." She wiped at her eyes. "After Joseph died, I let them continue to bully me and do as they please. Now they don't have a clue about real life. I am tired and I want to be with family that loves me. You all do love me, don't you?"

Again, silence. And then Eliza and Colette both rushed to their *aenti*. "Of course we love you," Eliza said. "This . . . this is so kind, so considerate of you. Levi will find comfort in this gesture and so will I."

Colette bobbed her head. "I always knew you had a heart, Aenti. Now I can see it with my own eyes."

Miriam frowned. "I have always been a loving *aenti*."

Abigail cleared her throat. "*Ja*, a loving, wise, and sometimes firm *aenti*."

"And you'll be even better now that you have us to spoil you and help you, too," Eliza said. "We must go find Mamm and tell her the *gut* news."

The partially opened door was pushed wide-open. "Tell Mamm what?" Sarah asked, her hands on her hips. "That you all decided to have a frolic without me? I'm going to pout."

They all started laughing and wiping their eyes. Eliza sat back and smiled, her heart bursting with so many newfound feelings. Who would have thought stern Aenti Miriam would come to her aid—to help the man she loved?

She couldn't wait to tell Levi about this, and tonight she'd write in her journal about Aenti Miriam, and about how much she loved Levi. But right now, she laughed with her sisters, Mamm, and Aenti Miriam. This was a *gut* frolic, the best kind. Now that she'd accepted her love for Levi, she would smile a lot more often. Just like Aenti.

CHAPTER THIRTY-ONE

Levi saw the note attached to the porch door.

From Rebecca.

Just what he needed today.

Levi, I came by with a freshly baked pound cake. Your brother took it and did not invite me in. He said your mamm isn't feeling well. I hope she'll be better soon so I can visit with her again. She's a delight. Also, my oncle wants to talk to you about doing some work for him. We have several fine horses, and I hear you are the best at what you do. Oh, and your home is so quaint.

Quaint. Why did that sound so condescending to him? Rebecca's *oncle* and *aenti* owned a large parcel of land and had several silos of grain, not to mention a produce market that stayed busy all year long. And they did have some excellent horses. Mr. Speicher always paid well, too. Levi had gotten to know Rebecca when he'd first come back to Shadow Lake. She visited with her *oncle* and *aenti* several times a year, she'd told him. She'd been away, too, helping her *grossmammi* in Missouri, but had returned for the winter. She seemed like a nice woman, but she prattled on about nothing and flirted way too much.

He hadn't found her in the stables the way he'd found Eliza.

Neh, she'd been in her home getting ready for a big frolic. She'd invited him but he'd declined. She had not taken the hint.

Comparing her to Eliza, he was grateful that Eliza was not flashy or flirtatious like Rebecca. Eliza didn't take her blessings for granted the way Rebecca did.

But what did it matter? He didn't want to be around Rebecca, and he'd messed up being near Eliza. But Eliza had messed up, too, by hiding his mother's illness from him.

He went inside and let out a tired sigh. Then he smiled. The kitchen was clean, and he could smell something wonderful bubbling on the propane stove. James was at his desk, but he turned when he heard Levi.

"I fed the cows and goats, Levi. I cleaned the barn out and sealed up some holes so the mice will stay away. I know they keep coming back, but at least we have barn cats."

"You did just fine, James," he said. "I checked the barn, and it looks better than ever."

James grinned with pride.

His brother was growing up fast now. Levi had neglected his duty to teach his siblings what needed to be done, but they'd gone over everything this week, and James had taken copious notes.

Laura had hauled out cookbooks and recipes annotated with scrawling handwritten notes splattered by cooking stains. The stains of love, Mamm called them. He understood that much better now.

"What did Rebecca bring?" he asked Laura as she went about setting the supper table.

"Attitude," his sister said on a snort.

Levi hid his smile. "Laura, you weren't rude, were you?"

"James took the food, thanked her, and then shut the door. But it's a pound cake. Doesn't need to go to waste. Only, I don't believe she baked it."

"She left me a note."

"She can write?"

"You both know to be kind to visitors."

"*Ja*, but Mamm is resting, and she doesn't need that magpie chattering in her ear."

"How is she?" he asked, getting to the subject foremost in his mind.

"She has eaten some soup and I helped her bathe and put on a clean gown. I did the laundry after school and most of it is dry." She glanced down the hallway. "I think Mamm was reading her Bible earlier."

"I'll go check on her, and then I want whatever that is in the stew pot."

"It's not as *gut* as Mamm's cooking, but I did try. I suppose we can have some cake for dessert."

"*Ach*, it does smell appetizing."

Laura checked the pots. "Almost ready."

"What did you cook then?"

"Spaghetti sauce to go with the dumpling noodles I made. I found an interesting recipe."

Levi grinned. "That does sound interesting. I'm hungry."

"I'll have the bread buttered by the time you get back from the washroom."

Levi went to clean up. He read the note from Rebecca again and decided he needed the money. Mamm's appointments and future hospital stays would be costly. The hospital had set them up with a payment plan that was doable, but he'd be paying it off the rest of his life. He'd go work for the Speichers, but he'd have to fit them in between his other clients. And he'd try to avoid Rebecca. That girl was trouble.

Eliza waited for Levi in the stables the next morning, so full of news, she was about to burst. How could she tell him that she loved him, that she'd help him? First, she had to find out his true feelings. He'd said he wanted to marry her, but did he really? Had he talked to Connie and heard about the promise Eliza had made? Could he forgive her? So many questions.

Her sisters had packed her a picnic basket and she had a blanket ready. She had warm sandwiches wrapped in napkins and hot cocoa in a thermos from the inn. She'd take him to the jutting rock. That had worked for Abigail and Jonah. Maybe it would work for her and Levi.

It was chilly out, so she wore a wool cloak over her dress, and she had on sturdy boots to keep her legs warm. Fall was turning to winter. Thanksgiving would be here soon.

She paced the alley while she waited, checking on the horses, talking to them, giving them small treats. They were all healthy and happy because Levi did more than take care of their shoes. He checked their legs and then studied the horses and felt their stomachs for any type of pain or digestive discomfort. He walked them and rode them and talked to them. They loved him as much as they loved her and Jonah.

When she heard someone approaching, she whirled to find him coming toward her. "Levi!"

He didn't smile. Would he forgive her once she told him the truth?

"*Gut daag*," he said, still not smiling.

"How are you?" she asked. "How is Connie?"

He gave her a dull stare. "Mamm is fine for now. She has medicine and she has appointments set up. We will get by."

"I want to help."

"You don't need to do that."

He kept walking. She followed. "Levi, I have so much to tell you. I brought some sandwiches and—"

He held up a hand. "I have something to tell you, too. I have to work at the Speicher place next week. I was looking for Jonah to tell him, but you're here so you can let him know."

"I see." Her heart plummeted. "The Speicher place. You mean, Rebecca's place."

"Her *oncle*'s place," he replied. "Just work."

Eliza tempered her anger and jealousy. "Of course. I understand."

"I'm glad you do. I need the money."

"Of course. Can we eat while we talk? I thought a picnic would be nice."

"I can't, Eliza," he said. "I need some time to process everything that happened last week."

"I can visit Connie and sit with her," she said, hoping to tell him about Aenti Miriam's offer.

"I have put an emergency phone by her bed. She can call me or nine-one-one. I had to do it, for safety's sake."

"That's smart, but I don't mind sitting with her."

"Eliza, you are needed here."

Eliza gave up on being calm. "You are still angry with me, ain't so?"

He turned and gave her a heartbreaking stare. "I am. I need some time away. I still need to work here, but . . ."

"But you don't want to be around me anymore. You will not forgive me."

He didn't answer. His stark expression and the tired lines around his eyes told her the truth. He would not forgive her.

"I see," she said, nodding her head and biting back tears. "I understand."

Eliza turned and hurried up the alley to grab her basket. "Eliza?"

She didn't look back because she was crying, and she didn't want him to see her cry.

She'd lost him. She'd finally found the love locked inside her heart, and now she'd lost the one she loved.

He was going to the Speicher place, the one place on earth she didn't want him to go. And yet, she still couldn't break her promise to Connie. She couldn't tell him about his *mamm* wanting her to marry him. Not now. Because he no longer wanted to marry Eliza.

That afternoon, Mamm opened the door to the quilting room and walked up to Eliza. "Shouldn't you be helping Jonah in the stables?"

Eliza could hear the buzz of conversation coming from the café across the hall. Always busy and bustling around here.

"I thought I'd work on my quilt. Abigail drew some patterns for me on her break. I'm so glad she's feeling better."

"She's passed the first trimester," Mamm explained. "I'm watching her, of course." Then she sat down across from Eliza. "I'm more worried about you right now. Colette said you came back with a basket of food, not eaten, and that you've been in here for hours. Why the rush, Eliza?"

"I want to get this quilt finished," she said, her heart racing, her tears held tightly so she wouldn't sob. "It's important that I do. I thought I'd give it to Connie."

Mamm drew back. "That's a nice gesture, but it's your story and your quilt. Why wouldn't you want to keep it?"

Eliza finished a stitch and saw she'd done it wrong. "I'm messing up. I need to focus."

Mamm grabbed her arm. "Eliza, look at me."

Eliza drew her gaze from the two female figures she was stitching, two women leaning close and talking. A primitive attempt to convey her story but she could see it all there. The moment Connie had asked her to keep a promise. A promise that had destroyed Levi's love for her.

"I need to get it done, Mamm. I need—" She stopped, exhaustion taking over. "Mamm."

Her mother opened her arms and Eliza fell against her. "It's over. Levi is still angry, and now he'll be working all next week at the Speicher place. Rebecca will be with him, flirting, cooking, and dressing pretty, and we know what will happen."

Mamm patted her back and then drew away and put her hand on Eliza's chin. "Levi needs time, *dochder*. I think it's wise for you two to take a break from each other. The following week is Thanksgiving. Maybe things will be better once he absorbs all of this."

"It won't be better," Eliza said. "He is hurt, and he's confused and . . . I love him so much. I didn't realize that until yesterday. It's all about sacrifice, ain't so? We give up things we believe to be important for the people we love. Jonah did that for Abby, and you've done it for Daed. I never had to face such sacrifice before—I knew I was loved by my family and *Gott*, but I never gave that kind of love to someone outside of my cocoon here."

"And now you know that kind of love," Mamm said, nodding. "It is quite a revelation. That's how *Gott* feels when one of his lost sheep comes home. His heart is filled with an immense love. Now you know that feeling, Eliza. It will help you find your way, because now you will trust in *Gott* to show you the way."

Eliza wiped her eyes. "But why would *Gott* bring Levi home and then cause him to turn away from me? I made a promise to a sick woman who loves her family. Was that so wrong?"

"*Neh*, that was the right thing to do. But right now, Levi is not seeing it that way. He has fought to win you back ever since the day we hired him, and in his mind, you have hurt him and betrayed him. He hasn't hit on the why, yet. But he will."

Eliza didn't believe that, but Mamm was wise, so she clung to her mother's words.

Glancing down at her quilt, she said on a shaky voice, "I want to finish this. I need to finish this. Just in case."

Mamm nodded, then went to the door. "Abby, Colette, if you're not too busy, can you *kumm*?"

Soon her sisters were gathered at the door, whispering with Mamm. What was going on? Not another intervention?

Neh, not that. They all walked in and took their places around the quilting table. Abigail spread out the quilt and Colette gathered needles, thread, and decorative yarns.

They had come to help.

Abby studied the quilt. "You are almost done. We have the man with a horse—Levi and Rudolph. We have you in the kinder buggy, with Levi driving up to the cottage, and there are the mums Levi gave you—such vivid colors—and the books—brown, green, and yellow. We have you riding through the apple orchard, a man in the background behind you. And the newest—two women talking." Abigail looked up. "The secret promise between you and Connie?"

Eliza nodded, unable to speak. The faceless figures on her quilt could not tell everything in her heart. She pointed to the unfinished panels. Swallowing, she said, "Here is one with my open journal, the threads representing words. Then James and Laura with Levi and me. I haven't done that one yet, but I will. No matter what, I will. And once I'm done, I will take the quilt to Connie and let her keep it to show Levi. Maybe he will see the truth of forgiveness here in these images."

That was her only hope now.

"Then we'd best get started," Mamm said, her expression serene and sure.

CHAPTER THIRTY-TWO

Levi pulled his buggy up to the Speicher home. An impressive place. Seemed he was always working at big, elegant over-the-top properties. This one was nice. A big rambling white farmhouse with porches everywhere. A huge red barn and two silos behind it. A pasture full of healthy livestock, both cows and horses.

A pretty spot with a nice pond at the bottom of the sloping backyard. It made a lovely picture with the colorful burgundy and gold leaves falling as Rudolph clopped up the dirt lane.

He tried not to compare this to his home, or even to the Shadow Lake Inn. But he couldn't help the shard of envy that hit him. He'd never been one to worry about money when he was out there on his own. He'd always been fed by the people who hired him, and he'd lived in rental houses between jobs.

Now, he longed for his own place, a place where he could be at peace and know he'd done a *gut* day's work. A place with a porch, and Lizzie waiting for him to *kumm* home. Would that ever happen? He had to work through his feelings to see what was left. Did he still want her?

Pulling his wagon up to the massive barn and stable, Levi remembered the day he'd arrived at Shadow Lake. He'd had hope that day, even knowing Eliza wouldn't want him there.

They'd worked hard to make their peace. He'd helped her heal physically and she'd forgiven him his youthful transgressions. He'd believed they'd find their way back to each other. He'd been attentive, giving her small gifts, helping her when she needed help, trying to just be near her. But now . . . he wasn't sure he could be near her anymore.

"We came so close, Rudolph," he said to his horse. Rudolph shook his mane and danced impatiently.

Levi hopped down only to find Rebecca hurrying toward him.

"Levi, it's so *gut* to see you again," she said, her dark hair shining, her winter *kapp* neat, and her dark green dress fluttering around her calves. She was pretty; no doubt about that.

"Now, we have a room for you in the stables. It's nice and clean and you even have a washroom there. Oncle always thinks of everything. One reason I love coming here."

Levi shook his head. "I can't stay here, Rebecca. My *mamm* is ill, and I want to be home with her at night."

"But Oncle expects you here all this week."

"We did not agree that I would be staying over. I told him I needed to be with Mamm. I'll get here early each morning and stay until sundown."

A hint of anger flared in her dark eyes. "*Ach*, well, you are needed here day and night. He has a lot for you to do before winter."

"I will do my job, but I can't stay here for a week," Levi insisted. "I'll go talk to him right now."

"*Neh*," she said, her eyes flaring again. "I have made a nice noon dinner for us. I'm a pretty *gut* baker, you know."

Levi was beginning to sense a lot more than horseshoes going on here. "Rebecca, that is kind of you, but I want to get to work. Now where is your *oncle*?"

"He is out on business."

"And when will he return?"

"I don't know."

"How about Elsie? Is she home?"

"*Ja*, but she is sleeping."

"At this time of day?"

"Or she might be knitting. She likes to be alone when she's knitting."

"I need to find out what I'm to do today. I can't stand here wasting time since I only have a half day today."

"So being with me is a waste of time?"

Levi wasn't sure how to handle this, but he was sure that if she had her way, Rebecca would put him in a compromising position that could lead to all kinds of speculation.

"*Neh*, you're pleasant and pretty, but I came here to work."

"So you do like me?" She smiled and her eyes fluttered in a funny way.

"I like you, *ja*. But again, I have to get to work." He glanced around and saw workers out in the fallow fields, cleaning up. "I'll check with one of these fellows."

Rebecca pouted. "I guess I can take the food I worked on all morning and give it someone else. Maybe I could visit your *mamm*."

"*Neh*," he said, getting aggravated. "We enjoyed the

cake you baked, but Mamm has to rest. She has to limit her visitors."

"Does Eliza King visit with her?"

That stopped Levi cold. "Sometimes, *ja*. But we have known her all of her life."

"So I've heard."

Now he'd hurt Rebecca's feelings. "I'm sorry, but this has nothing to do with you and me, or with me working here. Eliza and I were close, growing up, and now—"

He paused too long, giving Rebecca an opening. Her eyes gleamed. "*Ach*, have you two had a spat?"

"You could say that, *ja*."

"That's terrible. She does seem a bit . . . aloof."

"Excuse me?"

"All of the King sisters are that way, you know. They aren't truly kind. They think running a stupid old inn is something special."

"They've always been kind to me," he retorted. "And they work hard. That old inn is their livelihood."

"Then why do you look so sad when I mention Eliza's name?"

Levi couldn't give her an answer. He motioned to a man with a wheelbarrow. "I have to get to work."

He hurried away, leaving a pouting Rebecca standing there. But he had noticed that gleam in her eyes. It could only mean more trouble for him.

Two days later, Eliza had finished the quilt. She laid it out on her bed so Abigail and Colette could see it. Mamm planned to take a look after supper. She usually enjoyed sitting with Daed and Jonah for a while before Jonah and Abby went home. But she was also giving her daughters their time together, Eliza knew. Aenti Miriam had gone to her own room, but not before discussing her plans with the entire family. Mamm was still trying to process that revelation, too.

"I think it is kind of you to offer to help Connie," Mamm had told her sister. "Let's not bring it up until we know more, but when the time is right, I'm sure she and Levi will accept your help." Then she'd told Aenti, "I'm glad you'll be closer to us, and I'm also glad you have found a nice place for yourself."

They'd all been touched by Aenti's turnaround. Mamm said her sister was preparing for the future. She didn't want to be alone.

Now Eliza felt the same way, afraid of becoming bitter and bossy like her *aenti*.

"Eliza, this is very touching," Abigail said, bringing her out of her silent pity party. "I can see your story unfolding. The fall colors are striking, and I love how you've sewn the leaves along the way, almost like a vine or tapestry that ties it all together."

Colette touched her hand to the panel that showed a man and woman holding hands, with two children—a tall boy and a smaller girl with them. "Your happy ending?"

"I wish," she said. "I haven't heard from Levi at all, but I plan to go and visit Connie tomorrow, after Jonah and I have finished tending the animals, of course."

"You have been kept busy working in the stables while Levi is away," Colette replied. "He really was a big help."

Abby nodded. "Daed and Jonah planned to ask him to stay permanently. But that was before."

Eliza gasped. "He needs the work. They can't fire him."

"We weren't sure you'd want him around," Abby said. "Besides, they haven't asked him yet."

"He needs the work," Eliza said again. "I will work around him."

"Then I'll let Jonah know," Abby said. "He had planned to talk to you about it anyway."

Mamm came in. "*Ach*, are you through talking secrets?"

"No secrets tonight," Eliza said. "Just the finished quilt. I plan to take it to Connie tomorrow afternoon."

Mamm studied the bright colors of mauve, gold, and burgundy, with navy and some red added here and there. The characters did not have faces, but they wore Amish clothes—black bonnets or *kapps for the women*, black hats for the men, dark, rich colors for the triangular-shaped dresses. All created with geometric squares, rectangles, and triangles and telling an intimate story if one looked close enough.

"It's lovely, *dochder*," Mamm said. "But maybe you should hold on to it for a while. Connie would love it, but it's yours. Yours and Levi's."

"I can't, Mamm," Eliza said. "I can't bear to look at it, and I want Connie to have it—so she will know I tried."

Her mother didn't argue with her. "Then I will go with you to give it to her," Mamm said, brooking no argument.

Eliza bobbed her head. "I will need the support."

They arrived at Connie's house the next day and found Rebecca in the kitchen making a fuss about a casserole she'd baked. Laura was trying to put it away, but Rebecca insisted on heating it to serve to Connie.

Eliza wanted to turn and run, but the look on Laura's

face made her change her mind. James was out in the barn, obviously avoiding the confrontation.

Mamm did her thing and took over. "Eliza, help Rebecca find a spot for that casserole. I'm going to check on Connie. Laura, *liebling*, *kumm* with me to sit with your *mamm*. Eliza has brought a beautiful quilt to show her."

Laura rushed toward the back of the house, leaving Eliza to deal with Rebecca. Which she would do, her mood being far from passive these days.

"So you've made a quilt for Connie," Rebecca stated. "Is that the one you've been secretly working on?"

"I have worked on it, *ja*, but not in secret. The people I care about see it all the time."

"Including Levi?" Rebecca asked with a squeak in her voice.

Eliza held her ground. "I don't normally discuss quilting with men. It tends to make their eyes glaze over."

Rebecca lowered her gaze and fussed with taking the wrapping off her casserole. "This is a chicken potpie, or at least my version of it."

"That looks . . . interesting. I think the casserole should wait," Eliza said. "And now that we're here, you can go if you have somewhere to be."

Rebecca dug in her heels. "Levi will be home soon, and I aim to give him a *gut* supper. I also plan to stay and enjoy it with him."

"That's awfully kind of you, Rebecca," Eliza said. "But you've probably noticed he works late a lot."

"I've noticed so many things about Levi," Rebecca said. "We are practically together all day long. He's shared meals with me, so he must like my cooking."

"He likes to eat, *ja*."

Eliza waited, expecting more. And she got it.

"He's interested in me," Rebecca said. "We are compatible."

"And he told you this?" Eliza didn't believe her, but it hurt to hear the words.

"*Neh*, not yet." Rebecca twirled her *kapp* ribbon. "But I can tell he's falling for me."

Eliza whirled to turn away, knocking her tote bag off the counter. Her journal fell out, but she quickly picked it up and dropped it back into her bag. Rebecca eyed her with interest and a smirk that made Eliza feel ill.

But she regained control. "If Levi is falling for you, then I wish you both the best," Eliza said. "I'm going to check on Connie. You can sit here and wait as long as you want."

"I'd love to see this special quilt," Rebecca said, smirking again. "Not that I'm in the group you care about, of course."

"It's for Connie," Eliza replied. "I'll let her decide if she wants to show it off."

She hurried down the hallway. She'd need to get Mamm out of here before Levi showed up. She couldn't stomach the thought of him coming home to Rebecca instead of her.

Levi returned to find two buggies in the yard, and he recognized both. Before he could go in to see why a King buggy and a Speicher buggy were both here, James came out of the barn and explained.

"Rebecca showed up, but Laura had come home early to check on Mamm. Then Eliza and Sarah came, and they are both with Mamm now, but Rebecca won't leave, so

Laura is getting supper ready. Rebecca brought a casserole, and she plans to stay and eat with us."

He'd never heard his brother speak so much at once.

"It's okay. I'll wash up at the pump and get inside to see what's going on."

"I might just stay in the barn," James replied, his eyes wide.

"A *gut* idea," Levi replied. "I might be back to join you."

Levi was headed to the door when Rebecca came out with something in her hand.

"What are you doing here?" he asked, tired of her games.

"I came to visit with Connie," she said. "But Eliza and Sarah have been with her for an hour now. I didn't want to leave until I saw you." She motioned to a large cloth bag on the chair. "I've been waiting out here."

"I'm here, so you can go."

"Levi, you need to see something. I saw it by accident, but I couldn't help but read it."

Levi saw the small leather-bound book in her hand. "That's Eliza's journal."

"*Ja*, and a very interesting one at that," Rebecca said.

"You read her journal?" he asked, anger spilling over in his words.

"It . . . it fell out of her tote bag and . . . I saw it."

"Give that to me," he replied. "Then you need to leave."

Rebecca's eyes filled with hurt, but her face showed indignance. "But Levi, you should read the page I marked with the ribbon attached to the book. For your sake, Levi, read it before you make a big mistake."

She grabbed her things off the chair and headed to her buggy. Then she smiled and waved to him. "I'll see you tomorrow, I'm sure."

Levi watched her go. He'd give the journal back to Eliza. He wouldn't read it. But the ribbon beckoned him.

And then he saw Eliza's handwriting winking at him. He skimmed the words, thinking to close the book.

But he didn't. He saw what she'd written there about him, about his *mamm*'s request, and he saw exactly how Eliza felt about marrying him:

> *Connie Lapp is sick, and she wants me to take care of Levi and his siblings if something happens to her. It will happen. Parkinson's is a bad disease. I studied up on it. She will suffer in so many ways. I promised her I'd . . . do everything to help Levi, James, and Laura. But I did not promise marriage. She wants us to marry. She wants to die in peace.*

> *How can I make that promise when I'm not even sure I want to be married? How can I accept such a change in my life? I don't know if I can do that. But I promised Connie.*

Now he understood why Eliza had avoided him. She didn't want the burden of him and his siblings. She was in there with his *mamm*, pretending to care. She'd held back the news of his mother's illness because she couldn't tell him about Mamm's request. A request Eliza did not want to accept. She didn't want to get married—at least not to him.

And knowing that broke his heart completely.

Eliza had seen Levi out the window, but she didn't get up to rush to him. She couldn't see beyond Rudolph and his wagon out front, but she heard voices. Rebecca—he must be talking to her, and he'd probably ask her to stay for dinner. If so, she'd have her answer. Eliza would have to accept that Levi and Rebecca belonged together.

Mamm heard him and James coming inside. "Eliza, go and tell the menfolk to wash up for supper. We'll get it ready, then we must go."

Connie sat in a chair with her feet propped on a stool. "Don't leave yet. I want to show Levi this beautiful quilt. I don't think I've ever seen anything like it. It truly is so sweet, and I can see joy here in all the *wunderbar* fall colors."

She glanced up at Eliza. "I can see love here, too. So much love in each stitch. I want my son to see that."

Eliza shot Mamm a warning glance. "I'll finish supper, but I agree with Mamm. I think we should head back since it's getting dark early these days. We don't want to be on the road too long after sundown."

"I will make sure he sees it, Eliza," Connie said, deep meaning in her words. "You have been kind to me, even after I made a request that you might not want to honor. I won't forget that."

"Connie," Eliza said, kneeling by her stool. "I would do anything for you and your family."

Connie nodded. "I know. But it must be your decision, not the misguided dream of a dying woman."

Mamm gave them a soft smile. "Connie, you are not dead yet. You could live many years. There are new drugs and new procedures that do help people with your condition."

Connie smiled. "Then maybe I will live to see that dream come true after all. But in *Gott*'s own time, not mine."

CHAPTER THIRTY-THREE

Levi was waiting in the kitchen alone when Eliza came in.

"How are you?" she asked, wondering where Rebecca was hiding.

He didn't answer. He just leaned against the worktable and stared at his brogans, the expression on his face hard-edged and dark.

"Did Rebecca leave?"

He finally nodded and then reached behind him. "*Ja*, but she found this before she left."

Eliza gasped. "That's my journal."

"*Ja*, sure is. She showed me a particular page."

Eliza's stomach roiled with despair and anger. Rebecca had seen the journal fall out of her tote bag, and she'd obviously gone snooping while Eliza was in the other room. "She should not have read something that is private."

"*Ach*, well, she did, and now I know everything."

"Everything? What does that mean, Levi?"

He touched a finger to the journal, jabbing at the leather.

"The promise you've been keeping for Mamm. You didn't tell anyone about her illness, but we found out because she is getting worse. And even after that, after I asked you why you'd been avoiding me, you still didn't tell me the truth."

Her eyes burned with a fierce heat, and her heart began to tear apart in a jagged rush of pain, but Eliza held her head up. "And what do you believe to be the truth, Levi?"

"That Mamm asked you to marry me and help me take care of Laura and James. And that you really don't want that burden, ain't so?"

She couldn't deny that she'd written words similar to that, but he'd taken her private thoughts and turned them into something unpleasant and untrue.

"I did write that, *ja*. Weeks ago. Before—"

He slammed the journal down on the table. "Before we kissed or after, before you started avoiding me, or before Mamm got so sick? Before when, Lizzie?"

She wanted to tell him before she realized with every beat of her heart that she loved him and his family, and she wanted to be his wife forever. But from the look in his eyes, she could see he would never believe her. And he'd never forgive her.

Taking her silence as guilt, he said, "You can't even tell me the truth now, can you?"

"It seems you and Rebecca have already beat me to it by reading one passage out of my journal. One passage, Levi. I'm going home now, but you can keep the journal and read it at your leisure. You gave it to me and now you can have it back. Because if you trust Rebecca's conniving actions over your feelings for me, then you need to know the whole truth. And you also need to know that I will not try to prove myself to you again. I have forgiven you seven times over, and yet, you can't seem to forgive me. I'm sorry."

She turned and whirled toward Connie's room. "Mamm, I'm ready to go."

Mamm must have heard the urgency in her words. She came hurrying up the hallway. "I'm here and ready myself." She smiled at Levi. "Hello, Levi. I hope you enjoy the dinner Rebecca left for you. She sure made a fuss about it."

"That's not all she made a fuss about," Eliza said, grabbing her things to head out the door.

Mamm followed, silent and serene. But Eliza saw a burning fire in her sweet mother's eyes. She felt that same fire in her heart.

"Men are so *dummkopp* at times," she said, tears slipping down her cheeks after she'd climbed up on the buggy seat.

Mamm got up onto the buggy and patted her arm. "Much too dumb for words, for certain sure."

Levi stood shocked and silent for at least five minutes. Only when he smelled something burning did he jump and open the stove door to remove the scorched casserole. Placing it on a pot-holder, he stopped and stared out the window, wishing things could be the way they used to be when Daed was alive and Mamm was healthy.

Did I bring all of this on myself? He had to wonder how different things would have been if he'd stayed here. He and Eliza might have worked things out, or they might have each gone on with their lives. Daed might still be alive with Levi there to help more and make sure he had proper treatments. Mamm might have been able to see a doctor earlier. No matter, he was here now, and things weren't going all that great despite his presence.

"Levi?"

He turned to find Mamm walking slowly up the hallway, using the wall to help her balance.

Hurrying to help her, he said, "I'm sorry," he said. "I burned the casserole."

Mamm nodded, her right hand shaking slightly. "I'm not that hungry. Sarah left some soup. That sounds better to me."

He glanced around and checked the small propane refrigerator. Inside he located the vegetable soup, and then he sliced the freshly baked bread he found by the stove. The *kinder* could dig deep into the burned potpie and possibly salvage some chicken and vegetables. Or knowing them, they'd toss it to the goats. They did not like Rebecca. And now, neither did he.

He'd have to forgive her, and he'd have to forgive Eliza. But things had changed between Eliza and him, and he wasn't sure how to mend their relationship this time.

"Where is everyone?" *Mamm* asked, bringing him out of his dark musings.

"Laura is out helping James finish the evening feedings," he said. "I got the hay bales checked and stacked in the barn yesterday afternoon. They are *gut* and dry, no dampness or mold. James was a big help with that. He and I will get all the equipment cleaned for winter, so we'll be ready for the first cutting next year. If I can stay on it, we should have at least three cuttings and plenty of drying time. Hopefully, I can buy some more cows and maybe a few pigs." He let out a tired sigh. "At least our livestock will have enough hay for the winter."

Connie nodded and sank down in her favorite chair. "Levi, let the soup simmer for a while. We need to talk."

He'd tamped down his earlier anger. He would not upset Mamm, despite her part in this. She was only trying to protect her family but asking such a big favor of Eliza had been misguided. He wouldn't bring it up unless she did. It was over now, anyway.

But Mamm had other ideas. She waited until he took a seat on the old sofa. Then she folded her hands and gave him a long, sweet stare. "What happened with you and Eliza?"

"Nothing for you to worry about."

"Levi," she said, shaking her head. "I know I'm part of the problem between you two and I'm sorry."

"You don't need to be sorry, Mamm."

"Yes, I do. I asked the impossible of her—a young woman who loves you so much, she is willing to do anything to help this family."

"Except marry me," he blurted. When he saw the sadness in his mother's eyes, he regretted that outburst.

"But you are wrong there, son." Connie's hand shook so badly, she put it in her lap and held her other hand over it. "I need you to go into the bedroom and bring me the quilt Sarah and Eliza brought me today."

"Are you cold?"

Connie shook her head. "*Neh*, I want you to see the quilt."

Thinking this was an unusual request, Levi did as his mother asked. He went into her room, lifted the quilt off the bed, and brought it back into the living room.

"Stretch it out across the sofa," Mamm said. "You need to see all the panels."

"Did you have them make this?" he asked, confused. Mamm never talked quilting with him.

"*Neh*." Mamm sat still, her hands cupped together in her lap. "Eliza told me she began this quilt when you first started working at the inn. She calls it her forgiving quilt."

Surprised to hear that, Levi did as Mamm asked and spread out the brightly colored quilt. "I knew she was working on a quilt. It's pretty." And a thoughtful gift. Had she planned to give this to his mother all along?

"Sit here by me and start with the first panel," Mamm said. "It tells a story that you need to see."

The door burst open, and James and Laura came in, laughing about something one of the goats had done. But they both stopped when they saw the quilt.

"Where did you get that?" Laura asked. "Levi, did you bring Mamm a new quilt?"

James studied it and smiled. "Quilting is an art, ain't so? I have read Amish quilts can bring a lot of money in the *Englisch* world."

"It is true," Mamm said. "But some quilts are priceless and not for sale. *Kumm* and stand here with us. Levi was just looking at the panels. It's a gift from Eliza."

Laura's eyes widened. "Look. A man with a horse. Levi, that could be you and Rudolph."

Levi studied the panel Laura pointed to. The faceless man was leading a horse with dark red around his nose, just like Rudolph. "It might be," he said, his eyes turning to the next panel. "The mums I gave to Eliza and the books." He found another. "We had ice cream after her checkup, and several other times after her therapy sessions." The two ice cream cones were perfect triangles, but the creamy material over the cones was cut in half ovals to look like ice cream.

Amazing.

"That sounds nice," James said. He pointed to the panel with a pony pulling a small buggy. "That's Peaches and the *kinder* buggy. You said you had it ready for Eliza when she first came home with her cast off."

Levi held a hand to his chin. "I did," he said. He'd tried to show her kind gestures after talking to Jonah. "I wanted her to forgive me." And he'd wanted to be near her. Had that really changed?

Mamm pulled James and Laura to her side. They remained quiet as Levi studied the work before him.

The apple orchard—trees in brown with red apples clinging to their branches. An apple pie in a dish stitched with tan threads that looked like a crust. A woman riding a gray horse—Eliza and Samson—prancing toward a man waiting by a fence. Him, the day he'd seen her riding through the orchard. And finally, a man and woman with two older *kinder*, all holding hands. These replicas needed no words and no faces. He could hear the words spoken between them, both good and bad. A panel that showed two women huddled together, one whispering to the other—his *mamm* and Eliza? Then he noticed a panel that shook him to his core.

A woman sitting on a rock, trees behind her, writing in a journal. Eliza. Writing in her journal. The journal he'd given her, the journal that now lay on a side table where he'd placed it out of the way.

She'd told him to read the journal to find the truth.

Levi gulped, held a hand to his mouth. How could he have been so insensitive, so harsh with his words and actions earlier today? Eliza had forgiven him his transgressions from long ago, and he'd pestered her with what he thought were wooing tactics. But all he'd done was pressure her to the point of frightening her all over again. And then, the promise and the secret between his mother and her. Even more pressure, more demands, when she was still confused and hesitant. And now, Rebecca, who'd tried to come between them, had actually given him the one thing he needed to see.

Eliza's words, from her heart, all written in the journal he'd given her for just such thoughts. She'd left it here to prove to him that she'd forgiven him and maybe to show him that she did love him.

He turned and looked directly at Mamm. "She loves me."

"She loves you," Mamm repeated, holding her children tightly. "She loves us, Levi. She loves us enough to discover that for herself, and this quilt proves it in every panel and every thread."

James tilted his head. "It's so easy to see now, ain't so?"

Levi nodded, grabbed the journal, and hurried to the door. "Go ahead with supper. I'll be in the barn, and I might be a while," he said, tears burning his eyes. "I have a lot of catching up to do."

CHAPTER THIRTY-FOUR

Thanksgiving. Eliza didn't know how she felt, but Mamm had come up with a plan to keep them all occupied.

"We will open the inn and provide meals for anyone in need," she'd announced four days ago. "We will cook everything in the inn and have Thanksgiving there. I know there are people in this community who won't have a *gut* meal that day. We are blessed with an abundance of food, and this community needs to *kumm* together and enjoy what we have to offer."

Daed had sat in his place at the table and stared across at his wife. At first, they all held their breath, wondering what he would say. Then he had nodded. "*Ja*, we could make that a tradition."

So now after much planning, a lot of cooking, and dozens of donated turkeys, some already cooked and some cooking in the big ovens and out on smokers right now, they were up early to prepare. Edith had agreed to help since she had no one to eat with her anyway, and she usually ate with relatives. She'd ordered her relatives to get here early to help if they wanted to eat a meal with her today. Most of the kitchen staff had agreed to work and bring their families. Everyone was in a thankful mood. Abigail was ordered to only do sitting work—peeling potatoes, fashioning cut-outs for piecrusts, chopping vegetables and folding napkins. Aenti Miriam was in charge of all breads, and she loved to bake bread, so Edith and she made peace for the day. Matthew and Colette would be in charge of the happenings out front, along with Henry Cooper, the *Englischer* who worked the inn's registration desk. Everyone had a place and a task. Some of the people who'd stayed at the inn heard about the event and volunteered to help, too, even though the inn was closed today.

Eliza worked to make tea and keep the coffee machines running. An easy task that she'd performed many times before. Jonah did the usual routine checks on the stabled animals and the chickens, then came to do his part with parking and crowd control.

He walked up to where Eliza was making tea. "How are you?"

"I'm fine," she said. But considering he'd found her crying in the stables several times, she figured he knew better.

"I haven't talked to Levi yet about working here permanently. I wanted to see how you would feel about that."

She'd thought about nothing else. Levi had yet to finish working at the Speicher place, and he could be having Thanksgiving with Rebecca and her *aenti* and *oncle*. Since he had not bothered to talk to Eliza, her heartbreak hurt ten times more than the first time they'd broken up. Mamm had told her to be still and wait, but Eliza couldn't bear to be still. She knew she'd lost Levi, and she'd have to find a way to live with that.

Today, she'd focus on feeding people who needed love and hope. Mamm was always finding ways to show her daughters the blessing they had, and this certainly had brought Eliza out of her self-pity. Keeping busy would take her mind off losing Levi. Again.

"Eliza?"

She looked up to find Jonah still waiting. "I told you, Levi needs the work. But he probably won't be back. He doesn't want to be around me, for certain sure."

"I'll get in touch with him next week," Jonah said. "If he refuses, we'll discuss hiring someone else part-time. It will help later when Abby has our *bobbeli*. I want to be with her as much as possible."

Eliza nodded. "I think that is a *gut* idea."

Jonah nodded. "You know, he does love you. I believe he'll *kumm* around in time. He returned here for you, Eliza."

"He returned here for his family," she retorted. "I will move on and . . . never fall in love again."

Jonah huffed. "Famous last words."

"True words," she said, grumpy and wishing she could be more cheerful.

Jonah walked by where Abigail sat and kissed her, his eyes only for his expectant wife.

Envy hit Eliza in an ugly green flash. She would never open her heart to anyone again.

Never.

Colette whizzed by. "Pie, sister. Pie makes everything better, and we have at least six dozen in all kinds of flavors."

Eliza rolled her eyes. "I plan to eat a lot of pie today."

But really, she wasn't even hungry.

Levi walked into his house and found Mamm and the *kinder* dressed and waiting. "So we're doing this?" he asked.

"We are," Mamm said. "We were invited and we're going. You know what you need to do, don't you?"

He nodded. "I've thought of nothing else since Eliza left the other day."

He'd read her journal. Read it, cried, smiled, fussed at himself for being such an idiot. He'd prayed, planned, prayed some more, and then he'd reached out to Jonah.

"I love her, and she loves me. It's so simple, but I need help to make it real."

Jonah had come by to visit, and they had developed a plan.

Today, Thanksgiving, he would find Eliza at the big dinner, and he'd tell her he loved her and wanted to marry her. He had other plans, but he didn't want to spoil them by telling anyone. He could keep secrets, too. *Gut* secrets that he prayed would bring the woman he loved back into his arms.

"But what if Rebecca shows up?" James asked, the look of fear in his eyes almost comical.

"Rebecca has been sent home," he explained. "Her *oncle* saw her being unkind to one of the workers and then found out she'd been distracting most of the others. And when he confronted me, I told him the truth. She is a pretty woman, but her tactics are not the best. I think it will be a while before she returns to Shadow Lake."

"Are you sure?" Laura asked while she fidgeted with her apron.

"I also talked to Rebecca and told her that I love Eliza and that will never change."

"That should do it then," Mamm said, beaming. "Now, I have my medicine and I'm feeling hopeful. I've talked to Miriam, and she will be a great comfort to me when you are working. She can cook and she can read to me or help me with quilting or mending. This is the best solution for now."

Levi nodded. "She sure gave me a *gut* talking-to. My ears are still burning. Miriam made it clear that Eliza and I belong together, and we have been *lecherich*." Ridiculous. He'd been guilty of that, no doubt. "We have a champion on our side now that I've told her I will mend things with Eliza."

"That should happen today," Mamm said, relief in her words. "Sarah has fixed a spot for me to rest all afternoon if I get tired, and she and Miriam will be my nurses for the day. Let's get going."

Levi helped Mamm up onto the buggy and made sure everyone was bundled against the cold wind. Then he smiled at his family.

"You are all my blessings," he said. "I'm so glad to be home for Thanksgiving."

They all smiled and clapped. Rudolph lifted his nose and shook out his mane. Apparently, everyone agreed with that sentiment. He just hoped Eliza would agree with him, too.

Eliza smiled as she handed an *Englisch* family their containers of food. Each family got turkey, dressing, and all the trimmings on a big paper platter. They could eat outside by a firepit Jonah had made or find a spot in the inn or on the porch. It was chilly, but the fire in the lobby was warm and some tables had been set up there, too. Some people wanted theirs to go, so they had provided covered containers for that.

She'd moved from beverages to the front lines, and so far, they'd had about a hundred or so people, some alone, and some with hungry families. The crowd was dwindling now.

She stood on the front porch, a shawl around her arms, and watched the lake waters lifting in choppy waves. Winter was here but the sunshine had made it tolerable today.

Jonah came out and glanced at her. "You're needed in the kitchen."

"I'm taking a break."

"But . . . this is urgent."

She huffed a breath and hurried away. When she got to the kitchen, Colette asked her to cut a few more slices of pie.

"Why?" she asked. "Everyone has gone."

"We still need to eat," Colette explained. "And we are expecting a few more people."

Eliza went about cutting pie slices, the activity providing a welcome distraction. But the poor pie slices were uneven and clunky. "I'm done," she told Colette sharply.

Her sister glanced at the clock. "*Gut*, now go back on the porch and tell Jonah to watch for the stragglers."

Confused and hungry, Eliza whirled and headed out to the porch, noting that the café had been set with one long table so they could finally eat.

When she reached the porch, Jonah was nowhere to be found. Then she spotted a small buggy pulling up the circular drive.

A buggy she knew well. And Rudolph was pulling it.

Her heart stopped when she saw Levi at the reins and his family smiling and waving.

"But—" She turned to speak, but no one was there.

What should she do? Run away . . . or face him and tell him what she thought? What did she think? Her heart pattered a rapid reply—*talk to him, talk to him*.

She decided to face him, to find out what *he* thought.

So she waited, noting the buggy was decorated with fall flowers and vines that reminded her of the trim-work on her quilt. Their quilt.

Her heart, so broken and frayed, started pumping at a fast beat. Levi looked handsome in his Sunday clothes and a black overcoat. He stepped off the buggy and grabbed a small container of yellow mums while his family scrambled out and hurried into the inn with only a quick greeting. Then he walked to the porch and looked up at her.

"I love you," he said. "Want to go for a ride with me?"

This can't be happening.

But it was. He waited, patient and sure.

She ventured a remark. "You're not mad anymore?"

He shook his head. "I read your journal, but before that I saw the quilt, Eliza. Our quilt. I'm *dumm* sometimes but I now understand that quilts do tell a story, and . . . I saw ours right there in the panels you created."

Eliza blinked back tears, her heart swelling with hope.

She wanted to run to him, but she was afraid this was a dream and she'd wake up. "I . . . I want you to be sure, Levi."

"I am sure," he said, walking up the steps. "I want you to be sure, too. No pressure, no secret promises, just sure of our love. I know how I feel."

Eliza wiped at her eyes and gently slapped at his coat lapel. "I'm for certain sure, Levi. I love you. I have always loved you. I want to be by your side, and I want to be your helpmate. I do not think of this as an obligation or a sacrifice. I see it as a blessing, the best blessing of my life."

"Can we go for a ride then?"

She nodded. "But first, I need to do something."

He looked surprised. "Okay."

She leaned up and took his face in her hands. Then she

kissed him, putting her heart into it, her actions trying to show him what words sometimes could not convey.

Levi kissed her back with a gentle touch and a soft groan, his hands holding her waist, his chest a haven of strength and warmth.

Eliza stepped back, tears in her eyes, a strong love in her heart.

Levi studied her face, her lips, her eyes. "What did you think?"

She laughed and wiped at her eyes. "That was perfect."

Levi smiled and took her breath away. "So we are sure and certain we are ready? Finally?"

"Finally and forever," she said, smiling up at him.

"Let's go then."

He guided her to the buggy and then coaxed Rudolph around the drive toward the back of the property. "I promised you a ride through the apple orchard, Eliza."

Bobbing her head, she glanced at him. "I'd love that."

She leaned against him and savored the warmth of his coat, and . . . the quilt he pulled out of the back. Their quilt. He opened it and spread it out over their laps and legs, the heavy material wrapping them in a warm cocoon.

Then he kissed her again.

They rode up the hill and down into the orchard, leaves kicking up as Rudolph trotted along. Eliza lifted her head to the wind and took a deep breath. Forgiveness was such a beautiful thing.

Levi stopped the buggy in a pretty spot where the apple trees met to form an arch over them, then drew her into his arms and kissed her again and again.

Then he whispered, "I love you and I will cherish you the rest of my days."

She bobbed her head, unable to speak what was in her heart.

Then he chuckled. "But right now, our families are waiting for us in the café, and I have to admit, I am hungry."

She nodded again. "I want pie. Lots of pie. And turkey and stuffing and—"

He whirled the buggy around and drove right up to the inn and found a hitching post. Then he helped her and her yellow mums down. They entered through the back way and hurried to the café.

To the sound of laughter and applause as everyone they loved gathered there to celebrate their many blessings.

Mamm cried and wiped her eyes. Connie cried and gave Eliza a grateful smile. Her sisters ran to hug her close.

And Jonah winked at her, making her laugh. Then *Aenti* Miriam nodded in approval and shot Levi a knowing smile.

Daed hugged her and shook Levi's hand. "I'm sure glad you two worked things out. I was afraid I'd never get my Thanksgiving meal." He sat down and said, "Let us pray."

After their silent prayers, they all settled in to eat by candlelight and to rejoice in their *gut* fortune. Platters circled the table while everyone laughed and told stories about the many people they'd fed, stories of gratitude and true thankfulness.

As everyone chattered around them, Levi held her hand and whispered, "Just to be near you, that is all I will ever need."

Eliza smiled and whispered back. "It's *gut* to have you home, Levi."

Abby let out a gasp, causing all of them to glance at her. "Sorry," she said, smiling. "The *bobbeli* must be hungry, too. I just got a strong kick in the ribs."

Jonah placed his hand on her stomach, his eyes going

wide. "We have to make him strong to be a member of this family, and that was a *gut* strong kick."

"Or her," Colette replied with a tart smile. "You'll want to make her a strong daughter."

Jonah rolled his eyes. "I'll need all of my strength for that. Abe, my hat is off to you."

"That is the truth," Daed said, smiling at Mamm. "And we thank Thee, *Gott*, for our blessings."

Please read on for an excerpt from the next
Shadow Lake Inn Amish romance!

THE CHRISTMAS QUILT
by
Lenora Worth

CHAPTER ONE

Her sister was getting married today.

Colette King watched as Mamm helped Eliza with her pretty mint-green wedding dress, her hands gentle as she tied the white apron sash and then pinned a mauve flower made from fabric scraps on the front of the apron. Then she adjusted the organza *kapp* she'd made for Eliza a few weeks ago. This was a sweet, solemn moment since Eliza would one day be buried in the apron and the matching white cape. But it would be a long time before that happened, *Gott*'s will.

And it might be a long time before Colette had to wear that traditional apron and cape on her own wedding day. Her man was not here where he belonged. Maybe she wasn't the marrying kind. Maybe she'd just stay here safe and sound with Mamm and Daed all her life. Find a cat to love. Or she'd be the library lady, loaning out her precious books.

"There," Mamm said with a satisfied smile, her gaze moving over Eliza and bringing Colette out of lamenting her own situation. Mamm patted Eliza's hand. "You look lovely, Eliza. I hope you and Levi will always be as happy as Daed and I have been all these years."

Eliza blinked back tears, her green eyes bright. "I've never been so happy, Mamm. *Denke*."

"I'll bring you a bite to eat," Colette offered. "You might forget to eat during the celebration."

They'd turned the quilting room into the bride's room for today. Eliza stood and looked out the window. "A happy day."

Today *was* a happy day. Well, almost.

After hugging her sister, Colette hurried from the room and went out to get some air. Although it had snowed a bit last night, the temperature was mild enough to get through the wedding and the sunshine helped with that. She glanced around the grounds of the Shadow Lake Inn, her gaze moving over the new pavilion they'd built earlier this year. It glowed a stark shimmering white, against the dusting of last night's snow. The huge structure was filled with rows and rows of folding chairs they'd brought in on bench wagons. If the early December weather held, Eliza would marry Levi Lapp under the shelter of the pavilion, two firepits burning on each side to keep the chilly air at bay. They'd all worked hard to string evergreens and white ribbons through some of the beams and posts to make it look festive for this wedding and for the few weeks left of the holiday season when tourists would rent out the inn for parties and get-togethers.

Today, however, the inn was closed because of the wedding. A private event with a mixed group of attendees— mostly Amish and some *Englisch* who worked here, such as Henry Cooper who ran the front desk and watched over the huge lobby, and others who were vendors that provided the necessities to run such an establishment. Mamm and Daed would preside over the event and Colette and her older sister Abigail would be in the wedding party. Levi's younger brother, James, and their sister, Laura, would also stand by him.

But would Matthew make it back in time?

Abigail called out to her from the inn's back entrance.

"Colette, *kumm* help me with Jon, please."

Colette pivoted, her dark burgundy dress and crisp white apron swishing against the leggings she wore underneath to keep her warm. Tugging at her black cape, she called, "On my way."

She entered to the bustle of the industrial kitchen where large pans of baked chicken and savory corn bread dressing lined up on the counter alongside macaroni and cheese, creamed spinach, and various other side dishes. They were having a huge dinner after the noon wedding. Eliza looked so happy as she and Mamm hurried back into the quilting room. "Let me take Eliza a small plate," she said, hurrying to gather cut meat, some cheese, bread, and a handful of freshly made wedding mints, so her sister would have a sweet taste after eating.

She offered her sister the food and nodded her approval. "I have to tend to Jon," she said, so she could escape before she ruined her sister's joyous mood.

But her heart hammered that familiar beat with each step. *I miss Matthew. I miss Matthew.*

Would he be home soon?

Her Mattie had been gone for six long months, due to an ailing uncle who'd needed help on his Missouri farm.

"I'll be back in a few weeks," he'd told her the night before he left. "Just through the harvest."

"You'll need to get back soon. Abigail has a baby now and Eliza is getting married in December. We need your help more than ever."

His gaze moved over her face. "And do you need me, Colette?"

"You know I do. I love you."

It had taken her a long time to say those words, but she truly loved Matthew Mueller. Last Christmas, after they'd flirted and laughed and whispered sweet nothings to each other, he'd given her a quick kiss after a youth singing and told her that he'd loved her since the day she'd been born. Two years older than her twenty-one, he'd known her as a baby, a toddler, a *kinder*, a teen, and now, a woman. And loved her all that time. They'd been together since that night.

But it had taken her too many years to finally realize she loved him, too. Wishing now she could take back all the times she'd ignored him or brushed him away while they worked side by side in the inn's kitchen and café, Colette had savored their brief time together away from the inn, but he'd up and left a few days after she'd declared her love.

"Stop pouting and take Jon for his morning nap in the nursery room, please," Abigail said, handing her giggling son, Jonah Junior, over to Colette when she entered the kitchen. They called him Jon, but he looked exactly like a Junior Jonah. And he was loved by the entire family.

"*Kumm*, little pumpkin," Colette said to the *bobbeli*, glad to have something to occupy her time before the wedding. "You'll have to sleep right through the best part, but don't worry, you won't miss out on the wonderful food we plan to eat."

Jon bobbed his head, his dark curls so like Jonah's, and babbled a response. At almost nine months old, he babbled a lot.

"Nap, nap," she replied. "Ruth Ann will watch over you

and read you a funny story, ain't so." Ruth Ann was the official nursery worker at the Inn, since so many of the women had children now.

Jon giggled and grabbed at the strings of her *kapp*.

Colette kissed his baby-sweet cheek. "What a joy you are."

Abigail let out a sigh. "Two more hours and then our sister will be married to the man who kissed her for the first time."

Colette danced around with Jon, making him giggle again. "*Ja*, and we well know how that turned out."

"She is marrying him—that is how it turned out," Mamm said as she came in with Eliza, both of them beaming. "Colette, stop worrying about Matthew. The man loves you. He will be back."

How did Mamm do that? She could take one look at any of them and know exactly what they were fretting about.

Eliza's eyes held a dreamy sheen, but she tried to commiserate. "I know Matthew. He wouldn't tell you he loved you and then never return to prove that declaration."

"It's been longer than I thought," Colette replied. "In his last letter, he said he'd be home in time for your wedding. What if something happened to him? The weather has been bad to the west."

Mamm and Eliza shot Abigail a speaking glance.

"What is it?" Colette said, her instincts on high alert. "Something has happened. Is he okay?"

Mamm took her off to the side. "Do not fret about Mattie. I have it from a *gut* source that he's on his way home. His uncle passed last week, Colette."

"Where did you hear that?"

"From your *Aenti* Miriam," Mamm replied. "You know

my sister is like a sieve when it comes to gossip. She can't keep it in."

"But who would be gossiping about Matthew?"

"Just someone who has relatives in the same community. That's all Miriam told me. His uncle died and Matthew would be home by Christmas at the latest. Don't ruin Eliza's big day, *dochder*."

Colette bit her lips. "I'm sorry. I won't mention this again, but once the wedding is over, I aim to corner Aenti and find out what's going on."

"Well, I wish you the best on that," Mamm replied. "Now I have to get finished with this busywork and get your *daed* bundled up and ready for the wedding." Mamm tugged her close. "You look so pretty today, so get that smile of yours into shape and let's celebrate this wedding."

Colette kept one eye on the ceremony and one eye on the lane leading up to the inn. Lined with buggies of all shapes and sizes, it looked like a strip of black quilting material. But she wasn't thinking about quilt patterns. She wanted to hear the *clip-clop* of one more team of horses.

Matthew had to make it back before Christmas. She didn't like feeling helpless, yet she had to show patience and grace because he'd done a *gut* deed. He'd answered a call for help from an elder in his family. He could be dealing with the estate or staying to winterize everything so he could shut the place down.

Then it occurred to her. What if he had to stay there indefinitely?

Colette saw her mother frown, so she went back to listening to the vows Eliza and Levi were exchanging. Vows to love and honor each other. They were short and sweet, but the minister would also provide a sermon to remind others that marriage was a sacred promise between a man and a woman.

Forever.

That thought scared her. Was that why she'd pushed Matthew away so many times? Eliza had struggled with the responsibility of becoming a wife, and now Colette saw the gravity and the finality of her decision to marry Levi.

Did she want that?

Could she do that?

What would happen when Matthew came home?

She didn't have to wait too long for an answer.

As soon as the minister finished, they all headed to the inn to get warm and have dinner.

As the crowd moved across the lawn, Colette glanced up to see Matthew walking toward her with a dour look on his handsome face. Then she noticed the young woman clinging to his arm, smiling up at him.

In the same way Colette smiled at him each time they were together.

Had Matthew found someone new while he was gone?